Touch of Clandestiny

CATIE O'NEILL

CAMO PUBLISHING

Copyright © 2025 by Catie O'Neill

For more information, please contact catieoneillauthor@gmail.com

First paperback edition April 2025

Book by Catie O'Neill

Copy/Line Edited by Juicy Details Editing

Proofread/Formatted by Hope E. Davis

Cover Design by Methyss Art

ISBN 979-8-9913858-0-0 (paperback)

ISBN 979-8-9913858-1-7 (ebook)

https://catie1024.wixsite.com/catieoneillauthor

Author Note Before You Proceed:

Enter at your own risk

This book contains the following:

- Explicit sexual content
- Foul and sexual language
- Violence
- Sexism/misogyny
- Death
- Torture
- Excessive drinking

Chapter 1

enry held me roughly by the hips as he pressed into me from behind, gently sucking on my neck and cooing sweet words into my ear—a stark contrast to the vigor of his actions. This wasn't making love. It never was with any of my dalliances. It served to pass the time, though he had long been my favorite. There had been many, but for the Princess of the Kingdom of Revell that shouldn't come as a surprise. Despite my father's disdain for me, my status would always have men lining up for me. Because I cared for him, I left my gloves on, not subjecting him to what so many feared.

Our bodies collided in the comfort of my luxurious bed, and sweat dripped down his forehead. We had been at it for almost half an hour when a crash resounded outside. I interrupted his attentions to cross the room and look out my window—which, thanks to my status, allowed me an excellent view of the entire kingdom from the front of the castle. It also allowed me to see the front door and the terrifying sight that stood there. He reached to pull me back into bed, but my horrified glare halted him.

"What's wrong, Princess?"

My throat closed around words I couldn't get out. Tremors wracked me. Though I had never seen it in my lifetime, I had learned of this dark magic. This type of magic had been banned by my great-grandfather ages ago. Not just in Revell, but in the entirety of the eight kingdoms. Somehow, a large undead stag stood at the castle entrance. No fur covered his ghastly frame, which was larger than I had ever seen. His muscles rippled with every attempt to slam through the door with his impressive antlers. Stifling my fear to protect us, I finally forced the words out.

"We need to get to the doors of my suite and lock them. It's here for me." But how? All the mages on my father's council had surrounded the castle with wards. We should have been protected. I wasn't sure how I knew I was its target, but I felt it deep in my bones.

Run, Cecilia. Run.

I could hear the voice in my head. Warning me.

"What's here for you?"

I pointed out the window as he rose from the bed—his tanned skin slick with sweat—to bear witness to what I was watching. His jaw dropped as the stag finally managed to break through the door. We were running out of time. I threw on my silk robe and made a run for it. Though my rooms were not as impressive as my father's or brother's, the king kept up appearances by providing me with my own wing. I exited my small bed chamber into my mediocre parlor, looking for anything I could block the door with.

Crashing in the halls outside was the only indication that, if I stalled any longer, I would be too late. Careening out the door into my hallway, I looked left to where my wing met with the main hall of the castle, and there it was. Luckily, the regal undead stag stood facing away from me. It was too close. So close that I could smell the stench of rotted flesh. The odds of making it to the door to lock it were slim. I silently crept backward into the parlor, eased the door shut, and bolted it as I continued backing into the room before I crashed into the wall of flesh behind me.

I pushed him back towards my bedroom and whispered, "I

didn't make it to the suite door, we're trapped." We were left with only the parlor, bathroom, and bedroom to hide in, assuming the creature didn't find its way in.

The panic began to show on his masculine face as his hands trembled by his sides. Henry was sweet, but he certainly wasn't brave or tough. "What are we going to do?"

I was scared too, but from a young age I had been prepared for the possibility of our enemies coming for me. They knew what an asset I was to my father, and he loved to use the threat of my abilities against them. They feared me. Most people did. Even the men who got a thrill out of their fear in my bedchamber on lonely nights. Once we were back in my bedroom, I lightly slapped Henry's cheek to stir him from his stupor. Though I could still hear crashing in the hallway, it didn't sound like it was getting any closer.

"Push the bed against the door just in case. I have an idea." He did as I asked, still naked. Though I had put my silk robe on, it was transparent and did little to keep out the chill of this breezy castle. But...it was better than nothing.

"What are you going to do?"

As confident as I was in my powers, I wasn't sure who had sent this thing or what magic it possessed, and I wasn't willing to risk everything betting on myself.

"We have to distract it. My father's council chamber is just down the hall—the stag went right past it. If I can lure it there, we can get to my suite door and lock it. I don't want to risk it getting in here, and there are plenty of highly skilled mages and armed men in there."

I walked over to my orb nestled in its pedestal on my dresser and ungloved my right hand, hovering my palm just above it. It began to light up, and though I couldn't hear it through the thick stone walls, I knew a lovely musical tone was emanating from its sister. My father wouldn't answer—he never did. I wasn't sure why he had even bothered to provide me with one, because every time I tried to use it, I got a reaming in front of the entire council.

It had sat unused for two years. But this time it would be worth it.

We listened intently for what felt like an eternity before we finally heard the heavy door of the council chamber open—the only sound that could actually make it through the walls. I smirked as I heard the reaction I was hoping for. The crashing in the hallways changing direction. It was headed straight for my father and his lackeys—and my brother. There would be enough armed and magically talented men in there to handle the situation. If they couldn't, I wasn't sure I cared.

"Go! Lock my suite door behind him, now! Hurry!"

Henry took off, and I prayed he wouldn't chicken out as I listened with my ear glued to the stone wall. I ungloved my left hand and placed it on the wall, which allowed me to see the events unfolding in the chamber next door. Warmth suffused up my arm and tingled in my palm. The picture wasn't quite what I'd see in person, but it was as if the wall were a glazed window instead. This was one of the many talents of mine my father didn't know about, or he would not have put his council chamber right next to my bedroom. Since he never heard anything from my side— regardless of my nightly escapades—I was sure he didn't think it was possible. Without my power, nothing but the door could be heard through the wall.

My father's most loyal henchman—the leader of his personal guard—Captain Thomas Lovelace, opened the door just as the stag was about to break through it, lured by the melody from my call. He was startled for only a moment as the stag knocked him back and barreled into the room. Drawing a dagger from his belt, he threw it through the stag's skull. It instantly dropped to a heap on the floor, but that didn't prevent most of the old men from quivering in fear and shock. A few had risen and held balls of fire, ice, or water in their hands. Aside from the captain, my father was the only one that didn't look frightened. I chuckled at the look on my brother's face. I was surprised he hadn't pissed his pants. This was the heir my father had selected...

"Well done, Captain. As usual, you are the only person I can count on. The rest of you lot, sort out what that thing is and who sent it. Captain, I'll leave it to you to check that the princess hasn't been harmed and to see why she interrupted our planning." The captain nodded, lips tight and face stern, as he spun on his heel to follow his mission. I smirked, hoping that Henry had secured my suite well enough to give the captain a challenge.

My lover reentered the bed chamber with none of his earlier fear showing. I dropped my hand from the wall. Only a single other soul knew of this talent, and I wasn't about to let it slip now. I had seen enough for tonight, and we were about to have a visitor. It was time to put on a show. Kneeling on my bed, I turned to face him. Henry was not a complicated man, and while I had always been kind to him, he often did exactly as I said, though I never knew if it was out of love or fear. Despite our recent ordeal, it seemed the adrenaline had put him back in a frisky mood, so my persuasions wouldn't be necessary.

"Well, seems like we're safe now. How about you get back over here?" I untied my robe and slid it off my shoulders, dropping it to the floor. He gave me a filthy smile and climbed onto the bed to kneel behind me, re-entering me from behind. He slid my long, wavy, blond locks off my shoulder to kiss my neck as he reached around to massage my breast with one hand and gently run the fingers of his other hand through my wetness. I tipped my head back into his kiss with a moan as my bedroom door opened.

My bedchamber was small, so when the captain filled the doorway in his armor, he was within arm's length of where I knelt near the edge of my bed. He stood there with the same expressionless face he always had. His light stubble covered a handsome face with chiseled cheekbones, marred only by his constant scowl. Even though he was always in armor, it was obvious how well-sculpted his body was from his rigorous training. He held his head high, knowing his power and fearsome reputation. His uniform always looked neatly pressed and his hair well-groomed, and I deeply wanted to mess it all up, leaving him disheveled.

Though he had never seen me naked before, my dalliances were no secret to the staff of this castle. Henry paused only for a moment until I gently pushed back into him, encouraging him to continue. His hands roamed my body as the captain looked on—so close that I knew he could feel my breath on him. Henry's musky scent combined with the mint and pine aroma emanating from Captain Lovelace. Though his face was stony, the bulge he shuffled to hide elicited a snicker as my eyes dropped to it.

His cheeks reddened slightly when he realized I had caught him—but if the rumors were true, he was no stranger to a naked female body.

"Well, hello, Captain. Get bored of Daddy's awful meeting and decide to come have some real fun? You're welcome to join in and lend a hand. I won't bite," I said as I looked at him through lowered lashes.

He eyed my gloved hands. Though most of my father's court did so with disdain or fear, his look was curious. "Your father sent me to see why you interrupted our meeting."

It was difficult to focus on the conversation, as Henry had picked up the pace, edging me closer and closer to the precipice with every thrust. Letting out another moan as I writhed under the building pressure of my oncoming pleasure, I let out a sultry chuckle. "Well, I thought that was obvious. That creature broke into my rooms, and the only way to get it out was to sic it on them."

I saw the faintest twitch of a smile on the captain's lips before he returned to the stone-faced, expressionless wall I was used to. "You do realize it could have hurt any number of high-ranking officials, including the prince and the king? Are you that much of a selfish brat, Princess?"

"Oh, absolutely. Can't you tell?" My smile turned mischievous as I gestured to my current predicament. "Exactly why I invited you to join."

He stood there silently, still staring, expecting me to say more as Henry nudged me closer and closer to culmination, his thrusts turning ravenous. As if he were trying to stake his claim on me in front of another man. I longed to grab the captain and close the small gap between us. I had never minded onlookers for my exploits, but I was pleased to find that Henry didn't either as his hands explored my body and squeezed with each surge into me. Perhaps if I conceded to the captain's questioning, I would get my way.

"I would never willingly put any member of this kingdom in harm's way. I think you are aware of that, Captain. I knew they had you in there, and I was confident in your ability to protect everyone. Plus, almost all of them have very strong elemental magic. I doubt anyone feared for their safety. It was the only way to protect myself, as you weren't here to save the day. I do, however, want to express how grateful I am that you saved my family and, in turn, me. So, please allow me to show you my appreciation."

Keeping my hands gloved, I reached out to remove his leather gloves and pulled him towards me, looking to him for permission and allowing him ample time to deny consent. When he didn't protest or put up a fight, I placed his hands on my breasts as Henry continued thrusting into me. I noticed the bulge in his pants grow even larger, though he did eye the entry door to my suite.

Through my lashes, I watched him like a piece of meat and slowly leaned in for a kiss. I had planned on a simple, soft press of my lips to his, but electricity coursed through me, just under my skin. He astonished me with a flick of his tongue, urging me to open for him. I relented as his grasp on my breasts grew more urgent, his thumbs and forefingers pinching my nipples as I tipped over the edge into my orgasm. I collapsed against his armored shoulder with one last moan as my lover held me up from behind.

Though Henry was my favorite of my dalliances, I had never felt sparks like those the captain had just sent through me with a kiss and a flick of my nipple. I couldn't help but wonder what it would be like for it to be him behind me instead. He seemed to have the same thought as he broke his stone face to smirk briefly and wink as he put his gloves on and left the room. He shouted over his shoulder, "I'll let the king know your call was a false alarm. Have a lovely evening, Princess." He strode from the room with more cockiness than I had ever seen him muster. Despite laying in the arms of another man that night, his momentary smirk lingered in my dreams.

Chapter 2

I closed the door to her suite and sighed, pinching the bridge of my nose. *How could I let my control slip like that?* I had done my best to avoid her these last few years because I knew how strong the pull between us was, and I hadn't been sure I could contain myself. I had been right to do so. I'd be lying if I said I hadn't enjoyed every second of it, but it had been a terrible idea. What a bizarre day—I had gone from the lowest moment of my life to the most pleasurable moment I had been yearning for in a matter of hours. I would cherish that memory, because I wouldn't let it happen again.

I returned to the council chamber, which was in chaos. Mages of every magical inclination leaned over the ghostly stag, arguing about who could have sent it and how it had been enchanted. Certainly, none of them could perform magic on this level. The king was the most powerful, followed by a handful of fire mages and, of course, myself. The rest were water, ice, or flora mages. Their skills came in handy, but their powers were weak. Most knew basic magic like casting wards, but the magic of the gods that had been passed down to the eight kingdoms had waned in power over the last century. Many of the kingdoms surrounding us had mages, but none were powerful enough to be capable of this. Except for some rumors of those in Hinch.

"Ahh, Captain. What have you learned from that brat of mine?"

"Your Majesty," I bowed graciously. "The stag had entered her suite, and she panicked. She made the call to lure it here instead to protect herself. It was a false alarm. She isn't in need of anything."

"Of course, she isn't; what could she possibly want? She is fed the best delicacies in the kingdom, housed in luxury, and has been kept safe from every danger she could imagine while she wastes away her days with the help instead of finding a suitable husband."

I knew better than to argue, so I kept my mouth shut and my hands behind my back until he excused me. I couldn't wait to get to my room and wash off the memory of this morning. Unfortunately, I'd have to wait for the King to finish his address to the council. As I tuned out his voice, my mind replayed the morning's events.

Before I saw her descending the dank and musty stone stairs to the dungeon, I got a whiff of her peony and rosewater scent. It was so out of place in this miserable dump. I remained in the corner, avoiding the slow drip of the mucky water from the ceiling. The always stoic guard, hidden from her during her arrival. That was how the king preferred it—mostly to keep my magic a secret.

"What is it, Father?" The princess asked with an exhausted huff as she came to a stop outside the cell. Two of his guards were tying a beaten man to a chair inside of it while Aldus stood in the corner, avoiding anything that might sully his pristine attire.

"My men have apprehended another spy. I need you to learn where he has come from and what he intended to do while he was here," the king ordered, extinguishing the flame in his hand that he had been using to brand the victim. King Aldus was a fire mage, but his power far exceeded any other. He could shape it more adeptly and throw it harder and farther than anyone else in the eight king-

doms. Except his daughter. Possibly. We had yet to see the full force of her magic, but he surely feared it.

She rolled her eyes and removed a single glove. Her father jumped back, and his two guards lunged in front of him, grabbing at their swords. She chuckled, "I'm just doing as you asked. I can't question him without removing at least one, can I? You paranoid old bat."

It was hard to contain my smirk. Though I had always been loyal to the crown, it had grown harder over the years as he had, in fact, become more and more paranoid. And ruthless. And less human.

She looked down at the beaten man slumped in the corner of the cell and sighed. I imagined she was trying to process whether he had deserved his treatment, because I absolutely was. She put her hand on his forehead and began to work her magic. She was always so delicate with these men he tortured, which pissed him off. I knew I'd be the one to pay for it later, but if it kept her safe...it was worth it.

"Who are you?" She asked, her tone dripping honey.

"My name is Elric, Miss," he whispered politely.

"That's Princess to you, you conniving scum!" her father shouted, now safe on the other side of the cell. He bared his teeth as his hands clenched the bars, as if he were squeezing the life out of the man himself.

She knelt in front of the man and continued, her hand on his shoulder now. "What are you doing in my father's kingdom, Elric?"

"I am a refugee, Princess." He viewed the king with fear and made sure he chose his words carefully. "The Kingdom of Engleheim has fallen. First with a plague, then with fires to destroy the infected. It got out of hand, and the few of us left fled for our lives. We were hoping for sanctuary here, but I was the only survivor to make it this far."

"LIES!" King Aldus shouted again.

"Father, do you forget how my power works? He cannot lie." She shook her head in disgust at his outburst.

He watched her suspiciously. "He wasn't pained by your magic.

You didn't intrude into his mind. With each new arrival I ask you to question, you seem to use less and less magic."

"It only causes pain when they try to lie. You keep asking me to question innocents. Bring me a true criminal and I will show you suffering, Father. Perhaps you would like a round? I'd love to watch you squirm."

"Leave now!" he commanded his daughter.

She rushed out of the dungeon. Right past me without a hint of recognition. But my heart felt the pang. One last floral whiff was all she left me with.

"Captain Lovelace, it's your turn." I wanted to argue that she had been right. Men could not lie under her touch. This man was innocent and had done nothing but try to survive. He'd be lucky if he made it another hour.

King Aldus evacuated the remaining guards from the room for a private discussion. He hid his fear of his daughter from the rest of the council for a good reason, but I had gained enough of his trust that he never hid it from me.

"Thank goodness for your shadows, boy. You shouldn't fear me if you ever need to intervene against her to protect me. Understood?"

I nodded, though I knew that would be the one command of his I would never carry out.

"I thank the gods every day to have you, Captain Lovelace. The entire kingdom knows how useless Entriken is, and Cecilia is a lost cause. I'm certain I can always count on you. Your father would be so proud of you if he could see you now. Now, do what you can with this mongrel. We need answers."

Aldus had me torture the man with knives and shadow magic until he passed out, before bringing him back with my healing magic—repeating the process over and over. Normally, using my shadows only made my skin tingle, but using it for too long drained my energy and left my muscles fatigued. It had been far worse when I was younger. Learning to control it had been agonizing. The worst part right now was how much blood and sweat stuck to my brown hair, like a paste against my face, making it look even darker. Most of my men kept their hair shorter, and I was jealous of that advantage in this moment.

The entire kingdom knew of my skill with knives and swords—as well as my healing magic—but only King Aldus knew of my shadows. Shadow magic was a dark omen to most, thanks to many prophecies, but an ace up the sleeve for the king. The princess may have been more powerful than I was, but he had made me ruthless. I abhorred it, but I was good at my job. I had to be. My stone-faced expression had become part of who I was, and I made sure never to let any emotion show, no matter what situation I was in. To the man being tortured, I'm sure I looked like I enjoyed it. Each time I did it I felt less, and I feared that one day I would grow to enjoy it.

My shadows wove in and out of the man, slicing his skin and battering his body into releasing screams and whimpers. Over time, I had learned to drown out the painful noises. I just closed my eyes and focused on a promise I had made. The reason I had to do this—I had no choice.

King Aldus finally dismissed me when I had taken the torture too far and was unable to bring Elric back. The only mercy I could offer was pretending I could no longer revive him. I was given just enough time to clean the blood off before I was summoned to the council room. Just when I regained my composure, the beacon for Princess Cecilia's rooms came to life. My heart sank and my stomach clenched. She was in danger. I couldn't just leave to go check on her—the king would have my head. Fortunately, he sent me to go check on her instead.

Without pause, I yanked open the door, and an undead creature barreled in. I removed a knife from my belt and whipped it at him, covertly firing shards of my shadow magic behind it. The creature dropped quickly, and I exited the chamber before the King had a chance to interrogate me, too.

I came back out of my reverie when Prince Entriken elbowed me in the ribs. Though we remained friendly out of necessity, he had changed in the last few years. As his father's puppet, he did very little thinking for himself, but I was grateful he had brought my attention back to the present. The king had been speaking to me, and I had been totally unaware. I had been too distracted thinking about how witnessing Princess Cecilia with another man had turned me feral. I had wanted to rip her lover's heart out and throw it out her bedroom window. The only thing that had stopped me was the sight of her naked. I had spent nights with many different women to distract myself from my agonies, but none of them compared to the work of art that was her body.

"Are you listening, Captain Lovelace?"

"I'm sorry, my King. My ears were ringing so loudly that I missed you calling my name."

"Of course, none of these idiots have been able to figure out where this beast came from or what kind of magic created it. The rest of the council will be adjourning for the evening. Can you handle cleaning this mess up, Captain?" His undertone wasn't lost on me. He wanted to know what my shadow magic could glean in privacy. I nodded my agreement, and the council left us alone to clean up the body.

"Should I find you in your rooms if I discover anything, My King?" I asked after the rest of the council had gone.

"No need, Thomas. Just dispose of it. Some things can't be solved."

I watched him leave with furrowed brows, wondering what the hell that meant.

Chapter 3

Cecilia

T he next morning, I sat in bed reading before I was interrupted by a pounding on my door. Henry didn't even stir after the exhausting fête we had had. He had attempted to elicit a second round from me in the middle of the night, but my mind had remained on Captain Lovelace. He had been my father's right-hand man for the past five years—succeeding his father when he passed—but we had known each other since we were kids. Sure, we had played together as children when my mother was still alive, but since reaching maturity he had become so serious and always seemed exhausted by my antics.

Most other men in the castle didn't hide their attraction to me. I knew how beautiful I was, and my status and powers aided my cause. Thanks to my love for food, I did have a little more curve, but I was proud of it. None of the men seemed to mind. But Captain Thomas Lovelace had never thrown me a second glance. Perhaps it had been the circumstances. What man could resist the temptation of the situation he walked in on, but the sparkle in his eyes and his smirk had stirred up so much confusion. He was an enigma.

Throwing on my robe, I tossed my book on the nightstand

and opened my door to find that enigma on the other side, arms crossed and wearing a fierce expression. Glad to see this wasn't going to be awkward. He was right back to his normal self. He didn't make eye contact, instead looking past me to the man out cold in my bed.

"Your father requests your presence in the council room, Princess," he said flatly, tucking his arms behind his back. Not even a twinkle in his eye in memory of what we had done last night. He glanced at the book on my nightstand and a pinch of confusion tugged at his brow.

With a sigh, I tightened my robe. "I'll be there in thirty minutes. I'm going to bathe and get dressed."

"I wouldn't recommend that. He is rather irate. Just get dressed and come with me." He didn't turn or leave the room to let me change. I wasn't sure if he didn't trust me to listen, or if he just wanted to watch, so I—of course—made a show of it. After untying my robe, I let it slip down my back, watching him over my shoulder as I dropped it to the floor in front of me. I bent forward slowly to accentuate my ass as I picked it up.

I looked back and caught him staring, but he was quick to avert his eyes and kept any emotion off his gorgeous face. I gave up, finished dressing, and threw on a nicer pair of gloves. Red silk this time. "Let's go."

He led the way, held each door open for me, and announced me to my father.

His council sat around the very large cherrywood table that consumed most of the chamber's space. It was round and engraved with the symbols of all eight Original Gods and their magic, rotating between fauna and flora gods and goddesses. The magic that had become more and more diluted over time. One of the older men sitting at the table—who I remembered to be a fire mage—smirked at me. It wasn't the predatory kind of look I was used to, but I didn't acknowledge it.

My brother Entriken stood next to my father's throne—the

side furthest from me—and barely lifted his eyes from the floor. We had been so close when we were younger, but after our mother died our father had separated us immediately. Our classes were separate—we even had different teachers—and he had begun having my meals sent up to me instead of letting Entriken and I eat together. I would sneak out of my rooms to look for my brother, but it seemed to be a one-sided attempt. After a year of that, I had given up trying to see him. I still loved him dearly, but I didn't know anything about him anymore.

His eyes met mine for just a moment, and a glimpse of the man Aldus had tried to have me torture yesterday flashed through my mind. He had the same defeated look in his eyes—the bags underneath them—and the shaky hands that he tried to hide by gripping the hem of his shirt. He looked away before I could even grin at him. I hoped he knew how much I still cared for him.

My father sat on his golden throne, clutching the armrests and seething. He was the epitome of a tyrant, if you asked me. "How lovely of you to finally join us, Daughter. Too busy sleeping in after a long night of doing nothing?"

So this was how today was going to go. Holding up a finger to make my point and get under his skin, I said, "Actually, his name is Henry. Though you know that, because he is one of your personal servants, and I'm sure his presence is missed most nights as you prepare for bed." I leaned my back against the gray stone wall farthest from him and began to pick at my smooth, crimson gloves, feigning boredom. This would be anything but boring. He hated when I embarrassed him in front of his council. Currently, their jaws were on the ground at my impropriety. It never ceased to amaze me that they still weren't used to my escapades. The mage that had smirked at me earlier covered his face with his hands to suppress his laughter.

My father's face reddened as he lurched to standing, his eyes ready to pop out of his head. "Enough of your insolence, child. You are a princess of this kingdom and my only daughter. You better start behaving like it." He had been trying to get rid of me since I was eighteen. For ten whole years, he had wanted to pawn me off to the highest bidder as a bargaining chip for more power or alliances with other kingdoms. Since then, he had taken to sequestering me away in my rooms to punish me for my avoidance of my "duties."

I rolled my eyes, then caught the captain's. Though he kept his face stony, I swore I saw a hint of mischief in his eyes. "Please, we're all aware I am not the favored child. There's no need to pretend in this room, Father. You have your heir, and you just keep me locked away—only letting me out to do your dirty work when you see fit. As such, I enjoy my leisure because it's all I have. Now, you've wasted enough of my time. Why did you bother interrupting my...activities to drag me in here?"

Had anyone else spoken to him this way, they would no doubt be headed for a flogging or a beheading. That wasn't something I needed to worry about, as my father and his men were terrified of me. I wiggled my gloved fingers to remind them, only making eye contact with a few to strike fear in their cowardly hearts. They all looked away quickly except for one. I never remembered his name, but it started with a *Z*. He was a fire mage, and supposedly a powerful one. In all the times I had watched council meetings through the walls, he had been the closest to opposing my father—respectfully, of course—but often had to concede to the despot. He held my gaze firmly, face only wavering to crack a tiny grin.

My father's face was overheating, and though he kept steady, the tone of his voice gave away his instability. My brother was standing next to him, making sure to avoid my gaze. Growing up, we had been inseparable until mother died. I assumed he and the captain remained friends. Entriken was taller and stronger than father, but he had no backbone. He had let himself go when it came to personal hygiene and health, and I feared for his mental health. His shaggy red hair had grown longer and matted, and his clothing was wrinkled like he had been sleeping in it. His once emerald-green eyes were now a pale mockery of what they had been, and he had been steadily losing weight. He would live in Father's shadow forever, and that was just how Entriken liked it. Except right now he looked terrified.

"This behavior is exactly why you are not the heir. You are useless. I demand to know why you interrupted my meeting yesterday. I've asked you repeatedly not to use the beacon unless it's an emergency." The insults didn't sting anymore. They were empty, and I was used to them.

"And I haven't in years. It was an emergency, as I'm sure you noticed when that monstrosity entered your council room. My life was in danger, and it was the only way to get it out of my suite. I figured you would prefer your number one defensive weapon to remain alive. Perhaps I presumed incorrectly? Did your captain not tell you this was so?" I scanned the room for reactions and noticed a few of the younger mages in the room hiding smirks.

"He did indeed, and luckily for you, he slew the creature before anyone was harmed."

"As I was sure he would. Have you figured out who sent the stag and why it was here?" I asked, examining my brother once more. His eyes dropped to his feet, and I could see his hand trembling at his side.

"Not that it's any of your business, but no. We don't know who sent it or why." He stared at me blankly but didn't speak again.

"Can I go now?"

"Do you think this is funny, Cecilia? Is everything a joke to you?"

My brother crossed the room to hand Captain Lovelace a piece of parchment. I slipped off one of my gloves as he blocked my father's line of sight. Reaching out, I grabbed his arm as he passed me. Those who sat around the council table that could see let out a loud, collective gasp.

"In fact, Father, I did find it quite funny. And I'm sure I'm not the only one who thought so. Tell me Entriken, did you find it funny?"

He squirmed in anguish as my most well-known power burned through him, sending tingles up my arm. It tingled more when they tried to fight it, and he was fighting it. He had no option but to be truthful, and the more he fought it, the more it hurt. "Yes," was all he whispered as he stiffened and his eyes filled with fear, a tiny hint of the formerly bold emerald flashing in them.

He wasn't the only one that looked horrified. My father had informed me repeatedly that my gloves were to remain on at all times within this room for that exact reason.

"Captain, subdue her now!" My father shouted.

I let go of my brother's arm and lit a fireball in the same hand. "There's no need for that, Captain. I've had enough fun for today. Assuming my father is done with me, I'll gladly go back to my rooms."

Captain Lovelace had moved a few steps closer but eyed my fireball warily, flicking his eyes back and forth between it and my father, and awaited further instruction with his hand at his sword. As if that would stop me.

My father's face lit with a menacing glower. "You may leave, but you've earned yourself a full-time babysitter who won't be leaving your wing until you can get your act together."

One of his soldiers raised his hand. "If I may, Your Highness. I'd like to volunteer to keep an eye on the princess for you."

"That's very kind of you, Caden. Unfortunately, Captain Lovelace is the only one capable of doing so. Do you think you can keep my daughter in line?" he asked, turning to his favored captain.

He nodded, the ever-obedient servant. "Yes, sir, I can handle your daughter."

I cackled loudly, pulling all the eyes in the room back to me. Except my brother's. I wondered if he would be punished for his admission, but he was the favorite. I was sure he'd be fine.

The captain glared at me as he gestured to the door and glanced at the fireball again, still lit in my hand.

"Thanks, Dad, always a pleasure. Can't wait to do this again soon." I sauntered out with hips swaying, making sure to look back and smirk at all the assholes watching me leave.

When we got back to my rooms, Henry had left to attend to his duties, which I was glad of. I was curious to see how tonight would unfold, given the new circumstances. I flopped down in the pile of pillows that my maid had arranged on my settee as she smiled at me and prepared to leave the room. "Thank you so much, Amelia. Are you feeling better?"

"Yes, Princess." She looked over at the captain nervously, as if afraid to speak in front of him.

"Go ahead, Amelia, you may speak freely."

"I appreciate you giving me the last two days to rest. It was much needed. I stopped at the library and swapped the books you finished for the next few on your list."

"Of course," I smiled at her. "I appreciate all you do for me. It was the least I could do, and thank you for the library trip. I'll bathe myself. If you could, just ask Alwyn to send my meal up, then go get some more rest."

She nodded and left the room, carefully closing the door behind her.

"So, you can handle his daughter, huh?" I raised my eyebrows at him.

"Poor choice of words on my part." He took up his position by the door, arms crossed behind him.

"For the record, you're welcome to handle me all you like. Otherwise, this whole 'locked in my rooms babysitting me' thing is going to be awfully boring for you. I'm sure it will be a pleasant break for you though, from always having to be so angry and serious all the time," I shrugged my shoulders and made a mock angry face to tease him. It didn't work. Tempted to tease him further, I instead picked up the top book of the stack Amelia had left and began reading quietly. "You don't have to stand by the door all day, you can sit down. I won't bite."

I could see the wheels turning in his head before he sat down in the chair across from me and clutched his hands together on his lap, sitting up so straight and stiff it was laughable. My eyes dropped back to continue reading now that I wasn't worried that he was uncomfortable.

His stare was so strong I could almost feel it burning through me, but then it turned to the cover of my book and his head tilted. "I thought you were reading smut. Is that a book on vegetable gardening?"

I snorted at his assumption, though I wasn't surprised. "I also read smut, but yes, this is a book on vegetable gardening. It's a very fascinating subject, and one that might be handy for the future of our kingdom."

"Huh," he said, but refrained from elaborating anymore.

"You're going to get awfully bored just staring at me. You sure you wouldn't rather do something more fun?" I asked suggestively.

"No offense, Princess, but you're not my type," he said rudely, like a slap to the face.

"I sure seemed like your type last night," I retorted, dropping my book into my lap and giving him the full brunt of my glare.

"Sometimes men have momentary lapses in judgment. I'm sure you're used to that, given your history."

My jaw dropped in shock and, for a moment, I was speechless. "Like you don't have a reputation too Captain Cock...Fuck what my father says, I don't need a guard to keep an eye on me. I'm not going to do anything stupid. Go find one of your trollops and leave me be." I jumped up to storm out of my suite when another knock sounded at the door.

I swung it open angrily to find Henry standing on the other side. "Princess Cecilia, I brought you breakfast before I have to go back to..." he trailed off and his face dropped when he noticed who was sitting in my rooms.

"My father's orders. Apparently, I need a babysitter now. But perfect timing, I'm starving. Do you have time to eat with me before you have to go back to work?"

He looked down the hall then back inside at the captain, and his face split into a wide grin. "Of course, anything for you, Princess."

Chapter 4

These two fucking make me sick. It's clear she has no feelings for him whatsoever, but he's staring at her with those doe eyes as she eats each bite of her food and it's pathetic. I took a deep breath as I put my hands in my pockets, having resumed my position by the door when he entered. *Every so often her gaze full of ire burns through me. I know he's been throwing me angry glares too, but I could care less about that. I swore to myself I'd distance myself from her, but locked in her rooms with her? This is going to be atrocious.*

When he had started placing morsels of food directly in her mouth, I couldn't help but roll my eyes. The bacon, eggs and toast had smelled delightful when they had first been delivered. But after watching that, there may as well have been ash stuffed up my nose. I couldn't deal with this. "Hurry up, Princess, I have places to be, and if I have to babysit you, that means you have to tag along. You've wasted enough of the morning."

Not even looking in my direction, she stated, "I sure don't want you here. You know where the door is, since you've done a fine job of blocking it all morning."

Tipping up one side of my mouth with all the cockiness I

could muster, I said, "Sorry, Princess, Daddy's orders. You have ten minutes."

"I haven't even bathed yet," she said, turning to me with flames in her eyes.

"No need. Where we're going, it'll be better to clean up after."

She sighed and turned back to Henry with a pout. "I'm sorry my dad is doing this to us. I promise I'll make it up to you."

He tucked her hair behind her ear and kissed her roughly before taking her plate and leaving.

"Change into something less...fluffy...and let's get going." She did look adorable in the frilly, light pink dress that hung from her shoulders down to her shins, but it wouldn't do for what I had planned. I crossed my arms as she huffed off to do as I said. Though I got to boss people around often given my position, it was way more fun when it was the princess. She came out in a brown tunic and pants, which were perfect for my plans. She followed as I led the way to the training grounds where I usually whipped my men into shape. And where I kept myself in shape.

I had spent the last year renovating these training grounds, ensuring my men had the best equipment the king was willing to provide. We had a rack of proper weapons as well as a few racks of practice ones lining the round dirt training area. A short wooden fence surrounded the entire thing, except for two openings on opposite sides for entry. The training area had once been grassy like its surroundings, but it had been trodden down into dirt from excessive use. We also had a few training dummies made of straw and adorned with the colors of whatever kingdom Aldus currently held in most contempt. Right now, the training area was full of my men.

"What are we doing here?" she asked, looking around in disgust.

"You lack discipline. Perhaps teaching you in the fighting ring will help you in other areas of your life. It has for most of my men. How much training have you had? Judging by the state of you, I'm guessing none." I looked her up and down. She was beautiful, no doubt, and I knew she was powerful. But it was clear she had never attempted hand-to-hand combat.

"My father doesn't believe in letting women train. We're weak," she teased, with a saccharine smile and sultry tone, as she ripped off her gloves and threw them on the ground.

I made sure to hold my ground and show no fear. The only truth I was afraid to share was how I really felt about her. She wouldn't ask that anyway, so I was safe—but my brain had forgotten to tell the butterflies in my stomach that. "Good, I was going to tell you to take them off. Hand-to-hand combat isn't exactly fair without the hands now, is it?"

With an intrigued look in her eyes, she asked, "You're not scared?"

As I shrugged off most of my lightweight armor, I did my best to prevent my shirt from lifting, but her eyes darted away after a peek. "Why would I be scared? I have no secrets you would care for. Let's gauge your fitness first with a few laps around the ring. Get those muscles warmed up."

She rolled her eyes at me but did as I said, doing her best to keep up with me. Given how much I towered over her, I wasn't surprised that she was winded after two laps at my light jog.

"We're going to test out some fighting stances next, and I'll show you how to throw a few different kinds of punches. No magic. I just want to see what you're capable of without it."

She rolled her eyes. "Isn't the running enough? I'm tired. Besides, when would I ever not have my magic?"

"Of course you are, because you don't do anything all day. This is why your father is so pissed at you. Why do you think he assigned me to watch you? And there are ways to stop magic wielders from using their abilities. You're just lucky not to have encountered any of them."

She plopped down on the ground and crossed her arms. "Because he hates that I talk back to him, but other than reading and Henry, what else is there to do?"

Waving my arm across the training field, I replied, "You could get yourself into shape. Since I took over as captain, things have changed. We let women train now."

She looked up at me and tilted her head, scanning my face. "Clearly"—she stood up—"I'm not cut out for this. I'm already exhausted."

Gods dammit was she stubborn. "Every day you'll get stronger and tougher. You just have to build up your endurance. And you have to give a shit."

"Maybe you should take your shirt off—it might entice me to put in a little more effort."

Fighting with every bit of my control to keep my composure instead of laughing, I said, "That's not going to happen. The other night was a one-time thing. I got caught up in the moment, and I assure you, it won't happen again."

"If you say so. Hey, how about we make a trade? I train, and in return you give me something I want?" She reached out to touch my arm with a bare hand and I held my ground, but my heart clenched and all the hairs on my arms rose. I swallowed but held her gaze. She smirked and looked me over, assessing.

"Not happening." Her power sent warm, zapping tickles up my forearm, but so far, no pain.

"Why?"

Keeping my face still as stone, I refrained from letting any answer enter my head for fear she would dig something out. But she didn't prod. Either she had forgotten I knew how this power worked, or she was taunting me and expecting me to fear her enough to just give in. Eventually, her hand dropped when she realized I wasn't going to answer. Thank the gods. But then my heart sank when I saw her face fall in disappointment. Although, that was good, right? It would push her away. I hated being an asshole to her, but it was for her own good. I couldn't keep looking at her frown though, or I'd crack in no time.

"If you're not going to take this seriously, then you can sit over there and watch us train each day. I'm not giving up my daily regime because I got stuck with the spoiled brat that's a constant disappointment to the kingdom." My words had struck—I could tell by the tears forming in her eyes—but I turned before I let it guilt me into telling her the truth. It was better if it stung, at least now she would stop trying to seduce me. There was only so much one man could take.

She moped at the edge of the ring for the first hour until my men began removing their shirts due to the scorching midday sun. I didn't think I would have to fight to get her here the rest of the days if her pleased grin at their sparring was any indication.

In the middle of sparring with Caden—one of my good friends—a piercing scream rang out. Whirling, I found a large, black bird attacking Cecilia. Caden and I both rushed towards her as she batted it away and attempted to throw small fireballs at it, which only set the few trees around us on fire. Mayhem erupted, as it was rare for any of the guards to have magical powers. The one who did have water magic tried to put out the burning trees as we approached the princess.

Upon closer inspection, the bird appeared to be afflicted by whatever had taken root inside the stag. Whether her fire wasn't working or she was just missing I wasn't sure, but it was my duty to protect her. Drawing my knives from my belt, I was careful to conceal my shadows as I sent sharp shards of them barreling at the bird alongside my knives. The bird dropped to the ground next to Cecilia, who had curled up in a ball on the ground and was covering her face with her hands.

I examined the bird and handed it to Caden. It had the same signs of decay and dark magic the stag had had. Black, oozing goo escaped where my magic had cut it, along with the stench of death. So not even Cecilia could hear, I whispered. "Bring this to Kai. I want both of you to look into it, but don't say a word to King Aldus. Be covert."

"Yes, Captain," Caden said. He looked around at all the soldiers scrambling to put out the fires and stuffed the bird into his oversized shirt before jogging away.

Kneeling next to Cecilia, I tried to pull her hands away from her face to assess the damage. She fought me at first, swatting me away as if I were the bird. "It's me. Relax, it's dead. I need to see how badly you're hurt."

She finally let me pull her hands away to reveal multiple scratches from the bird's claws, but luckily the beak had not made contact. There were no signs of poisoning or dark magic taking root in the wounds, which meant she didn't need to see the royal healer. With the commotion from her fires, I doubted any of the men had seen what had actually happened. I wished to keep it that way.

"Just a few scratches and bruises. Nothing I can't heal myself. Is it ok if I touch your face?"

A few stray tears ran down her cheeks as she nodded, still sitting on the ground and trembling. I smoothed back her hair as I placed both palms gently on her cheeks and let my healing powers permeate her skin. The cuts stitched themselves back together, and the bruises retreated.

"All better. We should call it a day. What do you think?" Her eyes met mine, and I felt a squeeze in my heart.

She nodded, and I gave her my hand to pull her up. "Thank you," she mumbled.

The way she was looking at me—as if with adoration—had to go. I wouldn't be able to fight it. "Perhaps if you took training more seriously, you would have been able to fend off a merc bird on your own."

"You're a dick, do you know that?" she huffed at me before she silently followed me back to her rooms with her arms crossed, avoiding looking at me.

Good. If she hated me, she would stay quiet, and maybe I'd get through this week faster. And unscathed.

<h1 style="text-align:center">Chapter 5</h1>

<h2 style="text-align:center">Cecilia</h2>

Thomas had witnessed many of my *investigative* sessions with my father, and I had always made sure to put on a good show. Even when it hadn't been obvious that he was there, I had known he was skulking in the corner. I also knew how the kingdom believed my magic worked. Though most of it was right—that I needed to inflict pain to dig around in their heads for the truth—I could get a read on them without it. There was something he didn't want me to find out. Something he was trying to block, and it was driving me mad. It was suspicious that he had withheld the information when I had questioned him about a bargain and implied it would be something sexual. But why was he holding back? We had already had one sexual encounter, and he was known to have had his fair share of women. Was he afraid of my father? I had a week to achieve my mission to break him, and I was going to enjoy every second of it.

When we got back to my rooms, I held my silence and stripped naked right in the middle of the sitting room. It was the least I could do after he had saved my life from that flying horror and healed me, even if he had been an ass about it after. He wasn't wrong though—I should've been able to fight off a bird, but I had panicked. I had never been in a fight or attacked by anything, and my brain had just shut down. It was time to take his training more seriously.

I left my clothes on the floor just outside the bathroom as I washed off the sweat from the day. Though the run had been miserable, it hadn't impacted me as badly as I had let on. I just didn't want him to make a habit of forcing me to endure this absurdity. At least now I could sit on the sidelines and watch the half-naked men fight. It was puzzling to me that Thomas hadn't removed his shirt as well. He had been covered in sweat by the end of it, and from the inch or so glimpse I had gotten of the hard planes of his lower abdominals, he certainly didn't have a body to be embarrassed about.

Exiting the bathroom naked after having dried myself off, I caught him looking before he turned away and yelled, "Gods, Cecilia, put some damn clothes on."

"My rooms, my body. Not happening," I said, crossing my arms over my breasts and pushing them together. He turned back with an angry glare to match my own but kept the rest of his face emotionless, eyes exploring my body before turning around to face the closed door. How was I going to get him to crack? I scavenged my dresser for a night dress that covered enough but would still catch any man's eye and fluffed up my hair before returning to the sitting room. Taking up my favorite spot on the couch, I crossed my legs and cracked open my book, the slit in my dress landing mid-thigh for maximum seduction purposes.

Thomas turned around slowly before he ensured I was decent and said, "Thank you for being an adult."

Keeping my eyes on my book, I responded, "Most adults are perfectly fine with nudity, but since you insist on acting like a child, I figured this would make you more comfortable. Now, if you'll kindly shut the hell up, I'd like to read."

A knock sounded on the door, and Thomas answered it without waiting for me to acknowledge it. Amelia entered with her head down and attempted to dash to my bathroom to clean up. That wasn't like her. I jumped up to get in her way and lifted her chin gently with two bare fingers. Her green eyes fought to hold the glistening tears sliding down her cheek. Her short, red hair did nothing to hide the swollen discoloration on her cheek. Normally she pinned it back, but it was hanging free today, which was the first thing that had given her away. Her fair skin made the bruise show even more. "What happened? Why are you bruised?"

She remained silent. She knew I'd never use my power on her. She was also one of the few that knew how well I could control it. A fire burned inside of me, and I was ready to turn on the culprit. Amelia wasn't just my maid. She was my best friend. And under my protection.

"Amelia, please. Tell me what happened and who did this?"

She took a deep breath, knowing I wouldn't relent. I doubted it would even cross her mind to think I'd force it from her. "King Aldus came to the kitchen for a midnight snack last night and caught me eating what Chef Alwyn was preparing," she whispered, glancing in the captain's direction.

That motherfucker. "I'm so sorry, Amelia. Please don't put yourself in that situation again. You're always welcome to eat here, and I can get anything you like sent up."

"I don't want to risk you getting in trouble, Princess."

"Please, I'm in trouble constantly. I'd rather my father focus his ire on me. Go take a nice hot bath, and I'll have the captain send for my meal. I'll make sure he tells Alwyn I'm extra hungry."

She nodded, knowing it was useless to argue with me. As she headed to my bath chamber, I remembered something.

"Captain. Can you please use your healing powers to heal Amelia?"

"And why should I do that?"

Glaring at him with all the ire I could muster, I said, "Because, I'm the Princess."

He hesitated. "Your father injured her. I would be going against him if I did so. I don't think that's wise."

Lighting a fireball in my hand, I tilted my head at him and grinned deviously. The warmth spread up my arm and into my heart, not quite as hot as the rage I held back most days. "It's a lot smarter than being dead, is it not? I'll keep her hidden. He won't know you did it if that's what you're afraid of. And...I'm the princess. I may have said please, but I wasn't asking. That's an order, Captain."

His eyes scanned me as his infamous scowl deepened. I enlarged my fireball and pulled my hand back ever so slightly, which did the trick.

"Fine. But if your father finds out, you best believe he will hear that you forced me into it. Threatened me with bodily harm, even," he said with a growl.

He stalked over to Amelia and placed his palms on either side of her face. She flinched away at first, but she knew I'd end him if he hurt her. Her shoulders relaxed, and she sighed with relief as his healing powers finished the job.

"Thank you," she whispered to him, before nodding at me and heading in to take a bath.

Extinguishing my fireball, I sat back down and resumed my reading without another look in his direction.

"You're welcome," he said gruffly. I heard his boots stomp back to his guard position.

"Threats aren't the same when you say thank you for them. You should know that after working for my dad for so long. Who do you think I learned it from?"

"He's going to be livid when he finds out how much you let the help get away with."

Excuse me? Absolutely the fuck not. I could feel my fire inside me, itching to get out. The flames were being stoked by my anger. "Get away with? I sincerely doubt he even remembers who he injured. He doesn't see faces or people, he sees property. They're humans. Just like us. Just because that asshole sired me doesn't mean I'm any better than them. But I'm in the position that I'm in, and there's nothing I can do about it. I can at least treat others with respect. Something you may want to consider with how much pull you have around here. Although I'm sure you and your men are no better. I saw the way she flinched. How many times have you struck her?"

His jaw tightened and his eyes enflamed, his cheeks reddening. He closed the space between us quickly and pointed a finger in my face. "I have never, and will never, strike a woman outside of war and the training ring. That is a coward's action. I cannot help it if people fear my reputation. That fear is integral to my position."

My brows raised at his slip. The way I could easily push his buttons did something in my lower belly I wasn't proud of. "Oh my, Captain. Did I just hear you call King Aldus a coward? How he would *love* to hear that."

"That's not what I meant..." he barely got out between gritted teeth.

"Oh, it was. But don't worry, your secret is safe with me. Now, if you don't mind, I would like to get back to my book. Be a dear and arrange for some food to be brought up. Tell them I'm *extra* hungry today." I didn't have to touch him to know he was telling the truth about never striking a woman, but I still enjoyed watching him get so irritated.

He may be the mighty captain, but I'm sure somewhere in there was the little Thomas I had grown up with. Aside from my brother, he had been the only child around. Since we were babies, we had played together and been educated together. On a daily basis, he had been kind, humble, and intelligent. When I had fallen and cut my knee on a stone, he had patched me up. When I had cried over something a teacher had said to insult my intelligence, he had yelled at her until she cried. Afterward, he hugged me and told me how wrong she was. But something had changed since then. Since my father had gotten his claws in him. I just hoped he wasn't too far gone.

Shockingly, he did as he was told and left the room to send one of his men to the kitchens. Amelia returned from the bathroom moments after the food arrived. She was healed and fresh but still wearing the same clothes.

"Please, take whatever you like from my closet, dear. No sense in wearing the same dirty clothes now that you're clean."

She nodded and disappeared momentarily, returning in one of my simpler dresses. "Thank you, Princess," she said as she tied up her hair.

"Of course, love. Now, come and sit with me so we can chat. You look like you haven't eaten in days."

"The king has cut down on our rations—we get one meal every other day now. Everyone but the royal family and the council members," she blurted, wringing her hands together before flashing her eyes to the captain.

"What?" I asked her, before I jumped up and whirled on Thomas. I marched over and poked him in the chest with a bare finger. "What the hell is going on that they are barely being fed?"

"That's none of your business, *Princess*," he spat.

I gripped his wrist roughly, daring him to try me. I let my fire power heat my hand a few degrees. Though he kept his face straight, I could feel his pulse picking up. His Adam's apple bobbed, but he was stronger than anyone else who had faced me.

"Oh, I think it is. This is my kingdom too. My people. I won't ask again. One last chance or we do this my father's way."

He took a deep breath and met my eyes. "Trade with most of the neighboring kingdoms has been cut off. We haven't had as much food coming in, and what we produce within Revell isn't enough. We have far more mages than farmers."

No tiny bursts of pain came back my way. He was telling the truth. "And the farmers and townsfolk outside our walls? Are they being starved also?"

He pursed his lips and paused until I amped up the temperature a few more degrees. The words flowed with rapid speed. "Let's just say, everyone in this castle has it a whole lot better than those outside of it."

"And you're just okay with this, Thomas? Do you not also have a duty to protect all those people out there?"

"I follow my orders. Your father is the king. His word is law."

"And you're a fucking monster just like him." I dropped his wrist with one last blast of heat, scorching a brand of my fingers onto his skin. Leaving him with a reminder of exactly what I thought of him. I turned to storm away, ready to run to my room and do my best to not throw up my last meal.

Chapter 6

If she only knew how much of a monster I had become. And why I had had to become one. She wasn't wrong, but it didn't hurt any less. Especially coming from her. But she knew the king. She knew there was nothing I could do to stand up to him. Only one person could, and she'd rather throw herself at every eligible bachelor in this castle than do a single thing about it.

She turned to storm away and avoid the argument, but I wasn't letting that happen.

"That's rich coming from the spoiled brat of Revell. You and your brother are the only two capable of making a difference in this Kingdom. Your brother is a fucking coward, and you're too busy humping everything to do a gods damn thing about it. So how about you get off your high horse and drop this bullshit act of caring about people, when we all know you don't."

Her jaw dropped, and I knew I had struck a nerve.

"That's not true at all, Captain Lovelace, the princess—" Amelia began, before getting cut off by Cecilia lifting a hand.

"You know nothing about me, Captain Lovelace. And as of this moment, I'm quite happy about that. Amelia, you're welcome to stay the night here, but I'm suddenly tired of our company. Have a lovely evening my friend."

Amelia nodded to her and took a seat on the couch as Cecilia stormed into her room and slammed the door. The young servant looked around awkwardly, occasionally peering at me.

"What is it?"

"Nothing, Captain Lovelace," she muttered, eyes flicking to Cecilia's door.

"Clearly there is something you wish to say."

"I'd prefer to not receive any more bruises, thank you."

"Do you really think I would strike you? Surely you've heard better about me from the rest of the staff?"

"And surely you've heard better about Cece than you insinuated. I have to be soft-spoken around the king for obvious reasons, but I will not stand by and let you smear her. She is my best friend, and she is the kindest person in this castle. Most days she is the only solace any of us have. I'll spare the details of her help for fear of the king's wrath, but I'm sure you've heard whispers. The princess is extremely powerful, riling her up would be..." Her eyes flashed up at me again and she huffed a laugh.

"What's so funny?"

"You like riling her up. I heard what happened the other night from Henry, and I didn't believe it. I never thought the princess would stoop so low..."

"Bite your tongue. Your time around Cecilia has made you too brazen, just like her." I wasn't sure if I was angrier at her boldness or the fact that she was right and had seen through me so easily. My shadows were hard to contain when I got angry, so I had to do my best to keep myself calm. This week had already been trying.

Her head tilted. Though her words were firm, her voice wobbled with a hint of fear. "Or what? You want the princess—hurting her best friend isn't exactly the way to do it. Maybe, just maybe, you should try being nice to me, and I can help you get into her good graces."

"That's the last thing on my mind."

She laughed again, a light tinkling sound that I imagined she didn't make outside of Cecilia's rooms. "Keep telling yourself that. When you finally come to your senses, I'm sure you're already aware she loves food, but she also loves books. Educational ones but also dirty ones. And flowers."

My blank stare didn't seem to deter her, as she smirked once more and pulled a blanket over herself as she readjusted to lie down on the couch.

"Suit yourself. Have a good night, Captain Lovelace."

"Goodnight, Amelia."

Another chuckle before she whispered, "See, now it's not so hard to be nice, is it?"

Chapter 7

Cecilia

After slamming my door, I held my palm to the wall to spy on their exchange. Amelia couldn't stand up to my father, but I wasn't surprised she was willing to stand up to the captain. Especially since I was right in the next room. And because she was the only soul who knew of my spying ability. She knew she was safe.

What surprised me was her insistence that the captain was goading me intentionally. Like he enjoyed it. Like he felt something for me. For a brief moment that night he had intruded on Henry and I, I had believed it too. Since then, I had convinced myself it had been a dream. I hadn't spotted a single sign of interest since. In fact, he had done his best to remain fully clothed during training while parading every other man in his guard half nude in front of me. But his reaction to Amelia's questioning was interesting. Maybe she was onto something? I should've used my truth powers on him.

Sighing, I climbed into bed and quickly drifted off to sleep.

I was startled awake bright and early the next morning by a knock at my bedroom door. Cracking my eyes open, I saw that the sun was just barely peeking through my window.

"Who is it?"

"Get up, Princess, we have places to be."

"Oh, fuck off. The sun isn't even up."

"Now!" Captain Lovelace asserted.

"Ugh, fine." I got up, grabbed a sundress, and headed towards the bathroom.

"You don't have time for a bath, you're lucky I let you sleep in as late as I did."

"Oh, relax. I'm just washing up quick." Though I didn't flat out lie, I took my time.

I expected him to take the same route as last time to the training grounds. Instead, he wove through the interior halls of the castle. As we passed the kitchens, each servant and chef assistant moved out of his way. They all at least nodded or smiled at me in acknowledgment, but many also greeted me by title and name, and I greeted them in kind. The castle had been well-staffed my entire life, but this was the first time—to my knowledge—that food rationing had been implemented. I'd make it my personal mission to figure it out.

"Do you know the names of every staff member?" he asked, turning to look at me with a raised eyebrow.

"Of course. I told you, they're all human. And they're all incredible human beings. Tamara for instance—the shorter lady with the blond hair we just passed—is assistant to Chef Alwyn. Not only is she one hell of a baker, but she is also raising four children alone. I couldn't handle that much responsibility."

"I'm not surprised your father treats you the way he does. You two are polar opposites in that regard."

"Not sure it's a worthy reason for my treatment, so that's quite brazen of you to say. But it's a fact I'm proud of."

"I didn't say it was a bad thing. I've actually mentioned to your father that having their backing may be beneficial to him."

My laugh was more of a cackle, but picturing that scene was the stuff of dreams. "I'm sure that went over well."

"Luckily for me, he thought I was joking. When push comes to shove, if we were attacked, I think the people within these castle walls would defend you over him. I'm not sure he's thought that part through."

Interesting. First, the comment about me being the only one who could take on my father. And now this? From the king's right-hand man no less. Perhaps I wasn't the only one that thought my father was a deranged maniac that needed to be stopped? He had said it so casually, but his grumpy façade held firm. Anyone walking past would assume he was only dragging me along at the behest of my father. None would suspect the treason he was insinuating.

"I really would've liked to see that. Such a shame I missed it." I also wondered when and where it had happened, because I spent a lot of time spying on them through my wall. "How are you torturing me today, dear Captain?"

"Every few days my men and I take a trip into the villages outside of the castle to report back to your father. You get to come today."

I halted and my heart leaped into my throat. Shit. This wasn't going to be good. I had worked too hard to keep my secrets, and I prayed that nobody in the town would let on that they knew me. It would destroy all the hard work we had accomplished if Captain Lovelace knew. "Are you sure that's a good idea? Seems like a security risk if you ask me," I said, trying to keep my breathing even.

He spun to face me. "That's why your hands aren't tied. You have my full permission to remove the gloves should we have any issues."

Well, hopefully everyone in the village was as smart as I assumed they were. "Fine. Let's go."

When we reached the end of the hall, he pushed the door open and held it for me to pass through. His men lined both sides of the walk, ready for him to lead the way. A few of the ones I was more familiar with winked as I passed them. Thomas noticed and rolled his eyes, increasing his pace to stay ahead of me after exchanging a few words with his cartographer. Tired of his power games, I slowed and greeted a few of the men. The one he had spoken to—a man named Kai—never paid me an ounce of interest. I wasn't sure what use Captain Lovelace had for a cartographer, but he seemed close with him. Kai was a muscular, blond man with a short and neatly trimmed goatee who was often around just before my attempted truth extractions.

"Good morning, Kai," I said with a sultry grin as he walked past me towards the castle.

"Good morning, Princess," he responded flatly as he continued on his path.

"Hurry up, Princess. We don't have all day," Thomas yelled from up ahead.

"You're walking too fast for me to keep up with. Go on ahead, I'll be right behind you," I said, taking the arm of the man next to me.

The captain's fists clenched at his sides, and I wondered if it was in aggravation or jealousy. I found myself hoping it was the latter.

The village was only about half a mile from the castle, but I was still glad I had worn sensible shoes. The captain slowed as we approached to allow me to catch up to him. The houses were small and arranged in little clusters. Their age showed in the thick layers of vines that had climbed them, reinforcing their strength. The roofs were littered with patches, but the village was otherwise intact. It smelled like freshly turned soil, and the sounds of hammering and livestock bounced off the homes.

"So what exactly do you do when you're here?"

"Talk with the townsfolk. See if they're having any security issues. Ask the merchants if they've heard any news from the road. Normally, when I return to the castle I provide a full report to your father."

I scrunched my nose at the mention of my father. Had my mother still been alive, she would've made these visits herself. But instead of gathering intel, her aim would have been to greet the villagers and ensure they were well taken care of. Well fed, well stocked, and in good health. I missed her so much, but I knew I could never live up to her standards.

We approached a small group of farmers working a field in front of a row of homes. Recognizing most of them, I widened my eyes and made eye contact with them, hoping they would stay quiet.

"The king sends us to check on your production. How are this week's crops looking?"

The older man, Gunther, nodded to me first. "Good morning, Princess Cecilia. It's an honor to have you in our presence."

I nodded back, grateful that was all he had said. "Good morning to you as well, sir. How are you and your family? Do you have enough for yourselves as well?"

The young boy next to Gunther had been standing as upright as possible with his hands clasped in front of him. At my question, his jaw dropped.

The captain scoffed and said, "This is a royal crop field. These crops are solely for the castle. All the families in this village are given rations out of a communal garden."

Shaking my head in disgust, I was sorely disappointed that the rumors reaching me were true. Gunther gave his report to the captain, who then stomped away to the next batch of citizens closer to the town center.

"How much do you need?" I whispered as I slowly followed, far behind any of his men.

"Don't worry yourself, Cecilia. We're getting by. Don't risk yourself for us."

"Gunther. Please. How much do you need?"

He sighed and quickly turned towards the guard. "We're going to run out within the next two weeks. The King has been asking for more than usual, and we haven't been able to skim any for ourselves. Too many guards here watching us lately. Anything you can do will be appreciated. We'll thin out our rations if we have to. You've been providing enough for us to get by without suffering, and we're forever grateful to you for that. Your mother would be so proud of you."

A tear fought its way out of the corner of my eye as I nodded, catching the gaze of the captain who had turned back to see what I was doing. "Thank you, Gunther. I'll see you within the week. Take care and tell Rebecca I said hello."

I sauntered my way to my scowling bodyguard just in time for him to ask, "What were you talking to him about?"

With a sad smile, I gave him my best performance. "He told me I looked so much like my mother. He claims to have known her, though I'm sure any villager would claim such. But he was a kind man. He deserves better than this bullshit you and my father are putting these people through. Working their asses off to feed us and not themselves? Surely, we can make an arrangement that benefits everyone."

Thomas laughed and took stock of how close his surrounding men were. None were close enough to hear our conversation. He crossed his arms and looked down at me from his towering height. A light breeze ruffled his dark, messy hair. "*We* could. King Aldus would never. This village serves the kingdom, and that's that."

"Those fields are almost barren. When my mother was alive, they were vibrant, lush, and teeming with vegetables of all sorts. I have some ideas on how we can improve the soil, too. We need to do something. Anything."

"Not unless the King orders it. Better start coming up with a speech to convince him."

I held his gaze with challenge in my eyes, and he tilted his head to the side.

"Nothing else to say, Princess?"

"Just one more question. Why did you really bring me here?"

Dropping his arms to his side, he chuckled. "I thought that was obvious."

Chapter 8

"I'm getting tired. How much longer do we have to stay, Captain?"

"My men can finish up here, so we can head back. Let's go." I offered her my arm, but she rolled her eyes and started walking towards the castle. The pain of that stung more than I'd ever let on.

Doing my best not to touch her as we walked, I said, "You surprise me."

She looked up at me and gave me an appraising look as I did the same. "What do you mean?"

"You're not the spoiled brat everyone thinks you are."

"I'm fairly certain only my father and those privy to his council think that."

I snorted because she was right. But they were the only people I knew, really. She *was* kind—and I had heard rumors of such from the staff—but it was a whole other thing to witness it first-hand. She genuinely cared for every single one of them. Knew their names, their roles, and their families. She also had immense power, and judging by the books that made their way through the rotation in her rooms, she was smart too. King Aldus had no idea what he would be faced with when she realized she was smarter than him.

My sole reason for forcing her to tag along was to see if it would inspire her. Enrage her. I had a feeling it was working if her glare was any indication.

"You don't approve of how I handle the village, I take it?"

"No, I don't. You're starving those people. For what? So, my father and his lazy ass mages don't have to lift a finger?"

"It's how you're fed as well."

She huffed and crossed her arms, picking up her pace to stalk ahead of me. I caught up easily with my much longer gait. "I've never seen you pitching in at mealtime in the kitchens or helping tend the crops."

Slamming to a halt, she spun on me, golden locks flinging over her shoulder as she ripped off her gloves, hands glowing red. "You don't know a single thing about me or how I spend my free time. You haven't since we were children, so don't you dare fucking judge me. If anyone is spoiled around here, it's you!" She jabbed her pointer finger into my chest, sparks flying where she made contact with my armor and left a tiny singe mark.

There was a reason we used this type of metal for our armor. Even with the other fire wielders on Revell's High Council, none could damage it. Power like Cecilia's hadn't been seen since the Original Gods had walked our realm. The current rulers of each kingdom were considered the New Gods, but they had given themselves that title. Each was more powerful than the other mages in their communities, but they had only a fraction of the power of the Original Eight.

I threw my hands up placatingly. "Whoa, whoa. Calm down. It's not your fault your father locked you away. I'm just saying it also helps you."

"Well maybe I don't want the villager's help. I can do just fine on my own."

Sighing, I stopped following her. This woman was exhausting. But as usual, she wasn't wrong.

Whenever I needed to think, I inadvertently found myself in the courtyard, walking among the statues of the Original Eight. I found myself there again, looking each of them over, trying to uncover which had blessed Cecilia with her gifts. It was the only explanation for her level of power. Or it could be part of the prophecy, but I stopped myself from going down that route.

It is said the statues had been erected while they had still walked among us. The time when Cecilia's great-grandfather had ruled. They were evenly spaced in a circle, each facing the middle, and alternated between God and Goddess, flora and fauna. Each of the Original Eight had a variety of elemental powers, though I couldn't remember which belonged to whom. We learned little of them in our teachings, other than their names and what they were the God of. Our king had been too fearful to tell us more. It was rumored that all eight now guarded the gates to hell, but others believed they had retired to another, more peaceful realm.

Amfai stood mid-height compared to the others, with a turtle in one hand and a snake winding its way up the other arm. His hair was long and tied back, and I imagined his robes had been green to match most of his reptile and amphibian creations. His eyes were cold and hard, and I was always disappointed his statue wasn't adorned with scaled armor. He didn't seem like the likely culprit.

Blathe was the smallest of them all, perhaps to be closer to the lush flowers and grasses she was the maker of. Her statue was topped with a crown of weeds and blooming flowers, and she wore a light dress, much like the ones Cecilia wore when not being summoned to her father's chamber. She held a single flower, but her smile reminded me of Cecilia, so much joy and warmth. I could understand her seeing herself in Cecilia, so my wages were on her.

Crann was the tallest of them all, not surprising for the master of trees and bushes. He was solidly built, like a warrior, and his armor had the texture of bark. He held a branch that split into a

"V" at the end, almost like a pitchfork, and looked ready to battle. I didn't see him connecting to our princess at all.

Feithida's wild waves were the first thing that drew everyone's eyes. It took closer inspection to spot the myriad of insects and arachnids crawling all over the statue's body. She looked unbothered, a sentiment I didn't think Cecilia would share in the same scenario.

Iasca's long, straight hair looked like it had been slicked down by water and stuck to her back. In both arms, she carried a large fish like a baby, the Goddess of all sea creatures. I had never been to the sea myself, but it surrounded all eight kingdoms. She looked too carefree, but I couldn't rule her out either.

Memach's statue had a kind and warm demeanor, despite his large frame. His plinth was the widest, with a wolf seated next to him and birds on his shoulders. Though I was sure he'd be tough in a fight, I had always guessed he was the type to wage a war of the minds. The woman who had my heart had certainly mastered the art of manipulation, but I had never seen her interact with animals other than the horses we had learned to ride as kids.

Muisa was beautiful, no doubt, and appeared fierce with her chin-length, pin-straight hair. She certainly had the sass and attitude to make the list of potentials, but fungus and Cecilia just didn't seem like the right pairing. Seven different mushroom types spotted the arms of the statue, and lichen coated her stone boots.

Thair was who I had suspected the most, mostly because of Cecilia's love of food. His arms were full of a variety of produce, and I could just imagine that warmth would radiate from him like sunshine if I were to meet him in person.

Though this contemplative visit had narrowed my suspicions down, I realized I needed to do some research to learn what their powers were rumored to be to get a more solid answer. But even if I had that, how would they have blessed her with their gifts? None had been spotted in our lifetime. How could any of this be?

The following morning, I decided to wake up Cecilia for another day of training. As I reached up to knock on her bedroom door, it flung open. She stood before me already dressed in training leathers and an angry scowl.

"I'm ready. Let's go. You need to teach me how to fight."

She elbowed me out of the way and headed to the castle hall as I just stared at her, dumbfounded.

"Are you coming?"

"Um, yes." I had no idea what was happening, but I followed her to the training ring anyway.

When we got there, she spun around and commanded me— my entire group of men taking in the scene. "Attack me. I need to be ready if something comes after me."

"With what? My magic, weapons, or fists?"

"All of it. I can't afford to get caught off guard and be scared like that again. Wait, you have magic?"

"Wouldn't you like to know, Princess. Let's start with the basics. I'll show you defensive stances first; then we can do some sparring. Stretch out a bit and we'll get started."

Shockingly, she acquiesced. I remembered her being a fine student when King Aldus had still allowed us to be educated together. It showed as she quickly took in the stances I taught her. She didn't argue, didn't complain, and was more serious than I had ever seen her.

"I think that's enough stances. I need to learn something real. Attack me and see if I can fight you off. I won't throw any dangerous magic at you."

"First tell me why. Why the sudden change of heart?"

She assessed how far away my men stood and glanced back at me, her cheeks turning pink. "Because I couldn't even stop a bird. What am I supposed to do against a dangerous enemy? You're right, Captain. I'd never survive if another kingdom came after us, and my father isn't exactly the best at making friends with the neighbors."

"Okay. Your best defense is to make a shield with your powers. It'll drain you of magic, but it will keep you safe until you can prepare your own attack. Or let somebody else reach you to help. We'll start with me running at you to attack you. Throw up a shield to stop me. After you master that, I'll try throwing knives," I said with a toothy, menacing grin.

She raised her eyebrows at me. "Fine. Try not to enjoy this too much," she said sweetly, lacing her tone with snark.

Taking a few paces from her, I faced her as she took up one of the stances I had shown her. I began to charge as she lit flames in her hands. Her eyes almost crossed in concentration as she tried unsuccessfully to force them into a shield, and I slammed into her. Knocking her to the ground, I landed on top of her. Disoriented for a moment, she looked up at me in surprise. A pang of lust hit me as I became aware of what parts of mine were against certain parts of hers and she shoved me off of her.

"You ran too fast," she said, breathing heavily as she stood back up.

"Oh I'm sorry, should I slow down to a bird's speed?"

"Not funny."

"I'm not trying to be funny. Your enemy isn't going to slow down. Or feel bad for you. You have to learn to concentrate and be prepared when things go wrong. Are you ready this time?"

"I've never learned how to make a shield before. I can only make small, pretty shapes. I have to figure it out first," she said, voice raised.

Taking a deep breath, I collected all the patience I could. "Close your eyes and forget about the fact that I'm about to crash into you. Light the flames in your hands and in your mind picture a bubble around you. Picture yourself funneling pieces of the fireball into the shield, like water into a bath, until it's a full bubble."

I gave her a moment to try it without charging at her, and she formed a square wall in front of her but not quite a full bubble.

She dropped her arms and whined, "I can't do it."

"Whether you think you can or you can't, you're right. Believe in yourself. This time, imagine pulling more of that fire from deep in the pit of your stomach until it's enough to surround you. If not, I slam into you again. Ready?"

I didn't give her a chance to answer as I launched myself at her, crashing through a bubble of flame that scorched my eyebrows but not my skin. I tackled her to the ground again.

"That was better. If I had given you more time, I think it would've kept me out. Let's go again."

I stood as I was speaking but startled when she jumped up, threw her arms and legs around me, and squeezed. "I did it!"

"Barely," I said, putting her back on the ground.

"Are you hurt? Did I burn you?" She looked me over and dusted the ash from my singed eyebrows.

"I'm fine, I had my own shield."

She pinched her eyebrows and crossed her arms. "What kind of power do you have?"

"None of your business. We go again. Get set, and keep me out this time," I said gruffly. I glanced over at my men—my two best friends, Kai and Caden, watched intently, both wearing shit-eating grins. "Gentlemen, run twenty laps. Now!" I ordered. They rolled their eyes and followed orders.

Over the course of the next few days, Cecilia let me train her. Some nights she drank after, some she went straight to bed. After about a week, she had mastered making fire shield bubbles that kept me out, and her confidence grew. Perhaps there was hope for this kingdom after all.

Chapter 9

Cecilia

Finally, one night after our training, Thomas didn't follow me back to my room. I raced back just in time to meet Alwyn for the supplies. I took the sack of food he had pilfered from the kitchen and kissed his cheek as he left. I stuffed extra blankets into my bed to make it look like I was asleep and left an empty wine bottle tipped over on the table. Utilizing my powers, I snuck out of the castle back to the village to deliver the goods.

Gunther shook his head at me when I arrived, "That was a close one the other day."

"I know. Thank you for not letting on that we knew each other. Captain Lovelace doesn't seem as horrible as my father, but I still don't fully trust him. Alwyn took what he could, but he said it's getting harder. I've asked Amelia to grab me some books on farming, and I've been saving some seeds. I know it doesn't help now, but maybe in the long run..."

Gunther rested his hand on my shoulder. "You're doing everything you can, Cecilia. All of us are eternally grateful. You are your mother's child through and through. We'll be okay."

I hugged him and returned to my rooms. Fortunately, Captain Lovelace was already asleep on my couch when I arrived.

His loud snores covered the creaking of the floorboards as I crept into my bedroom, silently clicked the door shut, and collapsed into bed. Every one of these trips drained me, but I had no other choice.

I awoke to the sound of birds chirping outside my window and smiled—it was going to be a beautiful day. My peaceful waking was interrupted by a knock at my main suite door and some whispering between Thomas and whoever had knocked. Shortly after, he came to announce that my father had requested my presence in the council chamber yet again. I was wrong. It was not going to be a beautiful day.

"What's wrong, Princess? Hungover from too much wine last night? I told you drinking is no good for you."

Snorting, I threw him a glare to convey how ridiculous he was. "I had two glasses. It takes a lot more than that to get me hungover." Turning away, I mumbled, "I'm used to drinking way more than that these days."

"Let's go. I don't want to be reprimanded by the king because you're taking forever."

"What does he want?"

"I have no idea."

Rolling my eyes, I threw on a shabby looking dress and slippers just as an extra insult to His Royal Majesty. Thomas scanned me and turned away. I swore I heard him chuckle. I reluctantly put on my red lace gloves and strode into my father's council chamber unannounced, with Captain Lovelace trailing behind me.

"Daughter, how nice of you to—"

I cut him off before he could give me the same old speech he always did. "Finally join you. Yes, yes, I know. You summoned me, so just get to it. What do you want?"

"Have somewhere else you'd rather be?" He questioned, one eyebrow raised.

"Actually, yes. Literally anywhere but here."

"I'm so glad you think so. In fact, that is exactly why I summoned you."

My brother looked uneasy standing beside my father's throne like a shadow. His hands shook as he wrung his fingers together. I hadn't seen him this worried since we were kids. When I spied through my wall, I often saw him getting berated by my father, but I had certainly had it worse. I could never figure out why the beloved heir always looked so scared.

I rolled my eyes. "Just get to the point, Father. You're boring Entriken." My brother's terror-stricken eyes shot up to mine. He searched the room, scanning each member of the council before dropping his gaze to his feet again.

"I'm growing sick of you, Daughter. You have contributed nothing to this kingdom. Your only value would have been what I might have traded you for, but you squandered all hope for those alliances when each of the princes came to visit."

"Contributed nothing? Tell me father, who is it that tortures the mages and mercenaries that spy on your kingdom to obtain information? I'm not so sure you'd be up on that high hill without me."

"Captain Lovelace is also very talented at extracting information from prisoners. You are quicker and have a higher rate of success since they cannot lie to you, but I'm starting to weigh how much that efficiency costs me, child. If you are not kept in line, perhaps I can learn to wait longer for fewer answers."

I shot the briefest glance at Thomas, whose face blanched under my scrutiny. My father had him torturing people? Was that what his hints were about? His lessons? Had he finally had enough? The kingdom knew him as a fierce guard, but he was an honest man. I hoped he was still a good one, trapped into doing the bidding of a maniac. He might be powerful, but I believed he would only use his power for what was right.

"And what is your threat, Father?"

"You have thirty days to wed, or you will no longer be housed, fed, or clothed here. You may choose from any suitable prince of a nearby kingdom or a noble of this one. But you have exactly one month before I toss you out on your ungrateful, perpetually inebriated ass."

The fire mage from my last visit here stood and addressed my father. "King Aldus, perhaps you are acting a bit rashly. We're all used to Princess Cecilia's antics, but none of them have warranted a threat to be kicked out of the castle. She is a far greater asset to this kingdom than an enemy of it."

My father glared daggers at him. "You do not sit on this throne, Zell. You have earned yourself a spot at that council table for your magical skill and loyalty to this kingdom, but that is a privilege I can revoke whenever I like. As you asked kindly, I shall let this one slide. Should you question me on my decisions again, it will be the last time you do so."

The fire mage sat down quietly, but flames burned in his eyes as he glared back at the king.

For the first time in my life, I was stunned into silence. My father had threatened me many times over the years but always with violence. Never with homelessness. I had nowhere else to go. He may have been an asshole, but I didn't think that even he could be this heartless. Marriage was a prison. Then again, so was being locked away in this castle. I wouldn't do it. If I said no—put my foot down—I'd be free. Free to live alone in the forest. I had my powers so I could keep myself warm, but I had no money and no survival skills. Was that why Thomas had wanted to train me? Had he known this was coming and wanted me to be ready to survive out there alone? I looked at him and his eyes widened as they flicked to me. He hadn't expected this either. But why did he care? He'd be rid of the spoiled brat he had been assigned to babysit.

Tears pricked my eyes, but I couldn't let my father win. I couldn't. I'd learn to make it on my own, without the luxury of the castle. I had to, right? What other choice did I have? Would Amelia or Alwyn run away with me? They were the only friends I had. Nobody else would even consider it. Surely, the fear that my father would come after them would outweigh their loyalty to me. Where would I go? All the villages were loyal to the crown as far as I knew. Could I use my powers to build a shack in the woods? Hunt for food? Resigning myself to a fate I knew I couldn't bear, I strengthened my spine and gathered my composure, ready to fight back. I couldn't let him see how much his words had affected me, because I knew how much he'd love it.

Captain Lovelace stepped forward, and my heart dropped. I steeled myself for the second berating.

"If I may, Your Majesty? I would like to speak."

"Of course, loyal captain. The floor is yours," King Aldus said, tipping his head in respect and flicking his fingers to go ahead.

Tilting my head, I observed Thomas cautiously. Though I had seen glimpses of the unexpected from him this week, he was still my father's most loyal guard. I had a feeling this wasn't going to be good.

Thomas turned to me with an unreadable face. "Princess Cecilia, I'd like to request your hand in marriage."

Quiet gasps and whispers echoed through the room—mine the loudest. My jaw hit the floor as the wheels in my brain started spinning. He wants to marry me? Did I want to marry him? Why would he agree to this? What in the fuck was happening? If the captain's proposal shocked the council, they were going to love what came next.

Taking a deep breath and holding my head up high, I smirked at him. "I accept, Captain Lovelace. I would be honored." I had always found him handsome, but I had abandoned hope years ago when he had taken to ignoring me. Whatever had made him change his mind, I was glad for it. Even more so because I knew how much my father would hate this, yet he would get exactly what he had asked of me. The perfect revenge.

I smiled grandly at my father, making sure all my teeth showed. He was a bomb ready to go off at any moment. There wasn't a chance in hell he had considered this outcome. If I knew my father, and everyone in this room, and even myself...we had all expected me to argue that this was unfair and unacceptable. But Thomas had offered me a second option. Though he hadn't been overly kind to me this week, his behavior in the village gave me hope that this was the right path.

"Why, Father, you're speechless! I assume you approve, seeing as Captain Lovelace is your most loyal servant. I'm sure he will keep me on my best behavior," I said, playing the doting daughter. I was having a hard time keeping the previous night's dinner down. And it was not the wine's fault.

He certainly couldn't argue this in front of his council. Though I was sure Thomas was going to get a private reprimand for embarrassing him. He finally responded through gritted teeth. "Of course, it is, after all, what I asked of you. I just didn't expect the captain to lower himself so. Nor did I expect you to acquiesce so easily."

Anger flared in Captain Lovelace's eyes, unbeknownst to my father, before he responded with dignity. "With all due respect, Your Majesty. Your son has been like a brother to me, and I've looked up to you as a father since losing my own. It would be a great honor to become your son-in-law. I think your daughter, rough as she may be, can be molded into the model wife."

Damn, he was good at buttering up my father, but the model wife part I could have done without. I'd love throwing that in his face later to get a rise out of him.

My father stood and circled Thomas, assessing him cooly before clapping him on the shoulder. "Valiant reasoning, Captain. You have my blessing. I assume her suite will be suitable enough for you both. It's much larger than you're used to, Captain, and more than the princess deserves. You may begin wedding preparations but do keep your budget in check. I'll have Henry move your things to her rooms. He will be taking up residence in your former rooms, since he will need a bed now that he won't be warming hers."

Of course he had to get in one last shot. "Of course, Father. Anything for the crown," I cooed in mockery. "I have but one request. I'd like to spend more time with Entriken. I miss my brother dearly."

Entriken looked up at me with longing, and I swore a tear formed in his eye.

"Denied. You'll leave the heir alone. You are both dismissed. Captain, please come see me later once you two are settled," Aldus ordered.

"Yes, of course, Your Majesty." Thomas bowed as I strode out of the room with pride.

I held it together until we made it to my suite, where I slammed and locked the doors with a huff. That was a close one. If it hadn't been for him, I would most certainly have been homeless in a month. Spinning to face my savior, I grabbed his face and kissed him roughly, stunning him into immobility.

"I don't know why you proposed, but thank you. I promise I'll find a way to get you out of this before then, but I'm glad I won't be on the streets for now." He had offered me a way out and that was it.

He shook his head in confusion. "You don't have to get me out of anything. It was my choice, Cecilia."

Chapter 10

It *was* my choice but not one I had thought I'd have to make anytime soon. King Aldus had forced my hand. I couldn't let him throw Cecilia out in the streets. She was powerful, but the loneliness...she'd never survive. Truth be told, I was glad he had done it. Selfishly, I wanted to marry her, but it was also the only way to do so and keep my promise.

"You could have any girl in this castle, and from what I hear, you have. Why the hell would you want the shunned princess? If the king catches you with another, he will sign your death sentence personally. Promiscuity is one thing. Adultery is still outlawed under penalty of death, in case you have forgotten," she said with a sad laugh.

"You're one to talk. I do recall walking in on you and one of your little lovers recently, did you forget? Something you'll have to do a better job at keeping secret, my dear fiancée." I hated how jealous and angry I sounded. "I intend to keep my vows to you, Cecilia. You didn't have to accept." Except maybe she had. I had offered her a way out, and that was it for her. Sure, she was attracted to me, but it was lust alone. She was the princess of the most powerful and wealthiest kingdom in the world. Why would she want to marry a lowly captain? I stood up taller and straightened my armor as I did my best to ignore the fluttering in my stomach.

There was a knock at the door before it swung open violently. Henry did not look pleased to be dragging my things into his former lover's rooms. He didn't seem to mind sharing her, but losing her was undoubtedly getting to him. He barely even got my trunk into the room before he dropped it with a huff.

Though there wasn't any sign of tears, she did look upset as she ran over to hug him. "I'm so sorry, Henry, I didn't mean for any of this to happen. My father—"

"I know, Cecilia. I heard the whole thing. I was in there, though I'm sure you didn't notice with all the commotion. You didn't have a choice. I'm not mad at you, I promise." He glared at me and made a quick exit.

Though Cecilia thought her wing small, it was much larger than the closet I had been living in. All I had in the way of belongings were a few items of clothing and a handful of heirlooms from my parents that sat in the single trunk Henry had dumped off. I had been minding her for only a short time, but I hadn't noticed before how many vases of flowers were scattered throughout her rooms. Perhaps Blathe *had* been the one to bless her. I still had research to do.

One of my men came to check on us after Henry's abrupt departure. "Ah, Caden, could you do me a favor?" Caden was the partner of my cartographer and a talented archer. He was responsible for handling our horses. He also had a unique power, providing energy to other magic wielders, which came in handy when their powers drained them on the battlefield.

"Of course, Captain. What can I do for you? Relay a message to Kai?"

"Actually, I was hoping you could stop at the library and grab me anything you can find on the Original Gods. Don't ask the librarian for help, just whatever you can scrounge up yourself."

Tipping one side of his lip in a smirk, he analyzed Cecilia and then looked back at me. He was a smart man, and I suspected he knew exactly why I wanted them. "Of course, Captain Lovelace. Anything else you'd like for your...research?"

"That will be all. Thank you."

"The Original Gods? What are you researching them for?" Cecilia's honey-sweet voice asked from much closer than I expected.

"Just staying educated is all. You inspired me, I guess."

She raised an eyebrow at me but said nothing more.

"You're welcome to take the guest bedroom if you like. I can ask Amelia to stay in her own rooms tonight. There's plenty of space and it's clean."

I wasn't sure if it was what she wanted, but it wasn't what I wanted. I *needed* to be close to her. But I didn't want her to know that. "If we are to keep up appearances, it's probably best if it at least looks like I'm staying in your room. We'll leave my stuff in there, but if it makes you uncomfortable, I'll sleep on the couch to stand guard."

"It's fine, you're welcome to stay in mine," she said nonchalantly.

We spent the rest of the afternoon cleaning up her mess to make room for my belongings in her wardrobe and dresser. I didn't need much space, but she did not keep a tidy bedroom. I was happy to leave everything in my chest in the corner, but she insisted I make myself at home. She even cleaned up her bathroom to make room for my items, but she was appalled at how little I had in the way of toiletries.

The cook—Alywn—dropped off dinner with a smile and congratulated us. I couldn't tell if it was genuine, but I doubted it.

"Please, Captain. Take a seat and eat with me. You're not just my guard anymore, you may as well enjoy the new lifestyle," she said, resting her hand on my bicep.

"Thank you, Princess." We both sat down, her knee just grazing mine.

"Of course. Welcome to your new life. Wined and dined and

bored to death! Cheers!" She clinked her glass against mine and popped a cube of cheese in her mouth.

We ate in silence as she flipped through a book. Judging by the cover, this one was dirty. And not the soil kind.

"Would it be alright if we call it an early night tonight? I noticed you've been staying up reading on the couch, but maybe you could read in your room so I could get some extra rest?"

"We just talked about this. I told you it's fine. Especially as future husband to the princess. You'll sleep in the bed with me."

"I'm not sure that's a good idea..."

"You've made it clear how you feel about me, Captain. I don't plan to seduce you. But you got me out of a serious bind with your kind proposal, so I'm not letting you sleep on the couch."

"Cecilia, you have no idea how I feel—" I started, but she stopped me with a palm.

"It doesn't matter. I'm also exhausted. I'll go wash up and let you change in privacy."

She did as she said and met me in her room. I had changed into a comfortable and simple set of soft pants and shirt, awkwardly running my fingers through my hair. "Which side of the bed would you like?"

She climbed in, sliding up against the wall. "I'll take the inside so you can keep guard and get up when you need to." She patted the spot next to her and I climbed in.

More sitting than laying in the bed, I crossed my arms and looked at her. "You sure you're ok with this?"

"You're not the first man to warm my bed, Thomas. I've made it very clear on multiple occasions that I'm perfectly fine with you touching me, and that was before I agreed to marry you. I can't help how much you despise me. But for whatever reason, I'm glad you found it in your heart to help me, so thank you. And yes, I'm sure." She leaned up and placed a hand on my chest as she kissed my cheek and gave me a pitying smile. "Goodnight, Captain."

I didn't remember drifting off to sleep, but I did remember her peony and rosewater scent enveloping me. I awoke alone in the middle of the night to a light tapping at Cecilia's door. Instinctively switching into guard mode, I jumped up and quickly strode across her bedroom to the doorway but halted when I heard whispers. Cracking the door open, I peeked out to watch the exchange.

"I'm sorry, Princess, it's all I could spare this time. I thinned out the stew to save enough potatoes and meat, but I'm afraid your father has been keeping a much keener eye on my stores," Chef Alwyn said.

"Don't fret, Al. I'm sure they will be thrilled. Lord knows it's more than my father sends. The seeds you saved from the squash and pumpkin last week will go a long way in the coming months. Thank you for taking all my research into account. They've been utilizing my new seed propagation technique, and it seems to be working. I can't tell you how grateful I am for your help, my friend." She patted his upper arm before giving him a kiss on the cheek and seeing him out the door. Once it was closed, Cecilia stood alone in the hallway until Alwyn's footsteps had trailed off.

Right before my eyes Princess Cecilia and the burlap sack she had been holding disappeared. Panicked, I raced out into the room where she had been standing and screamed her name until she rematerialized right before me.

"I was hoping you were still asleep," she said solemnly, her head sinking.

"Holy shit, Cecilia, you scared the hell out of me. You can turn invisible? No being I've ever met has that kind of magic. Only the Original Gods have that power, if you listen to the stories."

"And now you know why I keep it secret. I can't hold it for too long because it takes a lot out of me, but I'm able to hold it long enough to sneak out of the closest castle exit. I've learned the guard rotations well enough that I can meet my friend at the drop point and return with just enough energy left to get back to my bedroom. Then I have to sleep it off for a few hours."

"Do you have any idea how dangerous that is? All it takes is one guard or one obstacle that holds you up—your father—that's why everyone always thinks you're sleeping off the drink."

"Trust me, I know. But I can't let a whole village starve. And to be fair, half the time it is the drink."

"Spoken like a true queen. Now I know why your father is always going on about missing food stocks. I never would've guessed it was you. You get some rest. I'll deliver this to the village. Just tell me where to go."

She sighed and handed me the sack. "It goes to Gunther."

"Well, that explains a lot," I said, smirking down at her. "Friends with your mother, ay?"

"Look, if you're going to be a smartass, I'll just take it myself."

"I've got it. Go get some sleep. Can't have my future wife exhausted when it's not on my account." I winked, and her face flushed a deep red.

Thanks to my position, I was able to leave the castle and deliver the goods to a very surprised Gunther. He turned pale as a ghost when he spotted me.

"Don't worry, Gunther. Princess Cecilia sent me. I have some items for you."

He carefully took the sack from me, eyebrows furrowed in confusion. "I'm sorry, Captain. This is just so out of character for you. I feel like I'm being set up. What have you done to the princess? Why isn't she here?"

"I understand. She's safe, but I didn't feel right about her risking her own safety when I could so easily make the trip myself. I know my word doesn't mean much to you, but I assure you I mean you no harm. I've always carried out the king's orders, but after my recent time with the princess—who I am soon to wed—I've been seeing my priorities a little differently."

Gunther's jaw dropped. The news of our engagement apparently hadn't made it out of the castle.

"I should be getting back to her. Enjoy your night, Gunther. The princess sends her warmest regards."

When I returned to our suite, I cracked open Cecilia's

bedroom door to find her fast asleep. I made myself comfortable on the couch, and within moments, I joined her in the world of dreams.

The following morning I woke to a heavenly scent and discovered Cecilia setting up our recently delivered breakfast. Bacon and pancakes. Something I was only allowed to eat on holidays when the king treated his most loyal men. She must've been very careful to sneak in only Alwyn so nobody would see we had not been sharing a room.

"How did it go with Gunther?"

"Well, he certainly didn't trust me. He didn't look happy that we're engaged either. But he took the items."

She chuckled and took a bite of her bacon. "Well, you are kind of an asshole. Especially to people you think are below you. And princesses."

I raised my brows at her. "I'm starting to regret my proposal."

When we finished eating, her comms globe lit up yellow and began to play an angry melody. She peeked quickly at it before saying, "That's for you." I didn't know how she knew, but I guessed it was because her father never called her. I was used to being summoned by him, but normally he sent a servant to fetch me since I didn't have a beacon.

"Captain Lovelace, the wall guards brought in another spy for questioning. Meet me in the council room. Alone. I hope you slept well. It's going to be a long day for you."

"Yes, Your Majesty. I'll be right there," I said flatly.

"Looks like he's finally given up on me, huh? For the record, those men were all innocent. I wasn't pretending to use magic. I did as he asked."

"I know you did, Cecilia."

"What happened to them all?" she asked quietly. "I'm not sure I even want to hear the answer."

"That's not something you need to worry about. I can't keep your father waiting. I'll send my best man to guard your doors, but I think you can keep yourself safe. Use the globe if you're in danger, and I'll be back. If I'm not back by dinner, don't wait up for me. I have a feeling it's going to be all day and a late night. I'll have Kai and Caden switch off guarding you. Get some sleep tonight and I'll be back before you're up in the morning, okay?"

She nodded but ran over and stood on her tip-toes to kiss me on the lips. My hands instinctively grabbed her hips and pulled her closer to me before I realized what I had done. I let her go and she broke the kiss, leaving both of us with a smile. It was a sweet and simple gesture, but it felt so right.

I strode from the room with all the confidence in the world. I had the life I had dreamed of, but how long would I get to keep it?

Chapter 11

Cecilia

The next morning, Thomas was nowhere to be found. One of his men remained outside my door, only allowing Amelia and Alywn in when necessary. It wasn't until lunchtime that he finally showed. He plopped down next to me and began digging into my plate of food without asking. There were dark circles under his eyes and a redness that meant he had barely slept. Had he been aiding my father this entire time? I pushed my plate closer to him and leaned back against the couch. He gave me a sad smile and devoured the rest of the plate. My heart tightened in my chest as worry consumed me.

"Do you want to talk about it?"

"Not even the tiniest bit," he responded, spitting crumbs back on the plate.

"Fair enough. Want to hear how my day went?"

No response.

"If you're going to be my husband, you're going to have to get used to listening to me ramble about everything. I'm going to tell you anyway. I woke up and you weren't here. I worried about you for about five seconds, but then I saw how hot the guard you left was and decided maybe it wouldn't be so bad."

His lips quirked into a half-smile as he took a sip of my wine.

"I had breakfast, played with myself, read a book about irrigation, lunch showed up, and all of a sudden, here you are looking like some undead, dark, shadow magic kind of nightmare."

His arm flexed before he brought my glass back to his lips for another sip.

"It's odd. I always thought marriage was a prison. A life sentence. Who would've thought it would be my only salvation? Especially marriage to someone who has spent the last two decades ignoring me." I scooted forward to get a better look at him, brushing his sweaty bangs off his forehead. "I'm sorry, but you look like hell, almost-husband."

He finally let down his façade and chuckled. It was a cheerful, tinkling sound I hadn't heard since I was eight. That had been twenty years ago.

"It's nice to hear you laugh again. I missed that."

He ran his fingers through his hair before he responded. "My job isn't meant for fun. My job is to protect people, Cece." I smirked at my childhood nickname, which I also hadn't heard in ages. It wasn't like him to drop the formalities. Something was wrong, and I needed to figure out what.

After our meal, he resumed his usual spot at my door. Though I was dying to figure out what was going on with him, I knew the best way to attract a fly was with honey. Reclining back on the sofa, I hoisted my skirt up, knowing that from where he stood guard on the other side of the room, he'd be able to see I wasn't wearing panties. I ignored his presence as I held my skirt up with my left hand and began to gently play with my clit with the other.

I worked my way towards climax for a few minutes before I finally looked up to find his eyes boring into mine, full of heat. He didn't shy away from being caught, breaking his gaze only to follow my hand's progress.

"Enjoying yourself, Princess?"

"Hmmm, not enough. I could use a hand." I stopped for a

moment to unlace the top of my dress, dropping it to expose my breasts.

"I'm supposed to be guarding you."

"You told my father you would be 'handling me' and I'm sure you'll be able to protect me all the same naked should danger arise."

He chuckled, glanced once at the door and then back at me. He paused a moment longer, then locked the door and ripped off his gloves while holding my gaze. He raced over to me and dropped to his knees beside my settee. His calloused hand slid gently up my inner thigh. He ran a finger through my slit and groaned to find how wet I was for him. His eyes glowed with pleasure as he took my closest nipple in his mouth, flicking his tongue around the stiffened peak.

I cried out and gripped his hair as my back arched closer to him. His finger continued to run up and down my clit. "Oh my God." I had not expected that. This was not the Captain Lovelace I knew.

He chuckled around my nipple, backing off slightly to blow on it before circling it again with his tongue. "Tom is fine, Princess."

"It's not like you to drop formalities, Captain Lovelace. What's going on with you?"

He stopped the motion of his tongue and looked deeply into my eyes as he inserted a torturously slow-moving finger into me. Maintaining his silence, he began pulsing in and out in a smooth rhythm when a loud knock at the door startled him into jumping up. "Who is it?" he shouted as I partially redressed.

"It's Chef Alwyn, Captain. I have dinner for the princess and yourself. Is everything alright? Princess Cecilia never locks her door this close to mealtime."

Thomas made eye contact with me and sucked his soaked fingers into his mouth, licking off every bit of my juices before turning to unlock the door. "Everything is fine. It was just an extra precaution." He opened the door and motioned for the chef to enter. "Please, come in, Alwyn."

Chef Alwyn was one of the few servants in the castle who wasn't as thin as a rail—likely because he was one of my closest friends, aside from Amelia. He was in his fifties, and it showed in his salt and pepper hair. What was left of it anyway. He had lost his wife last year to a terrible sickness. It had taken me months to get him back to his current state of grieving but surviving. Most days now, he was even chipper, especially when I fawned over his cooking.

Father forced him to taste all the royal meals to ensure they hadn't been poisoned, so he was used to eating better than the others. I also snuck more food to him and Amelia.

The chef peered at Captain Lovelace with suspicion before turning on me in my disheveled state. That he was used to. Me being locked in a room with the captain—that was new for him. He knew of our engagement and had feigned happiness, but I was sure he knew we had ulterior motives. He flicked his eyes back and forth between us a few more times as he placed the meals on my side table.

"Thank you, Alwyn, my dearest. What delicacy have you brought me today?" I said, rubbing my hands together and practically drooling in anticipation.

"Your favorite, Princess. Roast duck with a cherry reduction, roasted potatoes, and steamed broccoli. Only the florets, none of the yucky hard stalks you hate." I chuckled and gave him a bear hug. He took the opportunity to whisper in my ear. "Captain Lovelace, really? Your father is going to be livid. How on earth did you crack him, my dear?" I swatted his arm as I dropped the hug and didn't offer any response other than a wink.

"And for me, Alwyn?" The captain had his hands tucked behind him, as if hiding evidence.

"Lucky for you, the same. A little better than you're used to the king feeding you, eh boy?" Cook tapped the captain lightly on the cheek and left the room.

Alwyn showing up had been like a bucket of ice dumped over me after such a heated session with Captain Lovelace. The only thing that gave me almost as much pleasure was food. The aroma filling the room was enough to pull my focus. I uncovered my meal and began to dig in ravenously, eliciting a raised eyebrow from the still-standing Captain. "What? It's delicious. You better dig into yours before I eat that too!"

"We were in the middle of—"

"We were interrupted, and I'm not letting this delicious food get cold. There's plenty of time for dessert, Captain."

He snickered and sat beside me, carefully taking his plate and neatly cutting the duck. "You seem to have Chef wrapped around your finger."

"Well, it doesn't take much around here—all the staff are so used to being treated like shit that a little 'please' and 'thank you' go a long way. Alwyn may not have fire magic, but this—" I held up a bite of duck with cherry sauce dripping from it to accentuate my point "—this magic is even better."

He raised his brow and took a bite, chewing slowly as he stared at his plate. He peered back up at me a moment later. "Just another reason your father fears you."

"What?" I asked, stunned.

He glanced at the door to my suite and lowered his voice. "He is the most powerful mage on the entire continent, but the entire council knows that you are stronger and that he is frightened of you. You also have the love of every member of the castle staff and all the citizens in the villages—something he doesn't. All he has are his brainwashed nobles."

"You mean the rich old guys with all the power. The only twelve people—aside from the king and my brother—in this kingdom that matter?"

He shook his head as he put a broccoli floret in his mouth. "I know you don't believe that, because I certainly don't. This kingdom wouldn't function without the people."

"Why are you telling me this?"

"Because a war is coming, Cecilia, and your father is a maniac who is going to get everyone killed."

I knew a war was coming, and I knew what my father was willing to risk to ensure he was the victor, regardless of how many died in the process. Including me. I was his number one weapon after all. It did shock me that his loyal minion was the one turning on him. But perhaps I had been right about Captain Lovelace after all. He had always wanted to do what was *right* as a child. I was glad to see that hadn't changed.

"And what am I supposed to do? I'm just a spoiled brat locked in her rooms with a captain as a babysitter." Sure, I helped the people out in small ways, but I knew nothing about war or being a leader. I had hit my capacity for how much I could contribute, and I wasn't going to kid myself into thinking otherwise.

He scanned my face astutely, "You're not surprised by this news?"

"In case you haven't noticed, I am right on the other side of the wall," I gestured to the wall between my rooms and the council room.

"But we can't hear your...nightly activities over there," he said, looking adorably puzzled.

I glared at him and let him ponder what he was missing. "I'm sure you, my father, and Entriken-the-favorite heir will be safe when he sacrifices me for the cause."

He scoffed. "Your brother is useless. He's just a puppet to your father. But you...you would make a great ruler. All the people would follow you in a heartbeat, and I think you'd be surprised at how many of the nobles would as well."

I furrowed my brow. "I don't get it. You've been my father's loyal servant for years. And you're my brother's best friend. Not to mention that you've ignored me since we were children. Why now? What changed?"

He sighed and roughly ran his palms over his face before there was another knock at the door. It was another of my father's guards who offered to relieve the captain from watching me.

"That's not necessary, tell the king I'll be taking 24-hour duty. I don't trust anyone else to protect the princess." The other guard leered in my direction before leaving. I was grateful I wouldn't be stuck with him. Thomas turned back to me. "I don't want to talk about this right now. Let's just say many of us have become aware of what a deranged tyrant your father is becoming. I'd rather enjoy our dinner and talk about something else."

I conceded and continued eating but gave him a coy look. "Fine, but only if you promise me dessert tonight."

He shook his head, stifling a laugh.

Chapter 12

Thomas

The rest of dinner was silent, but it was pleasant to not be eating alone and in the middle of the night like I usually did. As captain, I normally didn't get time to myself until the rest of the castle was asleep. This was a lovely reprieve.

Once Cecilia had finished eating, she stood and stretched. My heart tugged a little as her beautiful face scrunched up adorably. "I'm going to go take a nice, hot bath. I think it would be wise for you to guard me in there instead of out here, don't you?"

"As you wish, Princess." King Aldus had technically never said to stop guarding her, but he didn't seem concerned about the stag attack anymore. Regardless, I stood and followed her, stopping in the doorway and leaning against it. I was more agile in this light armor uniform than I would have been in my full armor, as long as I made sure my sword was out of the way. She dropped her dress to the floor in a heap and turned the water on, checking to make sure I was watching. I was most definitely watching. I gripped the doorway so hard my knuckles turned white. It was the only way to keep myself from joining her.

My heart tugged again, warring against my brain for what I wanted versus what was right. We were to be married. Surely that changed some things. But the promise I had made...Would this violate it?

She angled herself to ensure I got the best view and soaped up her partially submerged body as slowly as possible. I had never been jealous of suds before, but I was now as they dripped down every curve that I wanted to run my tongue over. She took her sweet time torturing me before she finally got out, dripping water all over the floor. "I think I forgot my towel. Do you mind grabbing it for me, Captain?"

"Not at all, and please, Tom is fine." Although I kind of liked it when she called me captain. I grabbed her towel from the hook in her bedroom, and she held out her arms.

"Would you mind drying me off, Cap—Tom?"

I hesitated. If I touched her, it was going to lead to more. Could I do it? I dried her as if she were a child and made sure to avert my eyes so I wouldn't be sucked in by her feminine wiles. I did well until I got a whiff of the scent I would recognize anywhere, only stronger thanks to its fresh application.

When my eyes locked with hers, she finally spoke again. "You realize I've given you permission to touch me however you like multiple times now, yes?"

That was all I needed to hear for that last string in my chest to snap. Fuck it. I dropped to my knees, my sword at my side a hindrance. Ripping it off, I threw it into the suite behind me. It clattered across the room before coming to a stop as I lifted one of her legs over my shoulder and ran my tongue up her center. I had wanted to taste her for ages, and she tasted even sweeter than I could have imagined. And I had imagined it many, many times. I licked her ravenously—unable to control how badly I wanted her — squeezing her ass with both hands as I pressed my face further in.

Her squirming and moaning confirmed she was enjoying it just as much as I was, but the icing on the cake was her grip in my hair and on the edge of the tub, as she clutched both to keep herself upright. I hoisted her up and placed her on the bathroom sink counter nearby to continue my feast, this time slowing down and taking my time to enjoy the taste of her. She was so wet, and it was for me. I licked around her clit as I slid a finger inside, pulsing slowly as I pressed harder with my tongue. I ran my other hand up her chest to knead her breast, gently flicking the nipple with my thumb.

I could sense her crescendo building from the frequency and increasing volume of her moans. It was the most magical noise I had ever heard, and I never wanted it to stop. Even the promise I had made shot to the back of my brain. There was no more fighting it. I didn't let up as she came but pushed harder with my tongue and quickened the pulses with my finger, adding a second as she exploded into my mouth. I lapped every drop, savoring the sweet, honeyed taste I had waited my whole life for. I stood and wiped my lips with a finger, sucking up the last remnants of her.

Her gaze burned into mine with a wild passion and she leapt off the counter to wrap her arms around my neck, kissing me fiercely. She pushed me into the suite until my legs hit her settee, and I fell backward as she climbed on top to straddle me. I massaged her thighs as she kissed me, pausing only to kiss her neck and suck on her nipples between kisses. *This is fine. We aren't having sex. This is just harmless fun. None of her other paramours have been executed by the king, and he knew of many. We would be wed soon as well. Surely that would save me, as long as I stopped...*

She placed her hand over my bulge and moaned. I didn't think it was anything special. Due to my profession, I had seen many men naked, but we did our best to avoid staring at each other. As far as I knew, I was slightly above average. She reached for the buckle to my pants, and I grabbed her wrist, halting her actions with a shake of my head.

"I think that's enough, Cecilia."

"But I want more," she pouted. I wanted to bite her lip and shove her down to suck my cock, but she didn't deserve that kind of treatment. She deserved a candlelight dinner and rose petals all over the bed. Not this. This wasn't just some woman I wanted to sleep with. This was someone I had cared deeply for. It wasn't right. It needed to be special. She needed to know how I felt, but if I did that now, I feared it would push her away.

"Not tonight. Not like this." She went to climb off me, but I stopped her, holding her in place. "I didn't say you had to stop *this*. This is nice; we can keep doing this."

She smiled and continued kissing me, dragging my hands back up to her breasts as she ground herself into my lap with taunting gyrations. This woman was unraveling me, and I wasn't sure I'd be able to stop it again.

Chapter 13

Cecilia

Thomas had been more honest with me this week than he had been since our childhood, but he was still keeping something from me. This engagement was a sham to keep me out of trouble—I knew that—but he had always been such a genuine person. I had never used my power to force the truth out of him, and I respected him too much to do that now but not enough to stop me from spying through the walls when my father summoned him the next afternoon. One good thing about Henry being gone was that I didn't have to hide this power.

I scurried into my bedroom, ripped off my gloves, and jumped onto my bed. I placed both palms on the walls to ensure I got a crystal-clear view of what went down. My father was in the council room, alone with Entriken. My brother's eyes were fixed on the ground, and his hands picked at the hem of his shirt as our father berated him.

"You're fucking useless, boy! I had so much hope for you when your water powers started manifesting, but now you can't even fill a glass. How are you going to lead this kingdom when I'm dead, Entriken? You need to toughen up!" He slapped Entriken across the face. It was the first time I had witnessed him harming my brother, but Entriken took it as though it had happened many times before. I had never noticed any bruises, but had I really looked hard enough?

With tears fighting to escape, he whispered, "You'll outlive me, Your Highness. You are a New God after all. Long live the King!"

The king smiled, pleased with his cowardly son's answer. The heir he would never have to fear.

There was a knock at the door, and the king called for whoever it was to enter. In walked two guards, holding a sagging man between them. He already looked to have been beaten, and I wasn't sure he was still breathing.

Thomas entered a few moments later, still wearing the smile I had left on his face. That smile vanished at the sight of what lay before him.

"Captain Lovelace can handle it from here, gentlemen. You may go."

They dropped the man to the floor with shaky hands and exited quickly—with Entriken following behind them—all three men watching the king warily.

"Where was he apprehended, Your Majesty?"

"Does it matter, Captain? He is suspected of spying."

"Of course not, my king. Are you sure you don't want Cecilia to have a go at him first?"

"She wastes my time and energy and no longer gets the information for me. Is there a problem, Captain?

"None at all. Always happy to be of service. I was just surprised. She's more powerful than I am, after all. Something she clearly inherited from you."

I had to give it to him; he excelled at stroking my father's ego.

Chest puffed up with pride, my father prompted him, "Proceed. Find out what he knows."

I watched as he double-checked that the doors were locked and drew his knives from his belt. The man began to scream as Thomas started to slice into him. The cuts were not deep—just enough to be painful as he drained him of blood. That pain was quickly eclipsed when shadows emerged out of Thomas' hands, piercing the man's skin and spreading apart the gashes there. He faced away from my father but angled toward me, and I saw every moment of regret and struggle as he endured his torture of this man. My heart was splitting in two as I saw how much it hurt him to hurt others. Especially those he believed to be innocent.

I was shocked that Thomas had this power, but I understood why my father had forced him to keep it hidden. Had anyone else witnessed this power, they would've had Thomas executed. It was dark magic, and it had been forbidden ages ago. If he had not been compelled by my father, there was no way he would have used this for evil. But why did he keep doing it? Why had he not fled? Escaped my father's clutches and made a life for himself elsewhere?

Perhaps he thought my father would hunt him down. King Aldus would certainly try, but anything was better than this. Now I knew why he had confessed to me. But what could I do to help? I had to help. I couldn't bear the thought of him being forced to bear this a single time more.

Each time the victim was on the brink of death, my father forced Thomas to bring him back to consciousness by healing him and start over. Tears streamed down my face, but I couldn't stop watching. If he had to suffer through this, so would I. Especially since we were to be wed. It may not mean anything to him, but marriage was sacred to me, and when I took this vow, I would mean it. I watched as this continued for over an hour, draining every last ounce of hope I had had for our kingdom along with my energy. Eventually, Thomas could no longer revive the man. I was sure Thomas hadn't tried his hardest, but he had put on the show my father needed and had still gotten no helpful information.

"Well done, son. Go get cleaned up."

I decided, once and for all, that I wasn't going to let him continue enduring this on his own.

Chapter 14

I dismissed my best guard from duty outside her—our suite. I quietly opened the main door and headed straight for the bathroom to wash up. I tiptoed so I wouldn't wake Cecilia. It had to be after midnight by now. I opened the bathroom door to find her kneeling just outside the tub, checking the temperature with her hand. She turned to face me with dried tear marks on her face. What had happened while I was gone?

My traitorous heart almost burst from my chest as my shadows flared with rage at whoever had made her feel like this. "Are you ok, Cece?"

"This is for you. Come here."

She was worried about *me*? Why? Had she heard? Even if she had, why would she care?

She took a warm, damp washcloth and gently wiped away the blood spatter on my face before taking my cheeks in her palms and kissing me sweetly. It was a loving kiss, without a hint of the sexual tension the others had held. She went to remove my shirt, and I stopped her. "I'm not trying to seduce you, Captain. I ran the bath to help you get cleaned up. I promise not to touch you otherwise."

"You should be sleeping, Princess. I can wash myself. How did you…" I trailed off, wondering how much she knew. Perhaps she had heard the man's screams. Distracted by my thoughts, I didn't realize that she had gotten my shirt off until her jaw dropped, while her sparkling blue eyes glistened with tears. I knew it wasn't my muscular physique. I was fit from my training, but the scars that marred my skin had always been the first thing that had caught the eye of the ladies who had been privy to my naked body. It was why I didn't remove my clothing during training, regardless of how hot it was.

"Was this my father?" She whispered the question, as if she didn't want to hear the answer. She ran her fingers over my scars, examining them but taking extreme care not to harm me. Her fingertips were warm and left my skin tingling as they moved. When she pulled away, I instantly missed her touch.

"No." I couldn't tell her it was from accidents while learning my shadow magic. The magic I couldn't tell her—or anyone—about. "Why did you run the bath for me, Cecilia?"

"I saw what happened in there and I—" She stopped abruptly.

"How did you see?"

No response.

"What did you see?" My breathing was becoming labored at the thought of her witnessing what I had done in that room, but surely there was no possible way. She would've kicked me out of her rooms the moment I entered and called off our engagement.

"Get in the tub and I'll explain. No more arguing."

The way she said it reminded me of Queen Isadora, and my chest tightened at the thought of my almost-broken promise. The queen had had a way of giving commands in a firm but warm manner that left the recipient unwilling to disappoint her. Cecilia looked so much like her, and her mother would be proud to know how much of the queen lived on in her. I did as she said, taking off my pants and climbing in. Though she didn't comment, I did notice her checking me out as I complied, which eased my tension a little. "Okay, I'm in. Now explain."

She dipped a washcloth in the sudsy water and began cleaning the blood and other bodily matter from me as she spoke in a hushed tone. "First, I understand why my father makes you keep your secret, and it's safe with me. I never believed those prophecies. You're the kindest man I know, and you would never use dark magic unless forced by the asshole that sired me."

"Princess…" I said through gritted teeth. My tone came across angrier than I would've liked, but she was used to being screamed at by her father. It didn't even faze her.

She raised a brow at me and spoke with an even but sassy tone. "No, let me finish. Now that I know your secret, it's only fair that I trust you with one of mine. But you should know that I have never told a soul about most of my powers. Especially not my father, but not even my brother or mother. Only Amelia and Alwyn know about a few of them."

She took a deep breath and held it as she looked me over. I worried she didn't trust me, and I wanted to scream at her that her mistrust was ridiculous. I'd never rat her out to her father. The way I felt about her—I'd do anything for her.

"In addition to forcing the truth from people, when my hands are bare I can use them to see and hear through walls. Stupid of my father to put his council chamber on the other side of my bedroom wall, don't you think?" She chuckled, but I was in no mood for laughing.

"That's why Amelia wasn't afraid of me. She knew you were watching and would protect her. And that's how you knew war was coming?"

She nodded. "Among other things."

"And you saw everything I did tonight. What a terrible person I am."

She snorted. "You are a good, kind man. My father is the monster. It's not just you. He berates my brother—the beloved heir—and forces many of us to do unspeakable things. He has to be stopped. I saw the anguish on your face, but you're not alone. You have me now. And if you want to run, we run. That's the only bit I can't figure out though. Why do you do it? Why haven't you fled?"

She continued to clean me up so gently and lovingly that I had no choice but to believe her.

Meeting her sweet gaze, I simply said, "To protect you."

Chapter 15

Cecilia

My dinner had been threatening to come back up since my father made Thomas torture that poor man, but Thomas's admission had it happening all over again. Chills ran up my spine, and all the hairs on my forearms raised in protest. "What do you mean to protect me?"

He had avoided making eye contact with me for much of his bath, but now his eyes dropped to stare at the water. He hadn't protested that my hands had been bare, either. Like he didn't fear me at all. There were only two other people who trusted me enough for that. My eyes welled up as I considered how much had changed between us recently. Had he grown to trust me as much as I now trusted him? I was certain I had fallen in love with him, but how ridiculous was that? Love was a sham. The only love between two people I had ever known had ended with one of them leaping from the highest tower and the other turning into a deranged tyrant. I didn't want any part of that.

"Thomas Lovelace, you tell me right this instant!" I kept my voice even but firm. He wasn't getting out of answering this one.

His gaze snapped to mine, probably because I had accidentally lit fireballs in my hands that gripped the edge of the tub, heating the water. My anger at the memory of my parents' failed love had consumed me without me realizing. I quickly funneled some of my ice magic into the water to negate it, and the coolness felt like a minty balm in my chest. His eyes widened at the next secret revealed.

"Sorry, sometimes that happens when my temper flares."

He smiled and reached out to cup my face. "You're incredible, Cece. Do you know that?"

I leaned into his touch, enjoying the warmth for a moment before pressing him further. "Nice try, now tell me what you meant."

"First, I need you to answer a single question before we play this back-and-forth. Did you agree to marry me because it was the only option?"

How many times had I considered asking him the same thing, knowing he wouldn't be able to avoid an honest answer? But I was too afraid to hear it. Still squatting next to the tub, I looked down at my bare feet and shook my head.

"Look at me, Cecilia. Tell me the truth."

My emotions warred within me. I was scared of pushing him away, but even more scared of him not feeling the same way. "No. I said yes because you are a good man, and I'd be honored to be your wife. But you deserve better."

He snorted and cupped my cheek again. "Touch me and ask me the same question."

I jumped back, terrified of what it would do to him, and shook my head vigorously. "No, I don't want to hurt you." Or worse, hurt myself when I realized he was in this solely for himself. That he didn't feel the same. That the one time I had let myself get too attached would break me.

"It only hurts when someone tries to lie to you. Do it."

I sighed and my fingertips grazed his forearm where it rested on the rim of the tub. "Why did you ask me to marry you, Captain?"

"I asked you to marry me because I've been in love with you since we were young, and I've never wanted anything more in my life. I knew you'd agree in the face of your father's threat, but it was selfish of me," he whispered, and his voice wavered for the first time I could remember.

Tears filled my eyes, and I was helpless to stop them from falling. "But what does all that have to do with protecting me?"

"I think it's time you heard a story from when I was ten years old. It's about the powers Queen Isadora kept hidden from the king."

Chapter 16

I was sitting in the soft grass on a warm sunny day when the smell of peonies and rosewater drifted into my nostrils. Moments later, 8-year-old Princess Cecilia came running down the grassy hill with her maid and tutor chasing after her. The former with annoyance, and the latter with a mischievous smile on her face. The castle stood tall and firm behind us, and the forest beyond swayed in the gentle breeze.

Light footsteps approached from behind me, and the queen fluffed her skirts to sit beside me. She was alone, surprisingly, but smiled as she watched me observing the princess. "Can I help you with something, Your Majesty?"

"Actually, Thomas, I think you're the only one who can."

I furrowed my brow in confusion. "What is it, my queen?"

"I think it's safe to say you care for my daughter. You're very close friends, am I right in that assumption, Thomas?" I nodded, and she continued before I could answer. "And you have a strong sense of what is right and what is wrong, am I correct in that as well, my dear?"

"Yes, Your Majesty. I always listen to the teachers, and I follow all the rules. And Entriken and Cecilia are my best friends. I'd do anything for either of them."

She chuckled and took my hand in hers. "Excellent, because I have some secrets to share with you that are very important, and they must be kept from everyone. Including King Aldus, Princess Cecilia, and Prince Entriken. Do you think you can do that?"

I looked down at my small hand in hers, deep in thought. After my mother had passed away, the queen had cared for me almost as if I were one of her own. The queen was kind and good, but it felt like she was going to ask me to do something terrible. "As long as it doesn't hurt Cecilia, I can do that."

Her eyes flitted over our surroundings before she turned back to me and leaned in conspiratorially. "Very good, Thomas. The first thing I need you to keep secret is that I am a seer, do you know what that is?"

I nodded again.

"I'm not sure how much you have learned of how they work, but typically seers can only see one future. The future as it is unless the subject of that prophecy makes an important decision that sets them on a different path. My powers, however, behave a little differently. I can see all the paths forward and how likely they are to occur. For instance, in all of them, you fall in love with Cecilia in your teens and continue to feel that way even in adulthood."

I blushed in embarrassment as my free hand flicked grass bits off my britches.

"The problem is that in all of them Princess Cecilia has powers that terrify many in this kingdom. I've already taught her to keep any she learns to herself, even from me. All the paths where her father learns of her skills lead to her demise, which is why I am tasking you with her protection. I know you will always care for her, as I do, but I won't always be here to guard her. Your mission is to ensure that you become the next captain of the guard, a position you will inherit from your father. You must do everything you can to keep her safe and to prevent her father from learning of her talents." She pinched the bridge of her nose and paused.

My father was the bravest man I knew, and he had always taught me that, even when we were scared, we had to be brave. Even more so when we were scared. One day, I would take over for him, and I would have to live those words. Surely protecting the princess would be my top priority. This I knew, and it would be an honor to continue my father's legacy. "I will make sure I become captain, Queen Isadora. I vow to always keep her safe and to make sure the king doesn't hurt her."

She gave me a sad smile before continuing. "One more thing, Thomas. In many of the paths the gods showed me she loves you too. However, many of those visions showed the king keeping a closer eye on her. So please, be that eye, and be careful. Take care of my daughter. My Cece."

She started crying, and I had no idea what to do or say. Was she leaving? It wasn't my place to question the queen, so I complied. "Your Majesty, I will do as you say. There is no need to be upset."

She chuckled. "Oh, dear Thomas, I'm confident you will. But in every path where I survive, Cecilia does not. I cannot let that happen to my child. This is why I am asking you to take on this monumental task. You're the only one I can trust. I know I've said it a few times, but I need you to be very clear. Do you understand?"

I nodded gravely, tears filling my own eyes. I would do as she said.

Chapter 17

Cecilia

The tears streamed down my face—the dam no longer able to hold them back. I remembered that day. I had known he was outside, and I had run down the hill in front of him with my maid and tutor behind solely to make him laugh. To get his attention. My mother had killed herself two weeks later by jumping off the top of the highest tower. Because of me. To keep me safe. Gods, I was definitely going to vomit. Why would she have done that? I wasn't worth it.

"Are you okay, Cecilia?" He asked, tears glistening in his eyes.

I nodded, but I wasn't. How could I be okay? My mother had killed herself to keep me safe. From my father. And my future husband had been in love with me all this time and had been too afraid to tell me for the same reason. He had kept his promise, and he had kept me safe. He had put himself in danger time and again and had endured torturing men for my father to keep me out of harm's way, all so he could keep his position for my protection. I didn't deserve this man in front of me. I didn't deserve any of this. I had been throwing my life away since...well, since she had died.

Jumping into the tub, I straddled him, wrapping my arms around him tightly and nestling my face into his neck while the tears kept coming. The water sloshed over the top of the tub and hit the floor, but I didn't care.

He slid his hands to cup my ass and relaxed back into tub, chuckling with a hint of seduction. "You could at least have taken your dress off before you hopped in here," he whispered into my ear.

"There wasn't time." I pulled back and kissed him over and over on the lips. "Thank you, for everything. This whole time I thought you hated me."

"I could never hate you, but I swore to your mother I'd protect you. I'm still not sure I understand exactly what I promised her that day—I was so young. But being with you...it almost feels like it goes against my oath, and I wasn't sure how to live with that. I just needed to keep myself away from you because I knew I couldn't resist your pull. You see how long my self-restraint lasted against it."

This poor man had suffered all this time to keep a promise to my mother. I still couldn't comprehend why, but I found I didn't care. Smiling, I rested my forehead against his as we both soaked up the silence. "I love you too. I have since we were teenagers," I finally said, earning another grin and another kiss.

"Well, I think I'm clean now thanks to you, but we have a mess to clean up before bed," he said, taking in the soaked floor.

I grinned at him and lifted my palms in the air, the pressure building in my stomach as I dug deep—it felt like marbles rolling around in my gut. The bathroom floor began to quake as tiny cracks split in the floor and drained all the water before I dropped my hands and the cracks closed up. His eyes filled with wonder yet again. "I think I still have a few more surprises left, but that one is probably my favorite."

"There haven't been seismic powers in 200 years, Cecilia."

"I know, and there still aren't." I got out of the tub with a wink. "Now, we need some sleep because I think you're seeing things, Captain." Building up pressure in my chest, I swirled a tornado around me with a flourish of my hands to dry my dress before flinging it to the floor.

Once his awe had worn off, he rose from the tub, and I got my first full view of his naked body. I wasn't surprised to find him in perfect physical shape, but I still wondered about those scars. I had shared many secrets with him tonight, but mine weren't painful. I wouldn't ask him to tell me just yet. He spun slowly and I took it all in. I enjoyed the exceptional view of his perfectly rounded ass.

"When your father learned of my shadow powers, he asked me to train myself in secret. I had to learn to wield them as weapons. I did. But I was just a child. If I had gone to a healer for aid, they would have known what had caused them. They never healed properly. I tried to heal myself, but I was too young and not as skilled with that gift as I am now."

"It's still my father's fault." Everything was my father's fault. I felt my fire power heat my insides and I fought to hold it back. Resisted the urge to blast the walls between us away and take him out. It likely wouldn't work anyway, and I'd have his entire cadre waiting to end me.

"It's not. I chose this. I chose you. I will always choose you."

Chapter 18

Thomas

"It's not. I chose this. I chose you. I will always choose you," I said as I brushed her hair behind her ear. I had forgotten I was naked until she reached out her bare hands to touch my hips. Hands I had longed to feel caressing my bare skin since I was a teen. Hands I had dreamed of gripping parts of me every night. So many others feared her touch, but I knew what was in her heart, and she would never hurt anyone unless they deserved it.

For the past few years, I had drowned my sorrows in the arms of other women each time King Aldus had forced me to torture someone. It hadn't rid me of the pain, but it had given me temporary reprieve and distraction. Every single time, I had closed my eyes and pretended it was Cecilia. It was the only way I had been able to find my release. But now it wasn't the arms of some other woman. It was the arms of the woman I was in love with. The forbidden fruit I wasn't allowed to taste. But now I had had a taste of her, and I knew it was going to be so much more.

Grabbing my hand, she dragged me towards her bedroom. I had wanted this for so long, but I didn't want it like this. Not after what she had watched me do. But how could I say no? Who was I to reject her? I should've known she wouldn't ask that of me. She changed into a thin shift and lifted her covers, climbing underneath before patting the spot next to her. She sweetly wrapped her arms around my neck and held my head to her shoulder, massaging my scalp before placing a kiss on my forehead.

"Get some sleep, Captain. It's time somebody protected you instead."

I hadn't cried in front of another person since I was a small child, and in my adult life I had only cried once in the confines of my room after having taken my first life at the behest of the king. But this time, I found myself forcing my tears back as my heart swelled. Having lost my mother at a young age, I had never known this kind of caring or tenderness. I had been raised to be tough. Firm. Strong. Stone faced. But with Cecilia, I could just be.

"I'm going to find us a way out of this. I knew my father was a tyrant, but I had no idea how he was treating you. There has to be something I can do," she whispered, running her lithe fingers through my still damp hair.

"Your father knows nothing of your true power. You could easily overthrow him, and I would be by your side without question. I would wager some of the council might be swayed, and I'm convinced every single person in this kingdom outside the castle would as well. Whenever I go into the towns the talk is always of your kindness towards them."

She snorted an adorable giggle before saying, "I know nothing of being a leader. I've been trapped in this wing for 20 years."

I sat up to look at her, momentarily distracted by her perky bosom that was very much on display. "Your father forced you to endure the same education as Entriken, and he has no backbone, yet even he would be better than your father. All the people want is someone with a heart, and nobody has a bigger heart than you. You don't give yourself enough credit for your ferocity either. You're the only person I've met who isn't afraid to talk back to him. It's in you." And I fucking believed it.

She shook her head and broke eye contact with me. "Even if I wanted to be queen, I'd have to take down my father and his loyal council members. That's a lot of magic to take on alone."

"And if I knew a siphon who could help?" I held my breath, wondering if I had gone too far. This particular piece of information wasn't mine to share. But if it boosted her confidence, so be it.

Her eyes widened, "There haven't been siphons in centuries. If there were, my father would flaunt that. He's never mentioned it when I spied on him."

"Because he doesn't know. One of my best men, Caden, has hidden that power from all but myself and his partner, Kai. The three of us are very close."

"I'm scared. I'm not sure I'm strong enough."

Nodding, I nudged her chin slightly to bring her gaze back to mine. "I hate that your father has belittled you for so long that you don't see how incredible you are. I've only seen a fraction of your powers and I have no doubt you would succeed. What if we keep training and formulate a plan together? Would you consider it?"

"Perhaps, but I still think running is our smartest option," she said, chuckling. The sound was like the tinkling of windchimes in a warm summer breeze. Sighing, she added, "I could never leave the people. If it weren't for the supplies that I sneak them, many of them would starve. I'm starting to have faith that your plan has merit, Captain. I'm not ready, but maybe with your training, I can be."

"As you wish, Princess." Grabbing her face, I pulled her lips to mine for a ravenous kiss. I knew she could do this, now I just had to convince her.

"My goodness, Captain. Are you finally trying to seduce me?" she teased, before her face paled. "I'm so sorry, I shouldn't be joking after what you went through tonight."

Running my thumb over her lips, I said, "It's fine. I find the pleasant company has erased the thought of it from my mind this evening. I would seduce you, but I don't want it to mar the memory of our first time. Our first time will be special, and it will be a day neither of us forgets."

With a pout she flopped backwards into her fluffy pillows. "You're going to make me wait forever, aren't you?" she joked.

"Well, I've waited 20 years, so it's only fair," I said with a wink before lying beside her and wrapping my arms around her warm, smooth body. It felt so right. For the first time in ages, I felt content. Happy. Like I was exactly where I was supposed to be. There was still that tiny piece of my conscience niggling at me that I had broken my promise to the queen. But she wasn't here to make me pay for it, was she? She'd never know. I planted a kiss on her cheek and added, "I do think we both need some sleep though. Who knows what hell your father is going to put us through tomorrow."

I wished we had all the time in the world, but King Aldus had really done a number on his daughter. I just hoped that when the time came, she would feel ready. Because I was sure that the time was much closer than either of us wanted.

Chapter 19

Cecilia

A light breeze blew in through my bedroom window, carried on the first rays of morning light. It was much cooler this morning than it had been last night, but perhaps it was the warm arms around me that were missing. Thomas must've been out on a morning scouting mission. As if summoned by my thoughts, I heard his voice outside, shouting to one of his men up on the parapet. "Find the king and tell him to meet me in the council chamber. It's urgent."

I placed my bare hand on my bedroom wall to see my father sitting alone on his throne, fingers tapping on the arms. A guard knocked and entered. "Captain Lovelace is on the way with news. He wants to speak with you alone."

"Very well, tell my council to meet me here in ten minutes. I'll speak with him first and then update them."

"Yes, sire."

The guard left, and a very frazzled Thomas walked in a minute or two later.

"Captain Lovelace, what news do you have?" the king asked, picking at his fingernails. I knew the sound of his disgusting habit better than anyone.

Thomas bowed before my father before saying, "The

Kingdom of Hinch is sending their entire army this way. My men spotted their caravan last night and I confirmed with my own eyes this morning. They're camped out in the woods to the west of the village. They have the most magic wielders of all the kingdoms. I recommend evacuating the townsfolk and securing our fortress. I think with all our mages combined we can put up enough shields to protect us and defend the city. I'd also like to take a small team for reconnaissance, including Princess Cecilia, whose skills will come in handy to determine what we are up against."

My father's face didn't show a single sign of surprise. "Absolutely not. The townsfolk will be our first line of defense, and my daughter will not leave this castle. You may take a small party, but she stays," he said authoritatively, his voice projecting throughout the chamber.

"Your Highness, I highly recommend—" Thomas continued before my father cut him off.

"I am the king, Captain Lovelace. You best remember that," King Aldus said sternly.

"Yes, Your Majesty," Thomas said, dropping his head.

"The council is on their way. I'll share your findings."

"I'll stay and head up formulating the plan. I think Cecilia would also be a great help."

"You may stay, but the plan is already formulated. We just need to inform the council."

That asshole. Had his council informed him ahead of time? Shit. My time was up. If something was going to be done, it had to be now. No training, no planning. No choice.

Racing towards the council room, I turned myself invisible the moment I left my wing. The door to the chamber swung open to allow in the last few council members, and I snuck in behind them. Turning invisible took a lot out of me, especially for long periods, so I had to use it wisely. My skin felt as though it crawled with invisible worms. The entire council was seated around the massive table, awaiting the king's announcements. I maneuvered myself behind the throne, where I would be able to safely drop my invisibility when the time was right.

"Gentlemen, our esteemed captain has confirmed the terrible news. The Kingdom of Hinch, with its large army of mages, is camped nearby. They're headed here to take control of our kingdom. Though they are strong, we also have an impressive amount of magical firepower. We cannot let them win. Our villagers will be the first line of defense, and you all will be our last. The time has come to fight for our home. Don't let me down." He did have a knack for convincing his minions to do his bidding, and they all seemed eager to abide in the face of danger.

I wasn't having it. Slinking out from behind my father's throne, I halted at his side and dropped my invisibility. Binding his hands to his throne with thorny vines, I gripped his forearm, prepared to force the truth from him. The room fell into stunned silence after a wave of gasps. Thomas almost had to pick his jaw up off the floor. My eyes scanned the room for my brother, but he was nowhere to be seen.

"Do you plan to run, Father? And leave your council here to deal with this on their own?" I asked with an eyebrow raised, already knowing the answer. I glanced over at Thomas with an unnecessary wink. He would know this meant I was ready. I wasn't sure I believed it, but I had no other choice.

Gritting his teeth and squirming to break free of my solid bonds, he quietly said, "Yes."

"And you plan to let the army of Hinch decimate the entire village outside the fortress to buy yourself time?"

His fiery gaze meeting mine, he confirmed with a forceful yes.

"Well, see, that just won't do," I said, shaking my head. My heart had never pumped this hard. I could feel my veins throbbing with energy and just a tinge of fear.

Three of his council members launched to their feet as Thomas moved to stand in front of me for protection, shadows weaving from his hands. One, whose jaw hit the floor in shock at Thomas's dark and forbidden magic, prepared a magical attack against Thomas, while the other two aimed at me. My shield of lightning lit up the council room as it formed around both of us and my father. Their pathetic attempts ricocheted off the shield and back at them. Four of the twelve council members ran for their lives while the rest stuck around to join the fight. One single member leaned back in his chair, enjoying the show with a jovial grin.

I shook my head, laughing at their efforts. My father groaned in irritation and started barking commands.

"I order you to take them down. Destroy her shield, what are you fools doing?" he screamed with clear panic in his voice.

"As members of the council, I'm giving you one last chance to stop your attacks, and I will let you live. Anyone that continues to fight will be held accountable." My voice boomed through the room. I spoke firmly—my powers requiring no visible effort on my part. The thrumming in my veins started to slow and I could feel the first tug of my eyelids wanting to close. The burn in my eyes was always the first hint that I was close to my limit. My energy was draining quickly, but I could keep hiding it a little while longer. It had to be enough. If only I had known this was coming. Perhaps Thomas could've brought Caden to replenish my energy. But then he'd have been killed if we failed and my father had discovered what he had been hiding.

The remaining attackers raced from the room, leaving only the seated man who had thoroughly enjoyed the commotion. I watched him wearily as I dropped the shield, keeping my father's arms bound to his throne. The man—a fire wielder named Zell— stood up and clapped, still wearing his smile.

"My dear, that was simply fantastic. Your mother told me you were capable of amazing things, and I knew it to be true, but seeing you at work is something else."

"You knew my mother?" I asked, still cautiously focused on him in case I needed to throw up another shield.

He took in the state of my father before turning back to

address me. "Perhaps we should chat once your father is dealt with, my queen." He sank to one knee and bowed his head.

"I am no queen. Even if my father forfeited the throne, the rules state I would need to marry first, and we have not wed. He has also formally assigned Entriken as the rightful heir. But you're right. Let's get my father to the dungeon and secure him in the anti-magic cells, then we can chat." I said to both Thomas and Zell.

"Those were your father's rules, Cecilia. This is your kingdom now," Zell stated, looking back and forth between Thomas and myself. "If you still wish to wed, I can perform such ceremonies. Would you like me to help you detain your father, or should I wait here and keep the council room secure?"

"I think Captain Lovelace can secure my father on his own until we can have a fair trial. You and I will speak alone." Using my magic, I bundled my father up in a binding cocoon of vines that levitated him off the ground in a mini tornado, which Thomas easily maneuvered out of the room. I turned back to Zell, who gestured for me to take the throne as he sat in one of the council chairs. I took another council chair instead.

Part of me had wanted to kill my father right then and there, but I wouldn't stoop to his level. I'd rather just take over his kingdom, but that would have to wait until we weren't under imminent attack. I hoped Hinch would do the dirty work for us. Then no trial would be necessary, and the problem would be solved.

"You asked if I knew your mother, and I did. I do. Your mother knew this day would come and knew you would need allies. She knew Captain Lovelace would protect you, but she thought you could use someone else on the inside."

What? He clearly said he does. Not did. Does. My arms tingled and bumps rose on my skin. "My mother is dead. I saw her body fall from the tower myself," I said, leaning forward to place both forearms on the polished wooden table.

One corner of his mouth tipped up as he said, "You did."

With my eyebrows pinched, I sent him a questioning glare. "A necromancer brought her back?"

"No. A god did. Your mother was their favorite seer, after all. When she sacrificed herself to protect you, they knew she didn't deserve that fate. But no one could know or the worst of her prophecies would come to fruition."

"She's...still alive?" I hadn't realized my eyes were tearing, but I patted them dry when he handed me his handkerchief. My stomach bubbled with hope—or nausea. "Where is she?"

"Ahh, that is the question I hoped you'd ask. We have a long trek to where she is, and we have another mission to undertake on the way."

"And I'm just supposed to trust a member of my father's council?"

He chuckled. "Impressive. You're so much like your mother." He pulled a few pieces of parchment out of his pocket and handed them to me. "These are letters she has sent me over the past few years. I've had to burn most of them in case your father found them, but I'm sure you'll recognize her handwriting. You may keep them to read on our travels. We must protect the villagers from the impending attack before we make our journey. We have to get you out of here before the Hinch forces storm the castle, which I'm expecting to happen two nights from now."

I took the letters from him and examined them. A single tear streamed down my cheek as I took in the familiar script of my mother's handwriting. Before she passed, she had insisted on giving Entriken and I penmanship lessons.

We had just over two full days to evacuate the castle and the handful of villages surrounding it. It was possible, but it wasn't going to be easy.

"I planned for Captain Lovelace and I to stay to defend the castle as long as possible to buy the villagers time to escape. Then we will make ours."

He shook his head, "You are the queen, but I do not think that wise. Your father organized this attack—it's a cover for your kidnapping. To let the village fall, the much-loved princess be taken, and be the savior that made peace with their leader. It solves all his problems at once. At least it did until you foiled his plan this evening. The council is now on the run, but you have the villagers on your side. But you cannot rule if there is no kingdom. I insist that we help the people escape and make our exit with them. I will help you and Captain Lovelace set some traps and shields, but I doubt the Hinch army will cause any damage. When they find the kingdom empty, they will leave a small battalion to occupy it, but I'm sure your father will convince them to let him remain alive. They will believe we all fled and that they have won. Your father will never admit defeat at the hands of his own daughter. It may be wise to either take him with us or to take his life."

"Our laws decree that a fair trial must be conducted before someone is sentenced to death. I know he's broken the rule himself, but I will not be that type of leader. If we bring him with us, I'm afraid he'll finish the job of killing me himself. I'm not sure what the right answer is here, but I'm hoping when Hinch finds how badly he has failed, they will end his life for him."

"I'm afraid that's not going to work, but I understand your decision. Make sure you read those letters on our trip. We'll leave him here and deal with the consequences as they come."

He was right, of course. My nerves were getting the best of me, and my head was spinning. My mother was alive. I might be queen. Another powerful kingdom was on its way here to destroy my home. And me. And all they were going to find was a maniacal king locked in his own dungeon. This was too much to deal with at once, and I wasn't ready for any of it.

Chapter 20

"We have to find my brother before we leave. Granted, we're not close anymore, but he's still my brother. I can't just leave him," Cecilia begged as we prepared to evacuate. How could I say no to her?

"Go with Zell to deliver the supplies to the caravan. I'll find him," I assured her, taking her beautiful face between my palms to kiss her.

She ran off as I had asked, and I headed back into the castle. My first reaction was to head for the council room, assuming he was still cowering there, but I didn't remember seeing him at all. My gut brought me back to his childhood hiding spot. Our classroom. He sat in the windowsill, shaking and peering outside at the ruckus below. He quickly pulled his rolled-up shirtsleeves down, but not before I saw the cuts and bruises marring his skin. Had he been harming himself, or had the king been torturing his beloved heir?

Voice even, I asked, "You're coming with us, aren't you?"

He turned and made eye contact with me only briefly before turning his gaze to the stone floor. "I can't. I can't leave Father."

"Yes, you can. Your sister and I will protect you."

"Nobody can protect me from him. It will never stop." He

ran his fingertips over his sleeves, as if he were soothing the damage.

"Yes, we can. His reign is over. If you stay here, the Hinch mages will kill you. I can't let your sister go through that, Entriken."

He didn't answer and made no move to follow.

"Fine. We do things my way." I hit him with a tiny pulse of my shadow magic and rushed toward him. I caught him just before he hit the floor and flung him over my shoulder before returning to the caravan.

Cecilia's jaw dropped and her hands fisted by her side. "Did you knock him out, Captain?"

"He wasn't budging otherwise. I barely zapped him. You'll thank me later," I said as I placed him into the back of a cart.

"I'm sure he'll be fine, Princess," Zell told her, resting his hand on her shoulder.

My right-hand man and cartographer, Kai, approached with a map. Though he was a fierce fighter, his particular magic made his main profession a no-brainer. He unrolled a map of our kingdom and the surrounding ones and pointed as he spoke. Images appeared where he touched and disappeared as he moved his finger across the paper, sparks traveling in his wake. "The army of Hinch is here, we know there are also some scouts over here. We only have one option for travel, and it's through our farming village."

"Good, we can evacuate them as we go. We need more carts for the rest of the refugees," Cecilia said with concern in her eyes.

"It will slow us down, love. The less we bring, the faster we get out of here."

"It was not a request, Captain. I'm not leaving my friends."

Nodding, I took the reins and prepared to mount my horse. "Fine. You ride in the cart with Entriken until he wakes up. He's going to need a friendly face, and you're as close as he's going to get."

It only took us a few minutes to reach the farming village.

Upon seeing the large caravan, Gunther dropped his equipment and ran over towards us. "What's going on?"

"Hinch has sent their army to take the palace. We have to evacuate, and we don't have long," I informed him.

"Where is the princess? Is she okay?"

"I'm fine," she said, climbing out of the back of the cart. "Gather your people and tell them to pack light. We have to leave right now."

"Where are we heading?" Gunther asked.

"We're not sure yet, but right now we only have one route out that Hinch hasn't blockaded. We need to hurry," I said, hopping off the horse to help them load what they could into the carts.

We packed as much food as we could take and put the women and children in the carts with the supplies. The villagers prepared quickly, quite the opposite of the frantic scrambling I had expected. Almost as if they were prepared to run at the first sign of danger. Gunther was smarter than anyone gave him credit for.

The men took turns riding horses and hanging off the carts as we travelled. The few of my men that I trusted had come with us. Those loyal to the king had fled during the showdown in the council room. I was grateful we'd be able to make our escape without them around to witness it. We had Kai and Caden and a handful of others that had been privy to our treasonous rumblings since Cecilia had begun to show interest in challenging her father. They and the stronger men from the village surrounded the caravan—all of us with our eyes peeled for any sign of danger as we headed through the only path to safety we had seen.

Kai pulled his horse up next to me, showing me his map. "Our best hope of refuge is Yelen, Captain. We're heading in the right direction already. It should take us about two days, but we're going to have to make camp in the woods. We have a decent head start, so I think we can afford it if my map is still reading everyone. I can't make any promises if they have any specialized mages, sir."

Fortunately, all the kingdoms were small and close together.

The road system was intricate but not used as often as it had been when trade had flowed freely. The last decade of reduced trade had left them desolate, but thanks to our spying missions, they hadn't fallen into disrepair.

"Thank you, Kai."

"You're welcome, Captain," he said as he picked up the pace to lead our group in the right direction.

Zell approached me next. "I thought you might like to be notified that Entriken is awake."

"Is Cecilia in danger?"

Zell laughed deeply and raised his brows at me.

"You're right, dumb question."

Chapter 21

Cecilia

The cart bounced gently as I stared at my brother. All these years I hadn't been able to look at him long enough or closely enough to see how bad the dark circles under his eyes had become. His belly didn't show his status like my father's. If I had to guess, I doubted my brother ate much at all. Our father had worked hard to push us apart after my mother died. He'd even gone so far as separating us for education sessions. But I hadn't stopped loving my brother. He was clearly terrified of the king, but I wondered what kind of hold he had on him if he hadn't been willing to come with us. Had I done something wrong in his eyes? Why had Thomas's shadow magic even been necessary?

While I awaited his waking, I pulled the letters Zell had given me from my pack. He had asked me to read them on our travels, and this seemed like the perfect opportunity.

My Dearest Cecilia,

Zell has kept me informed of the happenings in Revell since I left. I assured him you would need some token from me to convince you to come looking for me, and I knew letters would be the easiest to transport. I also assumed you'd recognize my handwriting. If you're reading this, it means he has succeeded in convincing you to come find me. I can't tell you how much I've looked forward to this day.

After my death, which I'm sure he explained how I was brought back, he told me how difficult Aldus had become. I'm so sorry you had to go through all of that without me. I'm even more sorry that you were completely alone. After my premonitions led me to the path that I believed we were on, I feared for your safety. The only solution I knew was to kill Aldus. What my sight didn't show me was that I would fail spectacularly. I tried poison first, then hired assassins. When both of those failed, I tried strangling him in his sleep.

I was lucky to be alive after he caught me, but he was convinced your powers had coerced me into it. He only knows of your fire power to this day, though I know of more thanks to my gifts, but he knew you would have others. Without knowing what the others were, he became paranoid. He feared you could use mind control or dark magic to possess other beings.

You see, the night before I tried to smother him, I had spoken one of my premonitions to him while I slept. Though it wasn't very detailed, it did inform him that only you would be able to end his life, and that he would be unable to end yours. The only way I knew to prevent him from hearing more was to take my own life, hoping to put you on the path that kept you safe. I left some helpers behind with just enough information, as I'm sure you've already learned.

Zell also informed me of what has become of Entriken. Zell learned that Aldus feared you would use your powers on him to control him—like he thought you had me—or to harm his beloved heir. I never thought he would be so cruel as to separate a brother and sister at such a young age, but I grossly underestimated his brutality. I wish I could tell you more, but I'm only able to transmit so much in one letter. I promise to write again, and I cannot wait until we are reunited.

Love, Mother

Entriken cracked an eye open, and I gave him a sad smile, my heart full and tight at the same time. "Good morning, sunshine. You feeling okay?"

He startled, then sat up straighter and flitted his eyes around to take in his surroundings. "Where are we?"

"Honestly, I'm not sure. We passed through the farm village, and I don't know where Captain Lovelace has us headed just yet. I wanted to make sure you were okay."

His head sank, but not enough for me to miss his frown. His shoulders dropped like his whole body was giving up.

"You're safe, Entriken. We aren't going to let Father hurt you anymore. He's locked up in the Castle and the Kingdom of Hinch is going to finish him off. It's all over."

His laughter held no humor, but at least he finally met my eyes. "No, they won't. This whole attack was his plan. He made an alliance with them and promised them titles and land when he takes over the other kingdoms."

"I know," I said, nonchalantly.

"You knew they were planning to kill you? How are you so calm about this?"

"What? That part is new. I thought it was to kidnap me."

"When the stag attack failed, this was his backup plan with Hinch. They were sure their dark magic possessing the creature would be enough, but you outsmarted them. He was pissed." He ran his fingers up and down his forearms very carefully.

"The stag was his idea too? I'm assuming the bird was as well, then. No wonder we never found out who was responsible."

He picked at the knee of his pant leg before whispering, "I never heard about the bird."

"You knew about the rest and didn't tell me or Thomas?"

Without hesitation, he answered in a very hushed tone. Like he was worried somebody would hear him. "Father would have killed me. Thomas told him the dark magic was clearly from Hinch and asked to be allowed to look into it. Father told him not to bother."

"Oh, but it was fine for him to kill me?" Unintentionally, my hands began to glow with heat and Entriken's eyes widened.

"I'm so sorry, Cece. You know what he's like. I just couldn't—"

"Oh, trust me, I know what he's like. But I've never caved to his bullshit." Fucking coward. He was just going to let me die.

"You tortured people for him. That sounds like caving to me," he spat, with more courage than I'd seen him gather in ages.

I bit my bottom lip to stifle all the insults I wanted to hurl at him, but he was partially right. "Sometimes. But most of those men weren't tortured. They were telling the truth. Daddy Dearest was just too paranoid to listen to me."

We sat in silence for a moment before he spoke again.

"Thank you. For sending Thomas for me. I know that was you. After all these years, I knew there was no way in hell he'd come for me otherwise."

"You're welcome. Do we have to worry about you, Ent? Are you still Daddy's little pet?"

He thought a moment and looked up into my eyes again. "No, Sister. It's nice to be able to be within a foot of you again."

I smiled at him and the corners of his mouth tipped up just a smidge. "Good. It'll be nice to have my brother back too. Did Father ever explain why he wouldn't let us see each other anymore?"

"He told me you were dangerous and that you had possessed mom to kill him. He also said you had possessed mom to kill herself. I never believed him, of course. I know you're powerful, but you'd never hurt me."

Could my own father really think so little of me? I handed Entriken a chunk of bread and cheese then pointed to a blanket. "Eat something and get some rest. It doesn't look like you've done much of either recently. I'll make sure you're safe, Brother."

The cart came to a halt, and I placed a kiss on his forehead before hopping out.

"Why are we stopping?" I asked Thomas, who was dismounting his handsome stallion.

"Zell told me Entriken was awake, how'd it go?"

Weird. Zell hadn't looked in the cart. Maybe he had heard us talking? He nodded to me from next to the captain. "He said King Aldus was working with Hinch to kill me, not kidnap me as we suspected. He made some promises to them in return. Oh, and the stag was them as well. Daddy Dearest knew about that too."

"You're fucking kidding me. Why would he tell Entriken and not me? I'm his captain for fuck's sake."

I raised my eyebrows at him. "Maybe because you're engaged to his target?"

"We got engaged after, and he thought that was just a political move. He doesn't know it's real."

Something pulled at my chest at his admission in front of everyone. That what he and I had was real. I hadn't known that until recently, and it had been kept secret since then. Zell and the captain's two men standing closest to him didn't show any surprise.

"He may be a paranoid old bat, but he's not stupid. The entire council knows you've been in love with Cecilia since you were younger," Zell teased. "Honestly, I was surprised he agreed to your marriage. He must have either been convinced Cecilia wouldn't follow through with it, or he had felt confident in your proven loyalty and expected you to turn her around."

"And none of us ever missed how much you checked her out whenever she walked by during training," his handsome cartographer said. "I'm Kai, by the way. It's an honor to formally introduce myself, Princess Cecilia."

"The honor is mine, Kai. Thank you for joining us. I appreciate your teasing of the captain, but the news of the captain's longstanding feelings was a shock to me. I had never noticed."

"You may have been the only one. My name is Caden, Your Highness," a shorter, stockier man with a long, red ponytail said, bowing to me in respect. I recognized him as the man who had offered to guard me when my father had first decided I needed a babysitter. He and Kai had also frequently watched Thomas and I as we trained, so I wasn't surprised at them being so close with him.

"It's a pleasure to meet you, Caden. I've heard a lot about you from Thomas."

"Oh gods, I'm afraid to even ask," he said with mischief in his eyes. "We'll leave the two of you to talk. Anything you need, Princess, both of us are at your disposal."

"They seem nice. I think I'm going to like them a lot."

Thomas' blush from the teasing started to fade as the three men rode away. "I know you were counting on the Hinch mages killing Aldus, or at least punishing him, but I'm not sure they're going to do as you planned. They don't believe in a fair trial like you or I, but I understand why you didn't have the heart to kill him. I should have. Or maybe we should've dragged him with us. It's too late now to speculate. They'll be coming for us. We have to pick up the pace."

Nodding, I left him to lead the men and started to walk back to the cart.

"Princess!" he yelled. "You're riding with me. Let's go."

Chapter 22

Thomas

Since I was a child, I had ridden a horse almost every day of my life. Though I always appreciated it, I had never enjoyed it as much as I did with Cecilia seated in front of me. As I took in the floral smell of her hair and the way she leaned into me, I realized what an odd set of circumstances had to occur to lead us to this. Had this been the queen's plan all along, or had we upset the balance of the universe and set some dangerous things into motion?

"I'm proud of you. Your mother will be too," I whispered into her ear.

"Thank you," she breathed.

"How are you doing with all of this?"

"Honestly, I don't think any of it has sunk in yet. It feels like some weird dream. Like it's not actually happening to me. I think when we stop to rest and the adrenaline stops pumping, I'm going to be terrified. I've never left Revell. Not even to visit any other kingdom. This is the first time I get to see the world, and we're on the run, so I can't even enjoy it."

"When this is all over, I'll take you wherever you want to go, love."

"If we're both still alive." Her voice held just a hint of a tremble.

"We will be. I promise."

Zell joined us atop his shiny mare. "What's the plan, my queen."

She looked to me in confusion. "I'm leaving that up to the captain."

I smirked. "You're the queen now. You're in charge."

She turned pleading eyes on me and then back to Zell. "I don't even know where we're going. I can put on a show for the others, but I need you two to handle this."

"Yes, my queen," I said with a nod.

Zell filled her in. "Kai said we're heading to Yelen. They've been an ally of ours for centuries, though they're not fans of your father. They fear him too much to fight him. We'll be welcome there, but we have about two days of travel before we get there. The forest can be dangerous, but we have no viable options other than camping out in the woods for tonight. We're going to get as far as possible to give us some distance from the Hinch army. Did I miss anything, Captain Lovelace?"

"That about covers it. We'll be safe in Yelen. I believe they'll be looking forward to your rule. It'll be your decision where we go from there, but we'll need a plan." I squeezed her hip so she knew we were in this together. Part of me didn't want to trust Zell. He had been part of Aldus's council after all, but Cecilia trusted him, and she was an excellent judge of character. He had always been on the right side of morality when things had come to a vote, and he had been quick to spill information when Cecilia had taken over that council room. Almost as if he had been biding his time for that exact moment. Regardless, I'd keep an eye on him.

"I agree. I don't want to spend the rest of my life running. What's our endgame? To take Revell from my father? To go back after Hinch leaves and put him on trial, hoping the council members that fled and the surrounding kingdoms will go along with it? He has a lot of powerful friends who are just as crazy as he is. My gut says our only option is to kill him, but then I'd be no better than he is. And as much as I thought I could, I can't kill him. I tried this morning, and I just...I couldn't. He's still my father. No matter the path, we can't win."

Her eyes welled with tears. I couldn't imagine they were for her father—the wretched beast—but perhaps it was for the idea of what a father and daughter should be and the knowledge that there was no going back. Luckily, she had never known what that bond could feel like. I had, and I would burn the world down to get my father back.

"I'd say don't cry, but I'm sure this must feel overwhelming. You're not alone, though. And we're going to figure this out one step at a time. Step one: get to Yelen and see what kind of support we have. Then we figure out what to do next." I squeezed her and kissed the back of her head.

"Your father is building an army and alliances because he knows you have the advantage. I'm sure Thomas has mentioned this to you already. The council knew what he was doing, but we could only speculate as to why. His plan with Hinch to attack has cleared that up. We still have the edge, and he knows it. We just need to dig and find more answers. Figure out how he plans to gain more power and exploit his weaknesses. Once Entriken is rested, perhaps we can glean additional information from him. He seemed willing to hand over the details about Aldus's alliance with Hinch. Perhaps he learned more while cowering in the king's shadow." Zell rolled his eyes and looked back at the cart that contained Entriken.

"I'll talk to him tonight when we stop. I'll see what else I can learn."

"That's an excellent idea. We do have more to talk about, but I'd like to hear what Entriken knows first. It's too much to dump on you with the way this day started. The three of us will chat some more in the morning. Is that alright, Princess?"

We both nodded and watched him pull to the front of the pack.

"I've always liked him. He seemed to keep your father in check when his plans started to get increasingly delusional. I'm just not sure I fully trust him yet."

"I do. With all my heart. If my mother shared so much information with him, she knew he had a kind heart and would look after me. Just like she trusted you."

"Maybe. I'm still going to keep an eye on him."

"Of course, Captain." She looked up at me with heat in her eyes, and I felt her body temperature rise with her fire power. The warmth was welcome in the cool, dark forest.

Chapter 23

e had been riding for what seemed like days, though it had only been a few hours. Thomas had the stamina for this from all his years in my father's guard. I hadn't ridden for more than an hour at a time, and that had been when I was a child and mother had forced my father to let me take riding lessons. Perhaps she had known I'd need the knowledge to escape one day. My thoughts on this trek often wandered to my mother. How much had she planned for? Did she know I was on my way to find her? Would she be embarrassed by who I had become?

My body ached, my lids were heavy, and my heart felt like it was suffocating and withering. I tried to distract myself from the heaviness of the day by taking in the beauty of the lush trees and multicolored flowers that lined both sides of the carriage road. The leaves swayed in the gentle breeze, a sharp contrast to the booming drumbeat of adrenaline that had been pumping through my heart throughout our escape. It was so peaceful and beautiful. Something I would have loved to see sometime in the past two decades. But right now, I felt like I didn't belong in such a harmonious setting.

Thomas tightened his grip around my waist, shaking me from my thoughts.

"You're thinking so loud I can hear it. What's wrong, love?"

"Just wondering how much of this Mother foresaw."

He let out a loud whistle, drawing the attention of the members of our traveling party ahead of us. "Let's take a quick break, I'm sure everyone could use a stretch."

"And a new ass," I huffed, as he hopped off the horse and helped me down.

Leaning down to my ear, he murmured, "At least it's good practice. You'll be nice and ready for me."

I elbowed him in the gut gently and pretended to stomp away, all the while grinning like a fool.

Our cartographer approached and unrolled a massive parchment. "Captain, I'm afraid we're not moving fast enough to reach Yelen as quickly as you'd hoped. Perhaps we should take a long break now, make sure everyone is fed, then continue for a few more hours and make early camp in the woods like Zell suggested."

Thomas scanned the woods for a moment before turning back to the cartographer with a nod. "Very well, Kai. That's an excellent idea. I don't want to push anyone too hard."

I plopped down to rest and massaged my thighs. Caden sat down next to me and offered me a piece of jerky. "I don't know about you, Princess, but I find a nice chunk of meat always rejuvenates me." He winked at me, then turned to ogle Kai.

Snorting, I said, "Oh, Caden, we are going to be such good friends."

"Oh, you're going to be so sick of me." His tone shifted abruptly. "Seriously, though. How are you holding up? Not just physically, but mentally. That was a brave and scary thing you did, going after the council. Especially your father." He shivered.

"I'm not sure yet," I took a bite of the jerky and chewed while I contemplated.

"You were raised to be tough, and I have no doubt that you

are, but even tough people have to deal with emotions. Captain Cocky over there isn't exactly the best at consoling, so if you ever need to talk, I'm here. And I don't judge. Well, I do, but not about having feelings or fears."

"Do you think I should've killed the king?"

He let out a long sigh. "If it were me, I would have. But...he's not my father. I've seen what terrors men are capable of, and it's hardened me. Hardened them too," he said, pointing at Kai and Thomas. "Your heart is still pure and kind. I'm glad you didn't, because taking a life takes a part of you that you can't get back. I hope you never know what that feels like, Princess."

We shared a smile, and I took another bite of jerky and some almost-stale bread before we headed towards the river on Kai's map. There, we took a break to liven up the horses with a drink.

Zell stood with me while the others checked on the creatures. "I'm going to miss your antics in the council room. I always looked forward to the times you came in, wondering if this might be the day you set someone ablaze," Zell joked.

"I'd be lying if I said I hadn't considered it. Often. Who would you have had me burn?"

Tilting his head in thought, he said, "Honestly, all of them but me. They were a wretched bunch."

"You were also the only one that ever stood up to my father for me."

"I'm afraid it didn't accomplish anything, but I did enjoy the look of disdain he reserved for me after that. I, too, loved aggravating him. I made sure to oppose him in almost every vote we took. The fact that I'm still alive is a gods damned miracle."

"For what it's worth, I'm glad you are. And thank you for being on my side." I kissed his cheek as he patted my back in return.

The way he looked around and watched the men with concern, and the way he checked on how I was doing, made him seem so caring. I didn't know much about the man, but I wondered what his story was.

"I'm afraid I don't know much about you, Zell, other than that you've been on my father's council since I was born. Are you married? Do you have children?"

His eyes met mine, and a sadness filled them that even a smile couldn't hide. "I've never married. Came close a few times," he said with a wink. "I had a child, but I don't like to talk about it."

"I'm so sorry," I said, placing my hand on his. "You just seem like you would make such a good father. I won't make you talk about it, but if you ever want to, I'm a great listener."

He turned his gaze to his feet, but before I could say more, Thomas was getting us ready to continue.

The next few hours were even worse, but Thomas did his best to keep me distracted. The temperature began to drop as the sun dipped below the treetops. He pulled a blanket from the horse's pack and wrapped it around both of us. He had been sneaking kisses to the back of my head and neck all day, but the blanket protected me from view and his inhibitions dropped. He slid one palm down the low-cut neckline of my dress as he gently caressed my breast. His distraction was working. My head tipped backward against his shoulder, and his hand slid further, a finger swirling around my nipple.

"We've only got another half hour of daylight in the woods, Captain. I suggest we camp here for the night," Kai said, startling me. I had no idea when he had gotten so close with his horse, but Thomas wasn't fazed at all.

"Thank you, Kai." He casually removed his hand from my breast and pulled the blanket tighter around me. "It's perfect timing, as our queen is beginning to tire and it's getting chilly. Let's get three men working on building fires while you and I and a few others set up the tents. Two will tie up the horses." He pointed out his selections for each task as he listed them.

I chuckled and lit a fireball in my hand, "I think you can let those three men rest, I've got that part." Deciding to be brave, I hopped down myself, covertly catching myself on a mini tornado for an elegant landing. Those assigned to start the fires gathered sticks and built pyramids out of them for me to set ablaze. They were roaring in no time.

The tents were erected in moments. Most of them would house four people each, except for ours and the one for Caden and Kai. Including the villagers, we were about thirty in total. Thomas, ever the guard, put our tent in the center and the other tents circled evenly around us for protection. It seemed silly to me, because I had significantly more power than anyone here except Thomas. It made more sense for me to be the first line of protection, but that wasn't the monarchy they were used to.

We sat around one of the fires with our party, snacking on cheese and fruit to tide us over until morning. We hadn't planned to camp in the woods, but Alwyn had come prepared for anything, and my spoiled rumbling stomach was grateful for it. He and Amelia had ridden in a cart with two women from the village and some children. After feeding us, they went back to helping the women care for the kids.

Thomas and I sat with Zell, and I saw Entriken look over with concern. "Come join us, Ent," I said with a smile.

Reluctantly, he joined us.

"Is it okay if we ask you a few more questions? We're trying to figure out what Dad's plan is."

"Dad didn't trust me. I only knew his plan about Hinch because I walked in on a private meeting by accident. If he had kicked me out, they would've known he didn't trust his heir and it wouldn't have ended well. I paid for it, and he threatened to kill me if I told anyone, especially Thomas or the council. I've never been privy to any other conversations."

"Do you know why he wants me dead?" I gave him sad eyes, hoping it would tug at his heartstrings and get further information out of him. My stomach churned with anxiety at the thought that my father had formulated such a heinous plan.

"He's never said, but my only guess is that you're his biggest threat. And you have no loyalty to him."

"Something he did to himself," Thomas added.

"True. Dad started pushing her away as soon as Mom died. At first, he was convinced Cece had killed her on accident with one of her powers. He believes you have more powers he doesn't know about. There were many witnesses that Mom was alone, and everyone could account for where you were, but a powerful magic could've knocked her off that tower. He was convinced you could do it to him too."

"I had no idea. How could he think I could do that?"

"He's crazy, and he's dangerous. Why would he think you wouldn't be? You're his daughter..." Entriken shrugged his shoulders like it was the most obvious answer.

"Is there anything else you can tell me? Any weaknesses?" Zell questioned.

"That's everything I know. He kept me in his shadow but out of every discussion. I'm sorry. If I knew something else, I would tell you. The only other thing I've ever heard was that he was looking for something, but I have no idea why or what it is."

The temptation to grab his arm and make sure he wasn't lying was overwhelming, but he was my brother. I knew him, right? I had to trust him.

"I think it's time for us to head to bed. Make sure you rest up, because we've got to go farther tomorrow than we did today. We need to get an early start, and we'll need to move faster," Thomas told our crew.

"I just need to...head to the little girl's room, and I'll be right there," I said modestly.

"Want me to—"

Cutting him off, I joked, "I think I can go pee by myself, but I love you for always protecting me."

I headed out far enough that nobody could hear me relieve myself, but close enough that I could still hear my party. The trees were spread out nicely, and the moon lit my path, so I didn't need a fireball. The stars twinkled as if the world wasn't going to shit.

After I finished, I turned to head back to camp when I heard a rustling and twigs snapping. Lighting a fireball, I slowly spun to scan the woods to figure out where the sound had come from. My breath caught as a large, furry head with sharp teeth popped out from between two trees. I pulled my arm back, prepared to launch, but the creature only took one more step before dropping to all fours. Widening its mouth to show me more teeth, as if it was grinning, it flopped over to show me its belly like a dog.

"Well look at you, Mr. Bear. You're very handsome, aren't you? And so big! Are you here to eat me?"

He rolled back onto his stomach and stretched his very large, sharp clawed paws. *No, I'm here to protect you, my queen.*

Jumping back, I slammed straight into a tree and lost my footing. I tumbled to the ground before scrambling to stand back up. "Did you just...can I...?"

I heard a chuckle in my head before a husky voice answered, *Are you going to finish any of your questions, Queen Cecilia, or would you like me to guess what you're asking?*

My jaw dropped, my mouth unable to form words.

You need not fear me. As I said, I am here to protect you. There are many things you do not know, but it is imperative that I help guide you on your journey. I am not speaking aloud—nobody else can hear me. Though you have many powers, there are some you are still not aware of. Zoolingualism is one of them.

"Zoo...like I can understand animals? I've never even heard of that power. I mean there are stories about some of the gods..." My mind was spiraling out of control. How had I never noticed this power before? Come to think of it, how often were creatures anywhere near me? Birds would look at me with curiosity but fly off before I could get any closer.

Curious how many of your powers are only known to the gods. Wouldn't you say? His chuckle reverberated through my head again, but this time it filled my mind with warmth and a tingling sensation. *Aside from being able to speak with us, we can also sense you. If we are close enough, we can hear your thoughts. It's why we stayed away from you until you were ready. And you are ready.*

His reasoning was sound, but the idea was absurd. How could

I have godlike powers? Sure, Mom had been favored by the gods, but my father was nothing but smoke and mirrors and fearmongering. Perhaps Zell would know more.

"But...I have ridden horses when I was a child. We've been riding them this whole journey. Surely, I should've noticed this sooner?"

You did as a child. You got spooked thinking there were ghosts when you heard voices. The horses vowed to remain silent in your presence from that point on so King Aldus would not be alerted to this power. My creator requested it. As he had requested of the rest of us.

I remembered the day he was referring to. Father had sent me for a lesson, but when I arrived, my trainer had not yet shown up. I took it upon myself to brush my favorite mare and I heard murmurs. I ran out of there screaming and refused to go back for weeks.

But then I got distracted by another memory. "The stag..." I mumbled under my breath.

It was possessed with dark magic, but a small piece of its true self remained. It tried to warn you to run. It had no control over its actions.

"How do you know about the stag?" My brows furrowed, and fear clogged my throat.

My master had the birds watching you and those around you. They were only able to get a few words from the stag before the darkness fully consumed him. A dark mage from Hinch attacked him and forced an immense amount of dark magic into him. He didn't stand a chance, and my master wasn't able to reach him in time to help.

"What do I call you?"

My name is Ursin, but I like Mr. Bear if you prefer.

I smiled at his teasing. Ursin and I were going to be fast friends. As for the rest of my camp—I wasn't so sure.

Don't worry, I will let you enter first to explain, but I insist on guarding you tonight. Others will be along shortly as well. But you need rest, for your travels have only just begun. Let's get you back to your camp.

I hadn't spoken aloud, so I was a little taken aback by his warning. "Well, that's going to get awkward tonight..." I whispered as I turned to walk back to camp with my new giant brown bear friend following.

Sexual intercourse is a very primal and natural experience, Queen Cecilia. You have nothing to be ashamed of. And Captain Lovelace is an honorable man and an optimal mate for strong offspring.

"I can't believe I'm having this conversation with a bear..." I said aloud, shaking my head. "Why do you keep calling me Queen Cecilia? I'm not queen. My father is still king."

A sad king with only one person in his kingdom. You will soon be Queen of humans, but you are already Queen of all animals, my lady.

Overwhelmed by the last ten minutes, I hadn't realized how quickly we had come upon the camp. Yelling echoed around us, followed by a number of people scrambling to their feet. Thomas, noticing the large beast following me, began to bark orders, prompting the archers to draw their strings, ready to fire on his command. Caden stood at the front, and I feared he would hurt my new friend. Instinctively, I threw up a shield around myself and my new bear friend, holding up my palm to stop them.

Raising my voice, I assured them, "It's alright, he's friendly."

Thomas rushed through the camp toward me and skidded to a halt at the sight of my shield surrounding myself and a giant bear. "Where in gods' names were you? You were gone so long that I came looking and I panicked..." I'd never seen him out of breath before, and the guilt ate at my heart.

Dropping my shield, I moved further into the camp and signaled Ursin to stay behind for a moment. I looked at the assembled camp. "I must speak with Captain Lovelace about some things, but we are in no danger from any beasts in the forest. This is Ursin—he is here to protect me. There will be others."

Thomas backed up my command. "You heard your queen. No creatures are to be harmed." He nodded awkwardly at Ursin, who moved to follow me into camp. When the three of us arrived at our tent, the magnificent creature curled up just outside to keep watch.

"Thank you, Ursin," I said, patting the lovely beast on top of the head. He nudged my hand with his head.

It is my pleasure, my queen. Enjoy your evening. You are safe.

Caden approached the bear with a bucket of water and some scraps of bread. Kai stayed behind, practically using Caden as a shield. Caden scoffed and said, "Oh, don't be such a baby. He's clearly friendly. Hey, big guy. I brought you some food and water. I'm afraid we don't have any raw meat, and I'm not exactly sure what bears eat otherwise, but I take care of the horses here, and I'm happy to help you too!"

Ursin rolled his eyes at me with a bear chuckle. *I can hunt for myself, but tell him thank you for the water.*

I passed along the message, then Thomas and I entered the tent, and he whirled on me in confusion. "How in all the eight kingdoms do you know the bear's name? I mean, I believe you because..." He held up his hand, gesturing in Ursin's general direction. "But..."

I sighed, plopped down on our bedroll, and recounted everything my bear guardian had told me. When I finished, Thomas rubbed his eyes roughly with his knuckles. I waited to hear him tell me how crazy I was, but when his hands pulled away, he looked at me with reverence.

"You're incredible, you know that? A fucking goddess," he said with a proud grin.

"We don't know that..." I trailed off.

"You haven't learned that yet, but I've known since we were children," he said, leaning in with eyes full of fire. "My goddess." He grabbed my hips and flipped me onto my back, climbing on top of me as his lips met mine.

My fingers gripped his hair as I urged him for more, wrapping my aching legs around him. I reached to unfasten his pants, "I need more..."

As his tongue swept mine, he pulled my breasts out of my dress to assault them in the most heavenly way. Abandoning our kiss, he moved to swirl his tongue around one peaked nipple before turning to the other, "It pains me to say this, my goddess, but the first time we make love will not be in a tent for all to hear, but I will ensure you sleep well tonight."

I was reminded of the bear outside, who surely would hear it all regardless, and the animal huffed a laugh in return.

Chapter 24

Thomas

The first rays of sunshine broke through the thin slits of our tent, lighting Cecilia up like a painting of a goddess. I had already risen for my watch in the middle of the night, returned to bed, and woken again to check in with my guards. My queen's protector had kept his promise and guarded our tent all night. Others had come just as she had said, and the various predators formed a circle around our encampment. An extensive assortment of birds had also gathered around our firepit and looked to be having a meeting. A ridiculous notion, but I somehow knew it to be true.

When she finally woke, she looked up at me and smiled, still curled in my arms. "Ursin says you barely slept. There was plenty of protection. You could have stayed."

"I slept long enough, and I'll be fine. We should get up and get going though," I said, and kissed her forehead. "And that bear is a rat."

She chuckled, and the warmth of it spread up through my limbs and into my heart. The more time we spent together the more often I felt this little tug, like a string tied around my heart. We changed quickly and exited our tent—the only one still up— and joined the ranks preparing to continue our trek. We mounted our horses and snacked as we rode so we wouldn't delay the group further. A horde of bears and wolves escorted our party, and a mixed flock of birds flew around us, keeping watch from above.

"We have another five hours to ride, Captain. If we limit breaks, we should make it to Yelen before dark," Kai informed us.

I nodded and checked the path of the sun. "We'll take one break halfway for the horse's sake. I don't want to push them too hard."

Cecilia startled a moment, then giggled.

"What was that about?" I asked her.

"Your horse—Toirneach is his real name by the way—says only a brief stop will be necessary. And the horses are very relieved that they can now break their vow of silence." She paused to chuckle again. "He said some of them had almost forgotten how to talk; they've been mute for so long." She gently scratched the top of his head.

After a single break and an otherwise quiet trip, the tower of Yelen came into view above the trees in the distance. Yelen was one of the smallest kingdoms of the eight—if you could call it a kingdom, considering they hadn't had a king in decades—but it was the most physically protected. The stone walls were aged and marred with small cracks but stood strong—a testament to the skilled workers and mages who had fortified them. Dark green ivy provided a strong covering over the old rock wall that surrounded the town.

Cecilia finally broke the silence. "Ursin said the city is safe. The animals will hide in the woods so nobody gets scared. I'd like to leave by morning in search of my mother, now that the villagers will be safe here."

I nodded and shouted the orders. Upon entering Yelen through the gate that had been opened for us, we were greeted by a handful of nobles who bowed before us. Most of the villagers here were tradesmen and women and wore light brown tunics and pants. The noblemen were the aged members that had passed on the physical work to the younger generation and now used their knowledge to lead the community. The only way to tell the noblemen apart was the lighter color of their shirts, which no longer needed to disguise grease and ash stains. Yelen was an example of how I thought all the kingdoms should be run. The oldest spoke. "Queen Cecilia, you and your friends are welcome here as long as you need, and we are here to serve you. We heard news of your father's downfall from a message delivered by bird, and you have our loyalty. We are having a cabin made up for you, and the inn is available for your escorts. We'll get the refugees settled into homes around the village."

I helped Cecilia down from her horse, bowed to the group, and waited for Cece to speak. "Thank you, my lord, but I'm afraid I am not queen yet. My father still lives, and there are forces working against us. We will shelter here tonight, but a small group of us will continue on in the morning. We have a number of refugees with us. Are you able to take them in?" she asked, tipping her head in respect.

"Of course, Your Majesty, and you are queen in our eyes, regardless. We have plenty of accommodations and resources. The refugees will be welcomed here and provided for until they can get back on their feet. There are many tasks they can take on in return. My men will show them to the available rooms. I'm sure you'd like to get cleaned up. Follow me and I'll show you to your lodgings," he said, bowing again.

I had been to Yelen many times, and it hadn't changed since I was a child. All the buildings were made of stone and spread out evenly along the grid of their road system. Most of the homes had small gardens or pens of small livestock just off their porches. At the center of the grid was a water fountain surrounded by a miniature version of our eight Original Gods and Goddesses in statue form.

The refugees were escorted towards the houses ahead of us while our closer companions were taken to the inn for a hearty meal before they cleaned up and rested. Cecilia and I were escorted to a beautiful cabin containing plush seating, a fireplace, and a small dining set. The bathroom had a large tub and the bedroom was massive, filled with a cozy four poster bed covered in pillows and woven blankets. I grinned at Cecilia at the sight of it. Perhaps tonight would finally be the night. But first, the queen needed to eat. I knew better than to keep her from food.

After getting settled in, we headed to the inn to meet our crew for dinner. We joined Kai, Alwyn, Caden, Entriken, Zell, and Amelia, who were already seated at a large round table.

"What is the plan, Your Majesty?" Kai asked as soon as we sat down.

Cecilia smiled sweetly at my best friend. "Please, Kai. Cecilia is fine. I fear the only plan I have at the moment is to find my mother. I suspect the route will be dangerous. Thomas, Zell, and I will travel the rest of the way alone with my woodland friends. I'd like you and Caden to stay here to help everyone get settled in and to organize a protection effort in case Yelen is attacked."

I could see Kai's heart sink. He and I had become like brothers, and I couldn't remember the last time I had spent more than a few days away from him. I assumed he wanted to aid me, but he—and even more so Caden—already seemed so fond of our soon-to-be queen.

"Are you sure that's wise? Amelia and I can manage the refugees. I'd feel much better if you had more reinforcements. We have a full team here; I'm sure we can spare Kai and Caden," Alwyn asked.

"We'll be fine, old friend. I promise," she said, placing a hand on his forearm as he sat next to her. She gave him a smile then took another bite of her food before adding, "I think this tavern could use your help, Al. This food is not quite what I'm used to."

"It's far better than the rest of us are used to," Caden responded.

Cecilia's eyes filled with tears at this, and I stroked her back.

"I'm sorry, I didn't mean—" Caden started before she cut him off.

"No. You're right. It kills me to know how badly all of you

have been treated. It's not going to be easy, but I promise you that things will change. I'll make sure the whole kingdom is fed just as well as I am, no matter what I have to sacrifice. And treated better than I've been. I understand how you feel in that regard."

The rest of dinner was quiet and contemplative, but a much-needed respite for all of us.

"We have a long trip ahead of us. I'm going to call it an early night with my lady, gents. Have a wonderful evening." I took Cecilia's hand to head back to our room, only one low whistle following us out. She rolled her eyes at me and chuckled.

She headed straight for the bedroom and lit the small fireplace —the soft orange glow the only illumination in the dark room. The fire heated the cozy space to just the right temperature as the flames sent flickering shadows dancing across the bare walls. She turned to face me, skin aglow in the essence of her flames, and I was struck by how stunning she looked surrounded by fire. She always looked stunning, but the flames were clearly her element. The light to my dark. The good in the midst of this evil world. And tonight, her flames and my shadows would finally come together. I couldn't pinpoint the exact moment I had fallen in love with her, but it had been years ago. Granted, it had grown stronger since Aldus had assigned me to watch her, but I had always loved her. I had seen her naked a few times now, and we had been intimate, but I had never waited this long to bed a woman.

We had played the cat and mouse game for so long, but I wanted to make sure our lovemaking was perfect. Both of us had had our fair share of partners, but this was different. This wasn't just the joining of two bodies, but the joining of two souls that were meant to be together. Judging by the slowness with which she removed her clothing, I had an inkling she felt the same. It wasn't going to be like the rough ravaging I had watched her take from Henry as I joined in. She may have cared for him, but she loved me. The string tugging my heart told me that.

I approached her and took her wrists to stop her from undressing herself. "That's my job, Princess."

"I don't believe that was what Aldus had in mind when he assigned you to me," she said with a sparkle of mischief in her eyes.

Brushing her loose hair behind her ears, I kissed her neck. Her skin broke out in goosebumps, and I felt a shiver pass through her body. I doubted anyone had ever been this gentle with her. Yet another reason this time with me would be different. I released her wrists, and she immediately went for the ties of my pants. Chuckling against her skin, I said, "In good time, my love. We have all night. I want to make sure you never forget tonight. How your body feels against mine. How our hearts beat as one. How I kept you on the brink of orgasm for hours..."

It was her turn to chuckle. "Careful, Captain Lovelace. Unkept promises are a girl's worst enemy."

"Guess I better make sure I keep them then." I startled her by grabbing her by her voluptuous ass and carrying her to the bed. I set her down gently before standing back up to undo the ties to my pants. Her eyes darted between my hands and my eyes as I dropped my pants to the floor. Next, I slid my shirt up and over my head and tossed it to join my pants. I stalked closer to the bed, and she bit her lip as I neared.

I ripped her riding pants and undergarments off in one fell swoop, and a surprised screech escaped her before she launched into a fit of giggles. I stifled them by sliding my hands up the bare skin of her thighs. As my fingers reached the edge of her blouse, I grabbed hold to lift it up her body as my palms maintained contact with her body. I gave her breasts a hearty squeeze and continued pushing her shirt up until she sat up to let me pull it over her head.

When I flung her clothes to join mine on the floor, she said, "You take away all the fun. I wanted to take them off." Her bottom lip stuck out in a pout, and I wanted to bite it, but I had promised myself, and her, that I'd be gentle.

"Sorry, love, you're not allowed to do any work tonight. Now just lay back, relax, and enjoy the show." I ran a finger between her legs, finding her nice and wet for me already. I circled it around her sensitive bundle of nerves, making her back arch up off the bed.

"I wanted to hate your cockiness so much, but gods dammit is it hot. Please don't make me wait any longer. We have plenty of nights for foreplay."

Both of us now fully naked, I found that I didn't want to wait any longer either.

"Don't worry, I take contraceptive tea daily. We're fine," she stated, ruining the moment.

"I'm not worried about that. You'd make an excellent mother, I have no doubt. I was just taking a moment to soak in how lucky I am."

"Kiss ass. Just stick it in already."

I raised one eyebrow as I climbed on top of her. With my cock nudged at her entrance, I paused to take in her beauty and the pure elation I had in this moment. Slowly sliding myself in, I earned a pleased gasp. "I was trying to be romantic."

"Romance isn't really our thing, is it? Now call me a spoiled brat and teach me a lesson." She pushed me off her and flipped over to all fours, showing off her best assets.

"Gods, Cecilia. I don't want to just fuck you. I want to make love to you."

"And if that's not what I want?" The look in her eyes almost made her look scared, but I hadn't known her to have an ounce of fear within her and it warred with her words.

"Then I'll give you whatever you want, I just..."

She turned back over onto her back to meet my eyes and took my hands in hers. "I know. But I've never had feelings like this before. Sometimes I don't know how to handle it, so I joke. This scares me. It's never scared me before. How I feel about you scares me. Not all the time, but that's why I just want to do this. So my nerves fade away."

"I know," I replied with a tentative smile. "The way I feel about you scares me too. But trust me, I've tried for years to stop it. I can't. And I'm done wanting to."

She nodded and pulled me back on top of her. "Make love to me, Thomas."

"As you command, Princess."

I took my time and kept an even pace as I gazed into her eyes. I had never noticed before how they swirled with color, like a galaxy. Our hands explored each other's bodies as our pleasure built and our souls melded. With each thrust, her body rocked with mine, her breasts bouncing underneath me, just grazing my bare chest.

With more strength than I could've imagined, she rolled me over onto my back, managing to keep my length inside of her as she did so. She rocked front to back as my hand gripped her ass, thrusting into her harder each time she moved closer. She leaned back, gripping my ankles and rocking me into her harder and harder. I almost finished right then and there, watching the way her arched body coaxed her pleasure from mine. Entranced in my own bliss, I had forgotten my promise.

Flipping her back onto her back, I said, "I believe I told you to let me do the work. Just lay back and relax."

"You're going too slow. I need you, Thomas. Harder. Faster. Now."

I obliged, almost hammering into her with as much force as I was willing to risk so I wouldn't hurt her. After a few minutes, she began to tense up and I slowed down, not wanting this feeling to ever end, placing kisses along her shoulder. The string around my heart that linked me to her squeezed and squeezed, as if it was going to burst. Gods, I loved her. And this moment I had waited for was worth every moment we had put it off.

"Don't stop," she demanded breathlessly.

"I have a promise to keep. It hasn't been hours yet."

"You're a monster."

I chuckled and put my nose to her ear. "Only for you."

Each time she edged close to release, I slowed my pace or changed positions—teasing her but also fighting my own release. The warmth of the room and the occasional flicker of Cecilia's powers in the heat of passion had us both gleaming with sweat.

I built myself into a frenzy as I braced myself above her and looked deep into her eyes. I was determined to make her finish in the same moment I did and let my thumb swirl around her clit to ensure it. I regretted having held out for so long when my release finally overtook me, and I groaned with a final shudder into her. Her moans reached a crescendo at the same time, and a flash of light blinded me as I felt the temperature go up drastically. Instantly, I threw up a shield of shadows, protecting us from harm. I couldn't say the same for the room around us. Everything was ablaze.

"Shit!" she yelled, as she jumped up and shoved me off her. I watched as she used her ice and water powers to extinguish the flames. Not soon enough though, because everything was scorched. Both of us collapsed into the bed and each other in a heap of laughter.

"Good thing we stole a bunch of the king's money before we left, huh? We're going to need to pay for damages everywhere we stop."

Chapter 25

Cecilia

He had kept his promise. Just barely, but over two hours still counts as hours. It was also the best night of sleep I had ever gotten. I had set the entire room ablaze when he finally let me reach my release, but his shadows had protected him, and my ice and water had put it out before any real damage was done.

Bright and early the next morning, we left the safety of Yelen's walls to meet up with Zell and the others. We still needed to formulate our plan and check on the animals. Thomas checked in with Caden and Kai, leaving me to finally have more than a moment alone with Zell. I needed more answers, and he had them. "How do you know where my mother is? And how did you know she was alive?"

"She and I have had...ways of communicating since she was brought back. I'm afraid I can't tell you more than that."

"Then why now? Why didn't you tell me any of this sooner?" I asked him, my voice getting louder and shakier as my fists clenched my skirt.

He sat down on a log and brushed some dirt off his pants. "I've known Aldus for decades. He's a brilliant and fearsome man. Of all the paths forward your mother had seen, she did everything she could to avert the ones that ended badly for you. But she couldn't foresee every detail. This path we were on, it wasn't one where we expected him to try to take your life. But it was almost as if he couldn't do it himself, so he sent Hinch after you to do his dirty work. That plan has failed, but it was never his main goal. Power is the end game. My intel tells me he has learned of a way to gather more for himself. In his mind, he could surpass your power and be invincible. We have to find out what he knew and stop that from happening."

"Do we even know how he planned to do that? How do we stop something we don't know?"

He shrugged, then turned a curious eye to the approaching Captain Lovelace. "I'm sure his number one might have some knowledge we don't. That's why I mentioned wanting to talk to both of you once we were out of immediate danger. I see he hasn't lost that cocky swagger his position had given him in the castle. If anything, I think it's gotten worse since he landed you as a future wife," he said, giving me a mocking smile.

Laughing at his assessment of the captain, I agreed. "Maybe you should put him in his place more often. I think you'd make an excellent queen's lead advisor. I believe that gives you more power than head of the guard, does it not?"

"I'll make sure to point that out to him. Often," he said jovially before turning serious. "He is a good man, and he cares deeply for you. Love like that is a rare thing. Hold tightly to it." Zell analyzed Thomas as he approached us.

Once Thomas reached us, he planted a kiss on my forehead. "Everyone is accounted for and safe. The refugees have settled in nicely. Alwyn and Amelia as well."

"Good timing. We're hoping you can help us with some information."

"I'll do what I can. Not sure how much I can help, though. Cecilia knows everything I do already."

"You've been close to the king, young man. If anybody knows

what he knows, surely it would be you. Did he ever mention a magical object or something he was searching for?"

Thomas crossed his arms, thought for a moment, then nodded. "I wasn't sure what he was referring to at the time, because my father had just passed away and I was preparing to fill his shoes. I was still a child, but I remember him mentioning a lost divine object. I didn't think it was related, but recently he told me there was a prophecy the queen had mumbled in her sleep. He was convinced I'd be the one to help him when he had what he needed. He has sent me and my men searching several times in the past few years. We've had very little intel to go on. No idea what or where it is. He sent a mage with us who we believed had more information than us, but we've come back empty-handed each time, which really angered him. Why do you ask?"

"Zell believes my father is still looking for the item and that it could give him immense power. He plans to use it to become invincible—the only thing that will make him stronger than me. We have to find it first. Do you remember any of the prophecy?" I asked him hopefully.

"Of course. He made me repeat it every night.
Deep in the Blue Forest, there lies a ring,
That mixed with shadow, power would bring
Until the day darkness incarnate doth return
Humans, not Gods, would have their turn."
Zell let out a heavy breath and rested his face in his hands. "That was what I was afraid of. I had suspected he overheard the queen and I discussing this item. She had tasked me with helping you find it, Princess. We must get to it before your father does."

"Okay. Where is it? And what is it? And why didn't you just say that?"

"We needed to learn what Thomas knew of it first. I don't know where it is, but it's the Ring of Creidsinn. It is said to contain the powers of a god that the wearer would wield. Rumors say it can only be unlocked by the dark shadow magic that your ancestor banned and eradicated for this exact reason. He was a smart man. No one person should have that much power."

"But my father wants it, and he thinks he needs Thomas to use it because of his magic. Wait, how do you know about Thomas's magic?"

He chuckled. "Your mother was all-seeing, my dear. I know almost all of what she knows."

Zell spoke so warmly of my mother. I wondered if they had ever been a thing. What would it have been like to grow up with him as a father instead? Bringing myself back to reality, I said, "Thomas, did my father ever give you any hints as to where it was or how to find it?"

"None. He clearly had no idea because he sent his mage with us, searching every damn kingdom and torturing anyone he thought might have information about it."

"Well, that's shit. So how do we start? All we have is that it's in the Blue Forest, and that pretty much covers the whole continent. Why didn't you tell us about this sooner?"

Zell stood and placed a hand on my shoulder. "I wasn't sure who in our party could be trusted. Now that it's a smaller group, I felt better about having this discussion. Dropping on you that your mother was alive was enough for you to deal with to start. I think the ring should be our first stop. In regards to finding it, I think you'll lead us right to it, my dear."

Actually, that's why we're here, a gruff voice said in my head.

Thomas startled and hid behind me for a moment as an enormous wolf passed in front of us. "Fuck, that will never not be unsettling."

I was driven by instinct to trust this oversized creature and could feel his warmth radiating towards me. I ran my fingers through the fur on his back. "He says that's why they're here." The wolf sat down next to my feet and looked sideways up at me. "Do you know where it is? Or what it does?"

We know where it is. It will not be easy, but you're ready. Our master did not tell us what it does, but it was his. It will be yours now. That was his intention.

"Thank you...I'm sorry, I don't know your name." I frowned, scrunching my brows.

My name is Mac, Princess.

"Thank you, Mac." I smiled and tipped my head at him, earning myself a toothy grin and bow.

"Perhaps we should get our trek started," Thomas said, taking my arm in his.

I shook my head. "We learned too much this morning. We have to plan."

Zell stood and bowed his head down at both of us. "The captain is right. We have to get a move on to stay ahead of the king and any mages he has left. I'll do another sweep and make sure the others are aware of our departure."

Thomas bowed his thanks to Zell.

"Thank you, Zell!"

"You're very welcome, Princess."

We began to walk towards Toirneach, Thomas' horse, but I turned to smile at Zell one last time. He held out his hand to pet Mac, who gently nuzzled his face into Zell's palm. I turned back to face Thomas, who was also taking in the scene. His brows furrowed, and he looked back at me with a shrug before we continued to our animal escorts.

Kai and Caden approached, the former spreading out a map against the side of his horse for us to view. He slid his fingers across it, magically exposing the path we had followed here and showing no threats. "It doesn't look like we were followed, Princess. Which way are we heading so I can scope out the path forward?"

My instincts failed me, but the creatures all looked in unison in the same direction. I pointed towards the trail that headed west. "That way, according to our nonhuman friends."

He checked the direction I suggested, Caden holding his

forearm to replenish his magic expenditure. When he noticed me observing, I looked away in shame.

"It's okay, Princess. I just want to make sure he keeps his energy for the road ahead. We don't have any idea what we're going to encounter. How are you feeling? Do you need a little boost?"

"I've never...does it hurt?"

Caden playfully glanced at Kai. "Does it hurt, my love?"

"It tingles, but in a good way. It's like a burst of fresh, cool air in the morning," Kai said, kissing Caden before whirling to mount his horse.

Caden wiggled his fingertips at me, and I held out my hand. He placed a gentle kiss on my knuckles; then I felt a cool tingling spreading from his fingertips up my arms. Kai was right, it was like a cool morning breeze. I felt refreshed and lighter.

"Thank you, Caden. That felt lovely." And it really had. The stress that had been tightening my chest had even loosened. My fire power warmed me like the afternoon sun from the inside out, and my ice snapped my stiff joints. I had never felt so reinvigorated or alive.

"You should tell Thomas. He never lets me use it on him. Freaks him out to think his shadows are going to hurt me. If at any point you need more, don't hesitate to ask, okay, sweetheart?"

"I won't. Thank you, Caden."

When Zell returned from his check-in, we started in the planned direction. Thomas rode his horse, but Ursin insisted I ride him instead. Mac walked next to us. I didn't want to hurt Thomas's feelings, but this was way more comfortable on my behind than his horse had been. Aside from Zell, Entriken, Caden, and Kai, we also had a handful of other guards under Thomas' command. I was grateful Alwyn and Amelia had stayed behind though. I could feel deep in the pit of my stomach that the trek would be too risky for them.

My thoughts turned to our creature companions. "How did

all of you know where to find me? And can you understand each other? I didn't think different species got along this well."

The colossal bear's gruff voice entered my head. *We've been connected to you since your birth.*

Mac's slightly less gravelly voice came next. *Though all of us are connected to you, the Alpha and Luna of each pack—or the strongest and most fearsome in other species—have the strongest connection. All of us can communicate with each other as well, but it is easier for certain species to understand each other. For example, mammals find it easier to talk to other mammals and birds, versus snakes or lizards.*

"That's so interesting. I wonder why that is."

We've never been given an answer, but we bears assume it's because different gods created each class of animals. Mac and I were both created by Memach.

And we don't get along this well when the world is in balance. All the animals sense the war coming, and we know we must put our differences aside to protect you. The great wolf gave me a toothy smile then looked at Ursin with just a tinge of disdain.

Even when we think they're weak and tiny, Ursin added cheekily.

Better than being smelly and uncivilized, you great brute!

"Okay, okay. I shouldn't have asked. I appreciate you both, and you all have very different talents. There's no reason that should create a rift between you. I need you all."

Ursin preened under my touch as I stroked the top of his head. I held out my other hand to Mac, who nuzzled it. Mac shoulder-bumped Ursin then ran off ahead of the pack, the horses with their riders parting in terror at his approach. I chuckled at his childishness—such a contrast to the fear he instilled in grown men trained to fight.

When we paused for our first break, I sat down on a large boulder next to Entriken. "How are you feeling? Has the rest and food helped?"

The dark circles under his eyes had faded slightly, but it would take time to put some weight back on him. He gave me a sad smile and put a hand on my knee. "Much better, Cece. Thank you for looking out for me. After everything I haven't done for you, I'll never understand why, but I am grateful."

He almost jumped out of his boots when a large bird landed between us, making me chuckle. "It's ok, none of them will harm you. They're here to help." Holding a berry, I held out my hand, and he snatched it up.

The black bird with sharp talons stared at Entriken, tilting his head to the side as if analyzing him before turning back to me. *Not as good as meat, but thank you for your generosity, my queen. I will cherish this fruit.*

"You're very welcome. Did you need something from me, or are you just saying hello? I'm so sorry, I don't know your name."

Ean, if you please. I came to tell you that a lone mage from Hinch is much closer than your mapmaker can see. I lost him in the thick brush, so I think he cloaked himself. You must all be on high alert. If he's able to hide himself from the cartographer, he may be far more dangerous than you expect.

"Thank you. I'll inform the captain immediately. Please take a rest and ride on the wagon for a while. You must be exhausted, you poor thing."

Your kindness is most welcoming, Your Majesty. I'll do as you say. Perhaps I will ride on Entriken's cart and...keep an eye on him for you. He turned back to run his sharp gaze over my brother once more before taking flight.

Thomas approached us with the same evaluating gaze towards my kin. "We should get moving again."

"We should. I've just been informed there's a cloaked mage closer than we suspected. We have to be on our guard even more now."

"In that case, you should ride with me," Thomas said.

Absolutely not. She will ride with me, Mac said, as if Thomas could also hear him. *My queen, I can move faster than both these horses and the ambling bear. Should anything happen, I'll be your best bet to race you to safety.*

I'll escort you as well. Despite what the wolf says, I can keep up. Ursin bared his teeth and neither beast backed off from the stare down.

"I'm afraid the animals disagree. I'll ride on Mac for the time being, in case we need to make a break for it."

Mac's fur was softer than Ursin's had been, and he was a more comfortable seat, but the bear had been a much smoother ride. Both were still leaps and bounds better than the horses.

"Both of you are the leaders of your packs? Do you have wives? Children?"

They both rushed to speak at once, like children, and I worried they might start shoulder-bumping each other again. Since I rode the smaller mammal this time, I wasn't interested to see how that played out.

"Mac first, please."

My Luna is named Ceann. We've been bonded for twelve years and have 13 pups. A very lucky number indeed. She's an excellent mother, which allows me more time to manage our pack. I look forward to playing with all of them when I get home though. It's the highlight of every day, and I'm so grateful for her.

"That's beautiful and she sounds amazing. I'd love to meet her one day," I said with a fond smile.

You will, my queen.

"How about you, Ursin?"

I was mated, but my wife was killed a few years ago by one of your father's hunters. Fortunately, we did not have any children, so I don't have to worry about them being cared for while I'm away. Bears are lonely creatures, and it works well for us.

"I'm so sorry, Ursin."

You're not your father, Queen Cecilia. But it is the life of the bear. I grieve sometimes, but I'm also glad she's not around for the war that's coming. She would've hated this.

"I don't blame her. I hate it too."

Chapter 26

Thomas

Given my profession, I had never been one to let my fear show. It existed, but I'd never let others see it. That became a lot harder to do with a whole menagerie of beasts traveling with our caravan. Though I was unsettled, there was no doubt in my mind that every word Cecilia had said about them was true. They trusted her, and they clearly cared about keeping her safe. Zell and Caden were the only other two who appeared comfortable around them, or at least not terrified. Caden constantly tried to feed and groom them, and he and Cecilia had been bonding over them as she translated between the parties. He spent a lot of time with Mac especially but was fond of Ursin as well.

I just hoped they could help us find the ring before Aldus did. The animals were vague on the plan, just that they knew where the ring was and would lead us to it. So we followed. Kai checked the map frequently to see if we had any concerning obstacles, but we appeared to have put enough space between ourselves and Aldus's men. We had seen no sign of the cloaked mage the birds had warned us of, but I didn't doubt their intel.

My mood was soured by being separated from Cecilia the whole day, which was ridiculous. I had no reason to be jealous of her spending time with the critters. *Is she avoiding me? Perhaps now that she doesn't fear her father kicking her out, she doesn't need me anymore?* My worries were assuaged when we stopped to make camp for the night, and she rushed into my arms and planted a deep kiss on my lips.

"I missed you so much. At least I'm not as sore as yesterday though, so that's something," she said with a cheeky wink.

Chuckling, I brushed her windblown hair behind her ears and placed another kiss on her forehead. "I missed you too. I was starting to think you didn't need me anymore."

"Even if I didn't need you, which I do, I would still always choose you."

"And I, you, love. I'll help the men get set up while you get your forest friends organized and find Entriken. We'll have him join us and Zell for dinner before we get some rest."

She nodded and headed off towards the bear and wolf she was becoming so close with. I smirked as she gently patted each of their heads and they nuzzled into her. I was still amazed they hadn't ripped each other's throats out. In my experience, the two species hated each other. Even the animals realized something bigger was going on here, and I wasn't sure I wanted to discover how this played out.

I helped my men organize the layout of the encampment and then began setting up the tent for Cecilia and I before Entriken joined me. I didn't pause but glared at him as I continued erecting the tent.

He didn't make eye contact but fiddled with his trembling hands. In a low voice he said, "I wanted to say thank you. For making me do what I wasn't brave enough to do on my own. I'm pretty sure that saved my life, and I don't think I can ever repay you."

"As long as you're good to your sister, we're even. I didn't do it for you. She's the only person I care about at this point. Don't let her down again."

He nodded and walked away. Zell sidled up next to me a moment later, obviously having watched the exchange.

"Do you trust him?" he asked me.

"Nope. But Cecilia does, so I have to deal with it."

He raised a brow at me. "You suspect there's something he's not telling us? You think he was privy to more than he let on?"

"I do. I was the king's number one, but when I wasn't in the room, that blubbering snot was. I think the king has something on him, or I doubt he would've turned on his sister so easily. They were close as children. He clearly doesn't trust me, but he knows how dedicated you were to the council. I need you to keep an eye on him."

"Of course, Captain. You have my word."

Minutes later the camp was settled, and I took a seat with my lovely paramour, her brother, Zell, Caden, and Kai. In addition to the great bear and wolf on either side of her, several smaller critters gathered near Cecilia—the queen's own little council. We kept to small talk about the trek and learned from the wildlife that we were only days away from where the ring was hidden. They could sense it and assured Cecilia she could too, if she concentrated hard enough. We were so close, but none of us knew what to expect when we got there. Would there be some kind of test? What would the ring do? Would we even be able to find it?

We turned in for the night shortly thereafter, and I felt like I had just fallen asleep when I heard a beastly wail and high-pitched yelps. Before I could even get my pants on, Cecilia had run out of the tent towards the mayhem. By the time I caught up, our entire encampment was encased in a fog dome surrounded by powerful gusts of wind that barred everyone from the presumed danger outside. This was Cecilia's handiwork without a doubt.

I watched as Zell crashed through the wind towards her and whatever was causing the commotion. I fought to do the same, but it was too strong. I pushed and pushed before I finally forced my shadows to make a bubble around me to trudge through. When I came out on the other side, I walked into a bloody mess of strewn body parts and Cecilia crouched over Mac, her hands holding together an unfixable wound. Zell had his hands raised with fireballs aimed at the last surviving mage, who was beaten and barely breathing. Caden and Kai broke out of her dome right behind me.

"Thomas, help. You need to heal him. Now!"

I briefly looked to Zell who said, "I got him. Try to help her."

Ursin bounded to my side—flesh and entrails hanging from his maw—as I placed my hands on the gigantic wolf to assess the damage. He didn't appear to be breathing or have a heartbeat. From my first look, I knew it was too late, but I threw all my energy into reversing what had been done to him to no avail. "I'm sorry, Cecilia. It's too late."

She buried her face in the fur on the top of his head and whispered, "No. You promised me I'd get to meet your Luna. You need to wake up, Mac. Your kids need you."

Caden collapsed next to her, bracing his hands on my shoulders and pumping his amplification powers into me for the first time. I startled backward, afraid my shadows would leak into him. "I told you never to do that."

Caden's angry gaze met mine as he forcefully gripped my arm. "I don't care. Mac is our friend, and he needs help. If this helps, so be it. I can handle a little shadow. Just try to save him. Now!"

Mac still didn't stir, and Cecilia's tear-filled eyes looked up at me, breaking my heart. After a few moments of failed healing, I shook my head.

"What the hell happened? How did you get out of the tent so far ahead of me?"

"I could feel the beasts fear. It's the first time I've felt that connection. Their patrolling guards felt an approaching dark presence, but I wasn't fast enough. Ten mages attacked, all of them cloaked. The animals took out some of them, and I did the rest. Zell stopped me before I finished off the last one so we could question him. I was too late. Mac..."

"Died valiantly, protecting his queen. As any of us would

have. He knew what he was signing up for by joining us. He was an honorable wolf," Zell said, nodding at Ursin.

"We need to bury him," Cecilia said to me before she paused to hear out the bear. "Ursin said the wolves do not bury their dead. We have to bring his body back to his family. To his Luna. I know we don't have much room on the carts, but Entriken is in better shape. We'll let him sit outside the cart, and I'll ice Mac's body to preserve it. We have to do this for him."

I put up my hands in placation. "You'll get no argument from me. I'll carry him."

"Ursin wants to help. He said to put Mac on his back, and he'll bring him to the cart for you."

"I'll help," said Caden solemnly. Kai stroked his upper arm in comfort.

I never thought I'd witness a dead wolf on the back of his bear friend, but here I was. After I loaded the brave wolf onto the cart, I turned back to hug Cecilia, who broke down, sobbing harder than her tough exterior had let me believe her capable of.

Zell placed a hand on her shoulder, but the words he provided weren't the comfort I had expected. "Mac was the first to die for his new queen, but he won't be the last. You have a huge heart. It's why everyone loves you, but you're going to have to learn to live with this. You'll do well to learn from Thomas. You two head back and get some rest. I'm sure you're exhausted from how much magic you spent, so check in with Caden first for a refresh. I'll interrogate this one."

Pulling away from my embrace and taking a deep breath, she collected herself as she faced him. She stood tall. Regal. "No. I have to do this. This is war. I need to be queen."

She strode over to the remaining mage and gripped his wrist, a thin layer of ice forming around it. He was stunned awake and looked into her eyes, shaking with fear as he realized what was about to happen.

"Please, Princess. Please have mercy on me. We were only

following your father's orders!" His pleading was authentic, but it fell on deaf ears.

She tilted her head and stared down at him without pity. "Like you had mercy on my wolf? And I must've heard you wrong, because I swear you said 'Princess.' No. I am Queen Cecilia. Now tell me—" She squeezed him harder, gritting her teeth. As the pain of his resistance began setting in, she asked, "Who are you, and why are you here?"

He screamed in agony as her powers pushed through his brain. The bad ones always fought it. "I'm from Hinch. We freed your father from the dungeon you left him in, and he sent us after you to kill you. He can't let you find the ring first," he managed to spit out before he passed out from the pain.

A fireball grew in Cecilia's palm then shot straight through his heart, and a large sphere of ice froze around his head. There would be no mercy today. "All of them were cloaked, powerful, and using outlawed, dark magic. None of them had shadow magic, so my dad probably sent them to capture you. He didn't say it out loud, but I could see the truth in his head. Dad is scared, which is making him even more terrifying. There are more after us. We need to be vigilant. The beastly protection is not enough, and we need to pick up the pace. Be ready to leave before first light."

That was my girl. She could've easily broken down under the pressure of her loss. Instead, she was using the rage to fuel her fire and drive. My heartstrings squeezed tighter as it swelled in my chest.

"Spoken like a true queen," I said, smiling at her.

Zell also beamed with pride and nodded. "As you wish, my queen."

Chapter 27

What the fuck am I doing? Who have I become? Maybe Entriken was right. Father feared me because he thought I was just like him, and here I was showing no mercy to another human because they had killed an animal I had known only a few days. But Mac had been my friend. I doubted my father would avenge a friend. He was in short supply of those. His alliances made in fear were the closest thing he had to friendship.

I stormed back into camp without a word, leaving Zell and Thomas to clean up the mess I'd made. I let my storm dome collapse and snuck back to our tent where I washed up with the bucket of water that had been left for me. Then I collapsed on my bedroll and cried. I had never killed someone before. Hell, I'd never even punched someone. Sure, I'd threatened many, but I'd never had to go this far. I just had to let it out in solitude so our encampment wouldn't see how weak their princess was. Their future queen. What a laugh.

Remorse over taking a life is not a weakness. You did the right thing, but what you're feeling is normal. I'd be far more concerned if you felt nothing. I hadn't heard Ursin enter the tent—for his size, he was very stealthy.

"Thanks, Ursin. I think I just need some time." He laid down next to me and I rested my head on his shoulder, warm in the comfort of his fur. "How are you clean?"

Thomas offered, but he is still terrified of me. Zell washed me up after we got Mac in the cart.

We sat in silence for a bit before he spoke to me again.

It's okay to grieve. Mac was a valiant soul. He will be sadly missed, even by those of us that shouldn't like him. In my experience, situations like this can go one of two ways. Either you will spiral out of control with unhealthy emotions, or you can use your pain to fuel the fire to move forward. To press on. To win.

"I have no idea what I'm doing."

Nobody does. But unlike your father, you're willing to admit that. You learn. And unlike the king, you're not alone.

His head tilted, like he was listening, but I heard nothing.

Someone is coming. It's not Thomas, but he will be along shortly. I'll let you two talk. Just remember, nobody will see you as weak for being upset, but if you feel the need to compose yourself before anyone comes in, you have less than a minute.

Ursin left, and I chose not to clean up. It was Caden who entered. He took one look at my tear-stained cheeks and rushed to sit next to me, wrapping his arms around me and squeezing me tight. He let me sob into his shoulder and didn't say a word, but I could feel his power seep into me, and I took a deep, rejuvenating breath.

"I'm sorry I didn't ask permission first, but judging from that storm dome around us, you used a shit ton of magic. I have no idea how you haven't already crashed. I asked Thomas if I could check on you."

"Thanks, Caden. It took a lot, but I feel okay."

"And mentally? How are you feeling there?"

Pulling back from the hug, I looked into his eyes that gleamed with genuine concern. "I don't think it's sunk in yet. Mac's gone. And I killed someone." I whispered the last part, praying he wouldn't judge me.

"You killed someone that was here to kill you and the rest of us. It was self-defense. This is war, my dear. My heart breaks that you had to experience that horror, but you're so strong. It's going to sting, but you'll get through this. We're all here to make sure you do. If you start to fall, we will pick you back up. We'll be strong for you when you can't be. That's what friends are for."

Friends. Alwyn and Amelia had been my only friends for so long. Caden barely knew me, but I believed him. We were friends. I leaned back into his embrace and rested my head on his shoulder. "I'm really glad you're my friend, Caden."

Thomas entered, saw Caden's arm around me and smiled. I could easily read how much he cared for Caden and Kai, and I imagined that after he lost his parents, the two of them had become his surrogate family. Caden kissed my cheek and stood to leave.

"You did great, Cece. It's easier said than done, but remember that fact. Don't dwell on the bad. The rest of us are alive because of you and your quick thinking. You saved all of us. Sleep well." He and Thomas exchanged nods, and Caden clapped him on the shoulder. "Your turn, my friend. You know where to find me if you need anything."

Thomas took up the spot that Caden had vacated and let me cry silently into his shoulder for a while before he spoke, eyes staring into the far canvas wall of our tent. "The first time I had to kill was to protect my father. We were on the road doing a training exercise when a group of bandits tried to rob our caravan. The man lunged for my father, and I didn't think. I just reacted. I still remember what it felt like when my knife pierced his skin. I remember the color of his eyes and what it looked like when the life faded from them. I've killed many since then—some also memorable—but not like that first one. It takes a piece of your soul. I'd tell you that you get over it, but you don't. It does get easier to convince yourself you did the right thing though. When you're ready to talk about it, I'm here, but for now, just get some rest. I'm glad Caden replenished your magic for you, so you're not so drained."

I fiddled with the hem of my shirt and untucked myself from his embrace to look him in the eyes. "That's the weird part. I wasn't tired at all. When I was young, I felt the drain of magic use quickly. For the past few years, I only feel it when I go invisible. All that tonight—the storm dome, the fighting—it took nothing, Thomas. Nobody should have this power, and it scares the shit out of me. It was *easy* to kill them. Like a snap of my fingers."

"And you can talk to animals. There's no doubt in my mind you've been touched by the gods. There's no way they would have done that if they thought you'd use it for evil. There are reasons you're stronger than your father. The beasts leading you to the ring is just more proof of that."

Thomas didn't leave my side that night, and his embrace never loosened. I could hear Ursin and several other creatures surrounding our tent, their snores lulling me into a restless sleep where I dreamed of the poor wolf that had met an untimely end because of me.

The following morning, our party was silent. I had managed to hide most of my powers from them thanks to the storm dome, but there were still whispers amid the quiet. The whispers weren't of fear, as I had expected, but of respect. And hope. Finally, someone could challenge their king. I still hadn't shaken my grief or guilt.

"You're unusually quiet. Are you okay?" Entriken asked.

We hadn't told him what had happened last night, other than that we had been attacked. His nervous twitching had returned since he had heard the news.

"I'm fine. I'm just anxious now that we're so close to the ring. I have no idea how to wield it or even if we'll find it. I think I'm starting to feel its power."

"Feel it?"

"Yeah, the more we travel, the more I feel this...almost drumbeat in my chest. It's light, but it's there."

He looked like he was about to ask more, but Thomas and Zell joined us to see if we were ready to leave.

"How close are we?" Thomas asked.

"Ursin says we should get there in under two days. We need to ride hard. We can't afford any more slowdowns." I gave him a look that I hoped conveyed not to say more in front of my brother. I loved him, but I still wasn't sure I trusted him. I trusted both Thomas and Zell with my life. Caden, Kai, and the animals as well.

A large, fluffy owl landed on my shoulder and spoke. *The path ahead is clear, Queen Cecilia. We've kept an eye on it all night.* I nodded, and before I could say thank you, it flew off.

"Our route is clear. Let's get moving," I said, in a morose tone. I just couldn't get the sadness of losing Mac out of my thoughts.

Zell and Thomas looked at each other with raised brows as our company moved out.

It was hard for me to focus on our trek as we passed tree after tree, rock after rock, but the men were too concerned with keeping our caravan in order to notice me stuck in my own head. The first few minutes of our ride were silent, but the creatures couldn't ignore their connection to me.

Was your mother the only loss you've experienced before, my queen?

It amazed me how in tune with my emotions the noble beast beneath me was. "She was," I whispered. "I was only a child when it happened. This is my first actual loss as an adult."

You've been very fortunate. I am no stranger to loss. Do not let this loss take away your love and compassion. Your heart is what makes you who you are and what will make you a wonderful leader.

"Loss is one thing, but Mac dying is my fault," I said, wiping a tear from my eye. "That's something I'm having a hard time coming to terms with. I'm not worth his death, and I will not learn to live with it."

He huffed a laugh that probably sounded like a growl to the others, who turned to ensure my safety. I patted Ursin's head to assuage their concern.

If we did not believe you were worth it, we wouldn't be here. It is not just one or two of us, Cecilia. There are hundreds of us fighting for you. Even the humans have realized your worth, despite your father doing what he could to knock it down.

"I don't have what it takes, but Thomas does. I'm grateful he's been handling so much, as it's made it easier, but it should really be him. Not me."

Captain Lovelace is a decent man, but he was your father's mercenary for years. He never challenged him. He thinks he stands for what is good—and most of the time he does—but you consistently defied your father when his choices were wrong.

"He did that to protect me," I said, in an angry, hushed tone.

Aye, he did. But would you have?

"I just murdered an entire group of men to avenge a wolf."

Men sent to kill you and those you care about. Not innocent men that a paranoid king wanted to torture.

"I see no difference."

Which is why you are our queen.

I rolled my eyes at his reasoning, but regardless of what he said, I was never going to believe it. Around midday, we stopped to take a break, and I still didn't feel any better. My breakfast sat like lead in my stomach. Mac was all I had thought about the entire trek. He was my friend, and he was dead because of me. How was I supposed to lead an entire kingdom, never mind keep them safe, if I couldn't save one wolf? *Who am I kidding? I can't do this.* There had to be something I could do to stop this feeling.

Kai approached with his map spread to show me where we were. "My queen, there is a small village a few miles away. The captain does not think it wise to enter—too many witnesses. However, the village has a small trading post along the main road where we can restock for our travels. We'll only have to hit that road briefly, then we can reenter the woods and get back on our way."

Ursin confirmed that he was on board with the plan, then I requested Ean to have the birds scout our path. All was clear, and we made it to the trading post in good time. The villagers bowed or knelt upon seeing me and confirmed that they had heard the news of Revell. They refused to take any money for the wares we selected, saying it was their contribution to our cause.

We replenished our stores of bread, hard cheese, and water. Thomas and Zell purchased knives, and I grabbed two large jars of moonshine. I didn't wish to take advantage of their deal, but after losing Mac, I needed it. Ursin said I had to learn to live with it. This was how I lived with things. I snuck the jars into my pack, and we prepared to head back into the woods. All four men assured us our appearance would remain secret.

When our trip allowed, I snuck sips of my secret drink. After an hour, the pain and grief ebbed, as did my clear vision. I had missed the solace that I found in the bottom of a bottle, but I hadn't needed it in so long. Normally, I'd also turn to other forms of release, but the constant presence of Zell and Entriken left me plotting how to make that happen. When we stopped for the night to make camp, I dismounted Ursin and almost fell on my ass.

"Thomas, would you be a love and escort me while I *relieve* myself?"

"Of course, darling," he said, leaving Entriken and the mage with my furry friends.

When we were out of their line of sight, I shoved the captain against a tree and kissed him deeply. At first, he kissed me back, but then he pulled away to look into my eyes.

"Are you drunk?"

"What does it matter? Just fuck me, Captain."

"Oh, love. I've missed that so much, but I won't do that when you're in this state. What's gotten into you? We're being chased by danger, and you're drinking?"

My eyes brimmed with tears as my gaze sunk to my feet. "It's the only way I could stop feeling—"

"Mac."

I nodded, and he pulled me into his muscular arms, nestling my head into his chest.

"You don't need to drink yourself into not feeling. Talk to us. Me, Kai, Caden, Zell...We're all here for you. I'm sure even Entriken would listen. Let it out."

There was no more holding these tears in. They poured down my face as I sank onto the mossy forest floor. I could feel the dampness seeping through my clothing, but I didn't care. "I can't do this. I can't be queen."

He sat down next to me, gripped my shoulders, and looked at me sternly. "You already are. Look how you protected everyone yesterday and avenged your friend without question. You've made all the right decisions to keep us heading on the right path. Soon you'll have the ring too."

"And I'm responsible for getting that friend killed."

"Wars always come with casualties. You're no more to blame than the rest of us. But drinking isn't the answer. Turning our fury towards finding that ring and your mother...that's what needs to be done. Nobody said this was going to be easy. Don't be the spoiled princess I thought you were. I know you better now, and you're fierce, determined, and fucking unstoppable."

Chapter 28

I had cared for Cecilia since I was a child, but I had been in love with her since I was a teenager. Around that time, she had turned to alcohol and men to drown her sorrows. This was nothing new, so why did it bother me so much? I think I had hoped that being with me would help her grow into believing she was the take-no-shit, powerful woman I knew her to be. That her love for me would help her overcome her vices and confide in others instead of bottling her feelings. It broke my heart that I had been wrong, but I understood. The only person in her life she could truly trust had jumped off a tower to save her.

I was sure she had confided many things in Amelia and Alwyn, but neither of them had the power to help her. Zell and I did, but her unwillingness to confide in us appeared to hurt me far more than it hurt him. Each sip she thought she was sneaking, he eyed her and glanced back at me, but he didn't look angry. He looked concerned but unsurprised, and I suspected I'd be alone in the argument if I confronted her about it. *I'll let it slide. Or maybe I'll let Entriken be the scapegoat?* The thought had the wheels spinning in my head.

With Cecilia and Ursin at the head of the pack, I let Zell,

Caden, and Kai stay directly behind her. I started to fall back and gestured to Entriken to join me.

"Everything okay, Captain Lovelace?" he asked me.

I rolled my eyes at him. "We've known each other since we were in diapers, and the king isn't here. You can't call me Thomas?"

"As captain of the guard and future husband of the princess, no, I can't. It would be a great dishonor and would smear the good name of Revell."

My chuckle brought a smirk to his lips. He may have turned into a sullen creature, but he still had some of his childhood humor. Maybe there was hope for him yet. "I think King Aldus has smeared Revell's name enough on his own." After another shared smile, I turned serious. "I'm worried about Cecilia's drinking."

He tilted his head as he assessed me. "That's who she is. You had to know what you were getting yourself into. Why did you think Dad assigned you to babysit her?"

"I know. But...."

"But you thought you could change her. You're a fool if you think that," Entriken said firmly. He took one look at my concerned face and changed his tone. "I'll talk to her. She'll lose it if it comes from you."

"Thank you, Entriken."

He nodded and picked up his pace to catch her. I wasn't sure it was going to work, but whatever he said to her made her shoulders and eyes drop. Was she embarrassed? Hurt? Maybe I had made the wrong call. Selfishly, I hoped whatever he had said worked. She tucked the bottle away and then turned to glare at me, eyes full of ire.

Zell dropped back, leaving the others to guard my one true love.

"I take it that was your influence?" he asked, tipping his head in Entriken's direction.

I didn't answer, but I met his gaze.

"Slick to use Entriken as a scapegoat, but she's a headstrong woman. You're not going to get her to change with guilt. Just be honest with her. Tell her how you feel. You'll get a lot farther if you convince her *why* you worry about her. Otherwise, you're no better than her *father*." The emphasis he put on the word father concerned me, but he was right. I wouldn't bring it up again unless it really got out of hand. For now, it was clear that the drinking was part of her grieving process. When she was ready to talk, I knew she would come to me.

We had crept closer to the main road than I had realized, but I was glad the birds were keeping better watch than I had been. A whole flock of them dropped out of the sky and began to swirl around the four members of our party ahead of us.

"What's going on?" I shouted over the commotion, hoping Cecilia could hear me as Zell and I picked up our pace toward them.

The birds parted to let us into the circle, but we almost bumped into the larger mammals that had also surrounded her and the others.

When we finally got through, she turned to me with glazed eyes. "We were about to run into an encampment. Some of the men there are wearing Revell's military garb, and others appear to be in Hinch uniforms. We're trying to decide if we're going to go around them or attack."

Zell decided to point out what I was afraid to mention. "I suggest we go around, considering your state. We don't know if any of them have magic, and it's not worth the risk."

Caden and Kai looked at her and then at each other, both clearly expecting her to blow up.

"You're right. The animals will lead us safely around them."

The maelstrom of birds ditched their formation and rose to the skies again to keep an eye on the nearby danger as the mammals formed two lines and began marching in a new direction. All of us humans followed between them, two wide on our horses. Our entire party remained as quiet as possible as we continued our trek around them.

Just when we felt the coast was about clear, fate proved how wrong we were. I had been at the back of the pack but rushed forward when I heard screeches and howls, praying it wasn't Cecilia. I arrived to find her using her wind powers to barely hold a bear, a wolf, and two gophers above the spikes that lined the bottom of a magically-hidden pit. Caden had caught up to her before I had and was funneling his powers into her to keep her strong as she fought to get them out of peril.

A swarm of birds descended in a flurry of squawks, and I didn't need a translator to understand what that meant. Our commotion had caught the attention of the nearby army.

"Kai, Zell, Entriken. Over here, now!" She only needed Caden's help with her task, but the rest of us would need to defend against the second danger.

A troupe of twenty soldiers emerged wearing a mix of our uniforms, and one I had seen a few times before while traveling for the king. Hinch. I threw a shield of shadow around us as Zell surrounded us in flames. The twenty oncoming men and women stopped in their tracks. At least one of them had to be a mage to have set that trap, but most of them looked terrified to come up against us.

"As your captain, I order you all to stand down!" I shouted.

My former troop's eyes darted between me and the leader of the Hinch party among the group, like they were trying to decide who to follow. I hadn't met this particular man before, but I knew how the Hinch ranks worked. He had the most stripes on the shoulder of his uniform, so he was in charge.

"They no longer follow the great traitor to the crown. They are King Aldus's men first and foremost. And now they answer to me," the hefty man said and started hurling balls of ice at us. The rest of the group ran towards us, but our shields kept them out.

"Thomas, use your shadows to take out the mage. It'll be stronger than my fire against him," Zell said, voice unwavering.

"I'll keep us shielded. Kai and Entriken, prepare to fight just in case."

I began launching my shadows at the man, but he kept holding up chunks of ice to block them. Those who had previously followed my command stood stunned at my hidden and prophesized power. Those loyal to Revell took off, leaving just those from Hinch in battle with us. Out of the corner of my eye, I saw Kai draw his knife and chuck it at the mage's head as I threw more shadows at him. Too distracted to aim his shields at my attack, my shadows pierced his neck, dropping him to the ground instantaneously.

After the mage fell, the three of us took the rest of the army down as Entriken remained behind, taking in the scene. Not a single scratch had befallen any of us. Once we were sure they were all dead, we returned to where we had left the others to find that all the critters had survived as well. One had been badly injured, and Caden and Cecilia were bandaging it until I could come heal it.

"They're handled," Entriken told her as we stopped.

"No thanks to you," I quipped.

"You all have much more experience in a fight. I'm afraid I would've been more of a hindrance."

He wasn't wrong. He probably would've needed one of us to save him.

"And we would've joined you if I had been sober enough to get them all out without a struggle. I'm sorry I let you all down," Cecilia said as she climbed onto Ursin's back and let him lead her away ahead of us.

I used my powers to heal the wounded gopher, and we were back on our way. All of us were on high alert and ready for anything. I just prayed we wouldn't encounter something worse.

Chapter 29

Cecilia

My heart felt like it was being struck. Initially, I had thought it was just the alcohol, but after Entriken's guilt trip, I had packed the bottle away. The buzz had worn off hours ago, and I wasn't nauseous, so this wasn't the aftereffect. No. This was the pull of the ring. Maybe a little bit of the tug I felt towards Thomas too.

"It's reaching out to me. We're so close!" I yelled to my group. Closing my eyes, I breathed in the fresh air as the wind and Ursin's speed blew my hair behind me.

Thomas and I rode at the front of the pack. Normally, we had a few guards ahead of us, but we were confident the birds were correct and that the path was clear. I needed to be the first one there. The others followed behind us and did their best to keep up. The forest creatures would help guide anyone who fell behind. I just hoped no enemies were close enough behind us to hurt them.

We rode tirelessly for hours, taking only minimal breaks to give the animals water and our bodies a rest. With each stride, the beat in my chest grew stronger, and I could feel the direction of the ring. With only an hour left until nightfall, the pull grew so strong that I had to fight the urge to climb off Ursin and continue on foot.

The bulk of our journey through the Blue Forest had been through sparse trees, as Ursin had routed us where the entire caravan would fit. But here, the woods had thickened and there was a heavy mist covering the ground ahead of us. Most of the trees we had passed until now had been brown- and red-barked, but here, the moss coating the trees gave their bark a dark blue tinge. I had always wondered why it was called the Blue Forest, but here was the answer. The cool moisture clung to my skin and was a reprieve from the intense ride. The forest's aroma was mossy but pleasant and refreshing.

Only you and Thomas will be allowed through, Ursin said, bowing his head. *The animals will wait here, as our master commanded.*

Turning to Thomas and Zell, who had kept up, I repeated his instructions. "Only Thomas and I will be able to go through. Zell, please wait here for the others. The animals will stay with you to keep everyone safe."

Zell bowed in acknowledgement, and Thomas took my hand and led me to the only clear opening in the thick trees. We approached two large, blue trees that leaned towards each other to form an arch, like two lovers reaching for their last embrace. The path leading to it looked worn—as if many had tried to enter— but the scratch marks in the mossy bark suggested they had failed. Claw marks, antler marks, tool marks, human boot prints. Many had tried to enter this archway and failed. Would we fail as well? Perhaps it wouldn't even let us in. But the tug in my heart was almost dragging me in at this point.

I smiled up at Thomas as we prepared to enter. "We made it. Let's just hope I can do this." Had it been too easy? We had lost Mac, but the rest of us were still standing.

"We. We can do this."

Passing through the archway felt like passing through a water-fall. Coming out on the other side, we emerged into a small, round clearing with a pond in the center. Pastel flowers lined the perimeter where the trees stopped, and the floral smell was almost overwhelming. The silence stood out the most. Not a single twig snap, wing flap, or scurry could be heard—as if this clearing was its own little world.

We heard a popping sound, and then a ring of fire shot across the clearing at us. I threw up a shield of water and ice as Thomas threw a dome of shadow over us. The fire bounced off, but it was followed quickly by a ring of ice. We had barely caught our breath when the next onslaught—a tornado—came for us. My shield held strong, but Thomas's shadow dome began to flicker and fade into wisps.

"We need Caden. I can't take much more," Thomas barely breathed out.

"It's too late for that. Even if he had caught up to us, Ursin said he wouldn't be allowed in. Conserve your energy. I've got plenty left. As long as I don't have to become invisible, we can do this!"

He nodded and moved closer to me so I could shrink the perimeter of my shield.

A flurry of thorns sprouted from the ground and launched themselves at us like arrows, bouncing off my shield with an almost metallic clink. The clearing fell back into silence, but I held the shield just in case.

"Is it over?" Thomas asked, his breathing finally evening out.

"I don't know. I'm afraid to drop the shield or move."

"Keep the shield up, and let's take a few more steps," he suggested.

We took seven slow steps before the skies above us darkened and lightning struck the ground on the opposite side, shooting sparks into the air where it had hit a rock. The next strike was closer, and the third hit where we had previously stood, leaving a small crater in the grass. Thomas stayed close to my side but didn't show any signs of fear. He believed in me, and surprisingly, I believed in myself.

"Tell me if you need me to take over for a bit. I can give you a brief break," he offered.

"I'm strong enough, I think we just have to make it to the pool of water in the center."

He nodded, and we kept going. The lightning stopped, but I almost lost my balance when the ground began to quake. Ear-piercing snaps rent the air around us.

"I can stop this, but I can't hold my shield at the same time. Throw up your shadows."

His shadows surrounded us in a solid, unyielding mass. Dropping to the ground, I forced my fingers into the dirt below us. A crack split the grass between my feet and his, and I looked up to find his eyes wide with a hint of panic. Pushing harder, I forced my powers into the ground and tugged the two sides together until the crack sealed. Letting my power spread through the rest of the clearing, I closed each crack that had formed until the clearing was whole again.

Thomas's shadow shield had started to flicker again, so I lit mine up.

"This is one hell of a security measure for a place that only we can get into. How much more could there be?" he asked.

The darkness above us crept away, and the sky turned sunny. A mist I hadn't even noticed drifted out of the open area and into the woods surrounding us. Now that we could see the flowers around the clearing again, I was pleased to find that none of them had been damaged. All the craters, cracks, and scorch marks had disappeared as well. Our surroundings had returned to their original state.

Dropping my shield, I said, "I think it's over. We passed."

"You passed. I'd be dead without you. You didn't need me at all."

Thomas walked the perimeter as I approached the pool of clear, blue water.

"It's at the bottom. I can see it shining," I said, squinting to see the bottom.

Thomas walked over and bent towards the water to place a single leaf he had plucked from one of the trees into it. The leaf disintegrated as if it had been dropped into acid.

"Well, thank goodness for your quick thinking. I was about to hop in. What on earth made you try that?"

"Maybe that's why I'm allowed in," he joked, elbowing me. "I don't know, I just got a bad feeling about it."

Using my cyclone power, I swirled all the water up and out of the pool and tossed it away from us with ease, letting it burn its way through the empty clearing. The grass melted in an instant, and the few rocks the drops bounced on let off a dark, putrid smoke that smelled like rotten fish and eggs. I rarely used this power because I hated the way it made me feel—like drums were beating around my heart, spinning constantly and reverberating through my body. Over time, the painful resonance had grown weaker, but I still hated it. This time, it was so faint I barely felt it. Instead, it just felt like butterflies fluttering inside my chest.

Another gust lifted the ring up, blew off the remaining water, and plopped it down in my hand. The butterflies ceased their flight, and the tension in my chest disappeared. I put it on and... nothing.

"Well?" Thomas asked.

"I don't feel any different."

"The prophecy said it needed my darkness, right?" He held out his hand, and I gave him the ring.

He held it tightly enclosed in his fist, and shadows encircled his hand. I looked up at him, and shadows swirled in his eyes too, but he smiled sweetly at me, unaffected by the darkness. "I've never imbued anything with my shadows before. I'm guessing I just push them into it?"

"I have no idea. I've never tried putting my magic into things before, except when I force the truth from people. It's probably like that. Just close your eyes and picture pushing your power into it."

He closed his eyes and clasped it between his palms. "Okay,

try now. I wasn't sure if I was supposed to say some incantation or something, but we don't have much to go on."

I took the ring back, examining it to find that there were now marks shaped like shadows etched into it. I put it on once more. "Still nothing."

"Try putting some of your powers in there, and I'll wear it. Maybe we have it backwards."

I shrugged and did as Thomas had, holding it tightly and putting as much of my magic into it as I could. First, I tried pushing my truth power into it like I would a human. It wouldn't penetrate the material like it did skin. Lighting fireballs in my hands, I juggled the ring and then switched to ice. My powers felt easier to access and stronger, but I couldn't feel anything going into the now-cooled metal. I inspected it again before handing it back to him and found it now had small engravings of each of the powers I had used.

He put it on, and again, nothing. "Nope. Still the same."

"Maybe we did something wrong. Let's see what the animals and Zell know. We'll figure it out. In the meantime, we just have to keep it away from my father. I should've known this wouldn't work after finding the ring was so easy."

Chapter 30

Did I fuck up? Maybe I'm not strong enough. Or I'm not the one in the prophecy. I hated letting people down, but it hurt so much more when it was Cecilia. When we returned through the veiled archway where we had left Zell and the beasts, the others had arrived.

"You have it!" Zell cheered and pumped his fists in the air.

"We do, but it's not working," Cecilia said in a hushed tone. "We're hoping you can help us figure out what we did wrong. Caden, Thomas needs a boost. He used a ton of magic."

Caden did as she asked and nodded to me that he was okay as he did so. There was no shadow infection that he could feel from my end. I wasn't sure I had any shadows left anyway.

"Do you need any, Cecilia?" he asked, taking in her impeccable state with pinched brows.

"I'm alright, but thank you."

I scanned the woods around us for any sign of unease and said, "Perhaps we should get out of here first, in case we're being followed. Once we have a place to sleep, we can work on figuring out more."

Zell and Cecilia nodded before she climbed atop her hairy

friend. "Ursin says his cave is not far. There's enough room for all of us, and we'll be safe there."

I stayed by her side atop my horse for the brief trip. Other than asking Ursin if he knew anything about what they had to do next, she didn't speak at all. Her frown at his grunt revealed his lack of information from his master. Whoever this Memach was, he was kind of a dick. Then again, most gods were.

Ursin's cave was warm, immense, and pristine. It didn't smell like it housed wild animals but gave off an earthy scent. I wondered how he managed to keep it so clean, not having opposable thumbs. We tucked our cart and our whole entourage inside. Entriken sat with his sister, but I couldn't bring myself to get close to her after my failure. Kai and Caden met with the rest of our men at the cave entrance to decide watch rotations. I slid down it into a squat with my back against the cold, wet stone. Zell approached and plopped down next to me, giving me a knowing fatherly look.

"I let her down. My shadows aren't strong enough." I shook my head. I'd never been this disappointed in myself before. Except maybe when I had been an asshole to her to push her away.

He rested a hand on my forearm. "You didn't let her down. These things have a way of working themselves out exactly as they're supposed to. But the good news is we have the ring and Aldus doesn't."

"I'm not sure that's enough. How could Ursin's master, this Memach, not have given them a single hint for her?"

"Who are we mere mortals to question the decisions of gods? Maybe he thought she wasn't ready. Go to her. She thinks it's her fault. Don't let this push you apart."

Zell and I joined Cecilia and Entriken around the small fire she had lit for warmth. She looked up at me and said, "I have no idea what we should do now. Where do we go?"

"I'm too drained, we'll try in the morning. For now, we just have to stay ahead of your father and find a safe haven. They're following us, so we can't go straight back to Yelen. We'll head to the ruins of Engleheim. No one will look for us there."

Cecilia nodded and left us to prepare for bed. I wasn't about to let her give up. She laid down on her bedroll, and I snuggled up behind her and pulled a warm blanket over both of us. Ursin took up his usual spot on her other side. "It's not your fault. We'll figure this out."

"It's not yours either, but you're still blaming yourself, aren't you?"

I chuckled against the back of her head. "Fair enough. Let's just get some rest, and we'll do what we can tomorrow. I love you."

"I love you too," she said, wrapping her arms and mine tighter around herself as we drifted off to sleep.

She woke with a start in the morning, scaring the hell out of me. "It's gone. The ring is gone!"

I wiped the sleep out of my eyes and said, "What do you mean it's gone, how could it be—"

"Entriken is gone too," Zell growled.

I jumped up, enraged. "That godsmearer. He's dead."

"He wouldn't. They probably took him too, for my father. He wouldn't do that to me." She paused and looked at Ursin while the rest of us waited with bated breath for her translation. A tear streamed down her cheek before she spoke again. "Ursin says one of the other bears just communicated to him that he saw someone fitting Entriken's description riding a horse through the woods two hours ago. They couldn't catch him, so they rushed here to tell us. He was alone and heading back towards Revell." She turned and launched a single fireball at the wall of Ursin's cave, blasting a chunk out that sent shards scattering.

How the fuck had he slipped past our rotation of guards? I

should've left him to fend for himself when we left the castle and pretended that I couldn't find him.

Zell placed a hand on her shoulder and pressed his lips together tightly before consoling her. "If it didn't work for you, it likely won't work for Aldus either."

"Unless he knows more of the prophecy than he told Thomas. And my brother—he promised he was with me. I was going to have Caden amplify our powers today to see if that did the trick. Now we'll never know. Ean!" she shouted for her loyal bird, who quickly landed on her shoulder. "Have the birds follow him. Don't let him out of your sight!" The large crow nodded and took off.

I wrapped my arms around her, pulled her close, and nuzzled my nose into her hair. "I know, love. But he's always been a weasel. I'm glad you didn't trust him to tell him anymore about the ring, but I'm sorry he's hurt you. I'll make sure he pays for it."

"No," she said and pulled away to look into my eyes, hers flickering with dancing flames. "He's mine."

Chapter 31

Cecilia

We traveled in silence for the next few days. Not only had I let a member of our party die, now I had lost the most important object in the eight kingdoms—to someone I had loved and trusted. My own brother had betrayed me. My companions knew how badly I was hurting, but they were just as defeated and left me alone to sulk atop my bear. The pull to drink was strong, but my pull to Thomas was stronger. Each time we stopped, I let him hold me as I sobbed, but neither of us said anything. We all knew that there were no words to ease my suffering.

The only goal we had was to find mother. I had ordered the animals to send scouts to Revell and to track Entriken and requested the birds relay messages back and forth. Aside from our party, only Entriken knew I could speak with wildlife, and that bastard did an excellent job of staying out of sight from my creatures.

Tired and melancholy, we stopped to feed everyone, gathering around the fire I had lit.

Ean, a large crow, touched down next to me as I ate my breakfast.

The coward has taken the ring to your father. It took a moment to catch its breath.

"Shit," I said, as my bowl of porridge skittered across the ground. "Thank you, Ean."

Ursin rested his large head against my thigh and looked at me with sad eyes. *It's my fault, Princess. I did not detect the danger.*

"It's not your fault, Ursin. None of us could've known that Entriken was still on Dad's side this whole time. All of us, including the guard rotation, missed him sneaking out. I thought he was happy to be free. It's my fault. I should've used my truth powers on our party, especially on him." I hadn't wanted to offend those who had promised loyalty to me, especially my own brother. But if I had...

I wasn't finished, Princess, the crow crooned. *The ring didn't work for him either. Entriken wasn't aware that Thomas had imbued it, but regardless, the ring didn't work! That's excellent news. The bad news is that they're on their way here to force Thomas to imbue it. They also know that you plan to head to the ruins of Engleheim, so he's sending two parties.*

"Well, now we're one step ahead of them. Keep your eyes in the sky. We need to be prepared. I'll inform Captain Lovelace and Zell. And thank you, Ean. You too, Ursin. I couldn't do this without you. I couldn't have done it without Mac either."

With a smile, I patted both animal friends on the head and went to update the men. "My father has the ring, and it didn't work for him. Half of his men are on their way to join the scouts following us, and the other half are headed to the ruins of Engleheim."

"Well, I'm glad that little hint did us a favor. I had never planned to go to Engleheim—it was a test for Entriken. One he failed spectacularly. Now we've gotten rid of half of your father's remaining men. Fine by me."

"Where are we heading then?" Zell asked Thomas, who didn't have a chance to answer.

It was my turn to direct us. My turn to take the lead. Especially after having let everyone down so badly. "The plan hasn't changed. We're going to find my mother. She's seen all the outcomes, so maybe she knows how we can get this ring to work. Then we can worry about getting it back with her help."

"It's not going to be easy, and we're going to have to leave behind most of our escort. You, Captain Lovelace, myself, and the animals will travel to her. That's it."

There is a small village nearby that most of the kingdoms don't know about—they're well hidden. Your escorts will be happy and safe there, Ursin recommended.

I relayed the information, and we started packing up.

Chapter 32

Thomas

The village was only a few hours travel, and the villagers were more than willing to harbor our friends. Their population was aging, and they needed the younger muscle to keep the town going. The homes looked welcoming, but they were clearly in disrepair. There were no sounds of artisans making repairs, but there was the smell of cooking stew and roaring fireplaces. We stayed only briefly to help unload the cart and to ensure our party would be safe. The villagers' amiable relationship with Ursin was what assured Cecilia that they would be okay without us. She hugged each person goodbye and thanked them for their service before returning to Zell and I—who had been waiting with the other animals—with Ursin in tow.

"How are they not afraid of Ursin?" I asked as I took in the scene.

"He won't tell me, though I suspect a god's blessing is the reason they've stayed safe here. Or cloaking. Probably the same god who didn't give Ursin enough information about the ring to pass on to me," she said and glared daggers at the enormous bear, who huffed in return.

Zell chuckled and mounted his horse. "We have a five-day ride at a steady pace. The options for lodging won't be appealing. We'll be sticking to the woods, I'm afraid."

Kai and Caden approached us, each atop a horse, and each with a determined glare. "We're coming with you, my queen." Kai stated.

Cecilia immediately put her foot down. "It's too dangerous. You've both done enough. I can't ask you to do this."

"You didn't ask, my queen." Caden smiled at her with a sparkle of mirth in his eye.

"We might die," I said, hoping to talk him out of it.

"To die for such a queen would be an honor," Kai argued.

"You're not talking us out of this, Cecilia. It's highly likely you're going to need my powers and archery skills, and Kai and I are kind of a package deal."

"And I'm a skilled cartographer and swordsman," Kai added, earning a snarky eyebrow raise from Caden that made us all chuckle.

She rolled her eyes and turned back to me. "I'm going to give Ursin a break. Is it ok if I ride with you for a bit?" She looked up at me with a grin, which wasn't necessary to convince me.

"Of course, there's something I'd like to talk to you about."

"I'll give you two some space on the trek, but not too much. These woods are dangerous, especially under the circumstances. We're going to be entering the Black Wood soon," Zell said, reminding us all how serious this situation actually was.

"And it's something you can't say in front of Zell, Caden, and Kai?" Her eyebrows pinched adorably.

"I can, but it's something I should say to just you first."

"They're going to find out anyway."

I shrugged, took a deep breath, and prepared for what I hoped would be a romantic speech. I hadn't planned on doing it in front of others, but they had become family to us both. "I think we should have Zell marry us. We've been through so much these last few weeks, and it's made me realize not only how much I love you, but how little time we could have. I don't want to live another day without you as my wife."

Before Cecilia could answer, Zell jumped in. "As much as I agree the two of you should wed, I think we should wait until you get the ring back. It would be special to use such a divine object for your vows."

"I don't want to wait. The ring doesn't matter to me, just being his wife does. Please say you'll do it, Zell. It would mean so much to me for it to be you!" she implored him with wide eyes as she gripped his arms. I wouldn't stand a chance against that, and something told me he wouldn't either.

Looking down at her with the face of someone who knew he had lost the battle, he agreed. "Of course, I'll wed the two of you, but perhaps after we find a place to stay for the night?"

She launched herself at him, embracing him in an enthusiastic hug. "Thank you! Of course! I'm sure I can find something to fashion a ring out of on the way too," she said as she turned to face me. "I can break up some rocks to use as gems, and we can find..." she trailed off as I pulled the chain holding my mother's ring from inside my shirt.

"I've been wearing this since my mother died. Father said she had wanted me to have it for when I found my one true love. I was only two years old when she died, but my father told me so many stories about what a strong and fearless woman she was. I think she'd be honored to have you wear it."

Cecilia's eyes filled with tears that threatened to spill over. She nodded, her voice failing her.

Ursin brushed past me affectionately, and for the first time, I didn't startle.

Cecilia chuckled and explained. "He says he approves, but he's not calling you master."

"Noted," I said with a respectful nod in his direction.

We mounted our horses and were on our way, though we still had no idea where.

"Feel like giving us any idea of the direction we're headed, old man?" I asked.

"Not a fan of the new nickname, little boy. But now that it's just us, I feel it's safe to reveal where we're headed. For centuries, humans have feared the Black Wood. The rumors of its death and decay have spread far and wide, and they are true. However, they protect something very dear to this world, which is why it's so difficult for most to traverse. Even the gods-blessed beasts are not always safe, though if we stick close together and combine our powers, we'll make it to the Divine Hollow."

"What is the Divine Hollow?" Cecilia asked.

"When the Original Gods decided to leave this realm, they decided to seal theirs—The Divine Hollow—off from this one. Your mother now lives there, along with all those touched and protected by the New Gods that walk this realm. They only bring new beings in through resurrection, and with it sealed, none can leave. They still refuse to unseal it, but she is confident she and her new friends will convince them to do so when we make it there."

"How the hell do you know all of this, Zell?" I questioned.

"The queen has passed me messages sporadically over the years," he said to me before turning back to Cecilia. "There are animals there as well. You may be able to feel them as we get closer. It will help us hone in on the location as we enter the dark forest. Your mother knows we are coming. Now I just have to keep my promise and get you there."

Chapter 33

Cecilia

We rode for hours again, with only two short breaks to relieve ourselves, eat, and drink water. On the last leg of the trip, I switched to riding Ursin for the sake of my legs and ass. Despite the dire circumstances, it was hard to keep the smile off my face. Tonight, I'd become the wife of Captain Lovelace. Sure, most women would be more excited about the title of Princess, but being the Princess of Revell didn't mean shit right now. Each time I peeked over at my soon-to-be husband, the same silly grin was spread across his face. It bugged me that Zell looked disappointed—worried even. He cared for both of us, so what part of this was he upset about? Did some silly divine object really mean that much to him that it needed to be part of our wedding?

As dusk approached, the trees ahead of us grew closer together, and the forest darkened. The trees almost looked dead and decayed, with barely any sign of leaves or life. The bark was such a dark brown it was almost black, and I imagined if there were any sap left, it would ooze out in a dark and horrid-smelling goo. Whisps of mist floated around them and gave me an uneasy feeling in the pit of my stomach. My whole life I had begged to leave Revell to visit anywhere else—I would not have picked this place. We stopped at the edge to observe, but none of us looked prepared to enter just yet.

"We'll make camp here for the night. One last night outside the Wood. I don't want your marriage to be marred by its darkness," Zell said with a grim expression that made my stomach turn to lead.

"A little dramatic for you, my friend, but I can't say I disagree." Hopping off Ursin, I planted a kiss on his cheek in thanks.

Due to the increased fear of being attacked, we would sleep around the small fire we had built instead of in tents, and rotate watches with Ursin. Though we had left our human escorts behind, our animal entourage had followed us and now surrounded our mini encampment to witness the ceremony. When we entered the wood the next day, most of them would leave us. Only those brave enough—mostly the birds and Ursin— would continue. I was grateful so many had risked their lives thus far for me, someone who had done nothing but get one of their own killed. It broke my heart that Mac wouldn't be here for this, but neither would Entriken. Or my mother. Or Alwyn and Amelia. But Thomas, Zell, Caden, and Kai were my family now, and this was all I needed. If we sorted out whatever the hell was going on, we'd have time for a proper wedding. If we survived that long.

"I packed something special for the celebration," Caden said conspiratorially to me as he pulled some liquor from his horse's pack.

Zell's fatherly instincts kicked in as he yelled, "Not sure that's a good idea when we're running for our lives from a bunch of deranged and cloaked mages."

"It's their wedding, man. They deserve to celebrate a little bit," Kai chimed in.

"Don't worry, Zell, just a sip each will be enough," I assured him.

"Very well. We're going to need a few things. Thomas, you already have the ring for Cecilia, but you'll need a ring as well."

I used my powers to crack open the ground a few feet away and excavated a chunk of marble. I whipped my ice and wind powers around it until it formed a rounded shape, then blasted it with a precise and tiny ball of fire, piercing a finger-sized hole through it. The whirlwind spun it and dropped it into the palm of my hand. I passed it back and forth between both palms—hands glowing bluish white with ice—until the sizzling stopped, then held it up with pride.

"Nicely done, my queen. Your powers never cease to amaze me," Thomas said adoringly.

Zell also gave me a sweet smile. "Well done. The rings are set, and the ceremony will be simple, so that's all we'll need. I do wish we had a proper matrimonial archway, but we can forego..." he trailed off as I put my arms out to the side, palms up. As I lifted my arms toward my head in an arc, vines sprouted from the ground and met above us in a tall archway that sprouted with blooms.

I smiled at Zell and then at Thomas, who was looking at me with the heat of a thousand suns in his eyes. "Have to make it as close to perfect as possible. I never believed I'd take a husband, but I'm so glad it's you. We may be on the run, but I want to make sure neither of us ever forgets it."

"Don't worry my love, we'll have a proper wedding when this is all over. You deserve a glorious celebration. There's still time to back out. We don't have to do this now."

"I know we don't have to, but I want to. For the first time, I have something I want, and I'm not letting you slip away." Taking his hand in mine, I looked back to Zell. "We're ready."

"Never thought I'd see the day," Caden and Kai whispered in unison. Even the critters surrounding us huffed in laughter.

"Lady and gentlemen, and kind creatures of the Blue Forest, we are gathered here today for a momentous event that no one in the eight kingdoms could have foreseen. The marriage of Princess

Cecilia to Captain Thomas Lovelace. Please brace yourselves and make sure you're dressed warmly when the ceremony is over, because the chances of hell freezing over are very high."

Rolling my eyes at the fire mage, I said, "Very funny. Just marry us already."

Turning serious, Zell began again. "It is said that in the darkest of times, it is best to bring as much light as possible to the world. I can't think of a more suitable time for such an occasion. A celebration of love is exactly what the people of Revell need, and there are no two people I know more suited for each other. Except maybe Caden and Kai."

A round of chuckles and bestial huffs filled the crowd.

"It's my absolute pleasure to join the two people I care most about in this world in wedlock. Without further ado, Princess Cecilia."

One of my hands was held by Thomas, and I placed the other palm up in Zell's hand as he traced the ancient matrimonial symbols onto my palm. "Do you, Princess Cecilia of Revell, take Captain Thomas Lovelace to be your husband? In sickness and health, joy and sadness, in youth and in old age, to be your one true love and Anamchara for all of eternity?"

Anamchara. I had heard that word before, but I couldn't remember what it meant. "Yes," I said with a chuckle. "Of course I do."

Zell turned his attention to Thomas next, taking his hand for the same ritual. "And do you, Thomas, take Cecilia to be your wife? For richer or poorer, at home or on the run, and for exactly who she is standing before you, to be your one true love and Anamchara for all of eternity?"

Thomas eyed Zell at the use of the word I vaguely recalled from our studies as children. His pleased expression indicated he remembered the meaning. "Since the day I first laid eyes on her, I knew my answer would be yes."

"With the power given to me by the High Council of Revell, I pronounce you husband and wife. May the Original Gods bless this marriage. Thomas, you may kiss your bride."

Our marriage was sealed with a kiss and a resounding cheer from the two men and plethora of wildlife witnessing the occasion. Afterwards, we decided to rest and eat to celebrate. We passed around our drink, and even a few of the animals partook. As soon as I had Thomas alone and out of earshot, I was ready to pry.

"What does Anamchara mean?" I whispered.

One side of his mouth turned up as he leaned down to answer. "It's the Original Gods' term for soulmate, but it's stronger than that. It's reserved for a once-in-a-lifetime, divine kind of soulmate. Only the gods and goddesses had them."

"Was Zell being funny?"

"I don't think so, my goddess." He winked at me and cut off the conversation as we were joined by our friends. Caden held out his bottle for us to share.

I made sure I had only taken a few sips. There was no way I was going to let Thomas use it as an excuse to not consummate our marriage. I'm sure he'd have a thousand of them anyway with Zell still around. I waited until our party was fast asleep before I whispered my plan to Ursin. He reluctantly allowed me to lead Thomas away by the hand, but he assured me we'd be surrounded by animals for our safety whether we liked it or not.

Ursin kept his promise and kept them out of our line of vision, hidden by the thick brush and vines hugging most of the trees. I smiled at Thomas as I slammed his back into the nearest tree and kissed him roughly. "I went gentle on you at the inn. You won't be so lucky tonight."

He grabbed my hips and pulled me into his hard length that was surging to break free of his pants. He kissed me roughly and dug his fingers into my hair, then came up for a breath. "Oh, I think I'll be lucky tonight, wife." He hoisted me up and wrapped my legs around his waist, spinning us to put my back against the tree.

"Bark in my back is not the most comfortable, so maybe no promises of hours tonight, husband?"

He laughed as he lifted my skirt to find I wasn't wearing any undergarments. He opened the ties of his pants just enough to free his hard length and pressed into me. "Just as long as you don't light the forest on fire."

Chapter 34

When we awoke in the morning, it was eerily silent and still. Though the woods had been quiet the last few weeks, on the outskirts of the Black Wood, not even a hint of animal life could be heard. My new wife woke up groggily and nestled against me for one last hug before we rose.

"Thanks, Ursin. He says we should bathe at the stream nearby before entering and warned me that the waters within the dark forest can be dangerous, like the water guarding the ring was."

Kai and Zell were still waking up. Both nodded and rubbed the sleep out of their eyes before we joined Caden—who had taken the last watch—and followed Cecilia's bear to the nearby stream. I bathed with Cecilia while the other three stood guard, then we swapped and stood guard while they bathed.

Afterward, we prepared to undertake our foray into the treacherous wood. The horses informed Cecilia they would not be entering the dark wood with us but would wait here for our return. It looked like the rest of our trip would be on foot.

As we passed into the zone where the trees turned from vibrant and lively into dark and decayed, the temperature dropped, and the increased humidity meant our clothing stuck to us. The visibility decreased drastically—a combination of thickening mist and the increased density of the forest. I felt as if there were dozens of eyes on me. Cecilia shivered as she passed through and lit fireballs in her hands to light the way and keep us warm. Our pace slowed exponentially, the fear seeping into me, and I assumed it bothered them as well. I knew Caden and Kai so well, but I had never seen either of them this jumpy. All of our eyes darted around, cautious of every sound. I could feel in the pit of my stomach that something horrible was about to happen.

"We are so close to the hollow. I can sense it, the pull. I feel its direction. It's calling to me," Cecilia said, eyes trained hard toward the northwest. "We've lost most of our bird escorts—they bailed. Only Ean and an owl remain." She put out her arm and the large crow landed on it, tilting its head as it spoke to her before it flew off.

"What did the crow say?"

"Ean says the death and decay have spread every year, encroaching on the healthy forest. Most animals won't dare to venture within its confines anymore, except a handful of birds. He says the Original Gods first created this place to protect their hiding place, but they've been gone for so long that the darkness is no longer kept in check. He confirmed my instinct that we are to head northwest. They will scout ahead of us, but he says to tread carefully. There may be surprises."

She spun around, taking in our surroundings. She stood like the moon in the night sky, the darkness a stark contrast to her glowing beauty. She leaned down and dug her fingers into the dirt, black as tar. There were no flowers or moss—the only sign of life was the sporadic mushrooms breaking down the decaying matter. From where her hands had entered the soil, vibrant, green vines emerged and spread in all directions. Flowers in every pastel shade sprouted as they grew as far as we could see.

She stood and smiled. "There, that's a little better. Isn't it?" She started to walk again, beaming with pride, but with each step she took, the flowers wilted and blackened. The leaves fell off as the vines withered and turned to dust. Halting her steps, her shoulders sank and she shook her head. Even her power couldn't bring beauty to this much dark magic.

I wrapped my arm around her shoulders and kissed the top of her head. "Maybe once we get to your mother or get the ring back, we can combat this darkness. Let's just focus on getting there."

"See what happens when you try your shadow magic on it."

Aiming my palm at the ground where her withered vines had lain, I shot blades of shadows into the ground. "Nothing." We both shrugged and kept walking. I turned back and could have sworn I saw a black rose rise from the ashes, but I figured it was this spooky place playing tricks on me and kept walking.

Hours later, we felt more tired than we had on any of our previous days of traveling, like this place was draining us of our energy and magic. It probably was. Caden refreshed every one of us, and often, until Cecilia made him stop for fear it would drain him. Our first rest came more quickly than normal and lasted longer. We also learned that, despite his powers, Kai's map was completely blank within the confines of this ominous magical forest. Cecilia's pull consistently aligned with the direction Ean pushed us toward, so at least we weren't totally on our own.

As we ate our jerky and stale bread and attempted to rest, a ring of fire lit around us. A handful of mages—including Entriken—and the unstable king appeared in puffs of smoke within the circle. Cecilia jumped to her feet and threw a transparent dome of wind and fire around our entourage with one hand before lighting a fireball in the other. She stood as the only member of our party outside of it—prepared to strike down her father before the rest of us even realized what had happened.

"Hello, Daughter. I hear you've been busy," Aldus shouted over the whirling of her elemental dome as he gripped Entriken by the back of his shirt. He threw him on the ground between the two groups. "I brought your brother back to you."

The rest of us formed a semicircle behind her with our weapons, ready to fire our powers, but I was struggling to keep my energy up enough to do so. I wasn't sure how long we'd last.

Cecilia, on the other hand, appeared to be getting stronger. More energized.

"I don't want your little puppet, father. He's no use to me. He got you what you wanted. I'm sure he can still help you stab other people in the back."

Even through the shield, I could see that Entriken was battered and bruised. He looked ashamed too, but he always looked that way in the presence of the king.

"My men caught him sneaking away to warn you I was coming. His loyalty to me has finally died."

"That ring you're holding says otherwise. He was safe with us. Unreachable by you. He had no reason to bring it to you."

"Fear goes a long way, girl. Advice you never heeded from me."

"It came in handy against your council. They looked awfully afraid of me when they fled like the cowards they are. I'm sure these puppets of yours won't take much convincing either. Maybe if I had sent you back the remnants of your previous attack party, you'd be here alone. I'm just sorry I didn't end your life before we left. Clearly the mercy of a trial was a mistake."

"My council was nothing compared to the mages of Hinch. I'm afraid you don't stand a chance. Why don't you just hand over the captain? Let him imbue this ring with his dark magic, and I'll be on my way."

"Oh, Entriken didn't tell you? It's already imbued with Thomas's magic. And mine. If you look closely enough, you can see the mark from his shadows burned into the metal along with all the marks of my powers. I guess it just doesn't work for someone as useless as you, *Father.*"

Aldus examined the ring thoroughly, then handed it to a mage next to him for a second opinion.

"I can feel shadows within it, Your Majesty. She speaks the truth," the mage said before handing it back.

Entriken paused his scrambling crawl toward me to turn back and face his father. "I swear, I didn't know."

"That's because we knew better than to trust the rat. At least Thomas did. I thought my brother cared about me, but I really should've known."

King Aldus threw the ring at Cecilia and screamed. "That fucking thing is useless. You may as well have it! I'll settle for ending the lives of both of my traitorous children instead."

The ring easily made its way through her shield and landed right at her feet.

"Put it on, Cecilia!" Zell shouted as the rest of us fought to break through her storm dome.

Fireball still lit in her hand, she put the ring on her finger, and her whole body levitated, aglow in a bright and blinding golden light. Her hair flowed around her as flames licked up and down her body, followed by waves of water. A whirl of air spun around her like a tornado and vines shot from her hands, taking root in the dark wood around us, supporting her in the air. The string that tied my heart to hers squeezed my heart harder and harder until I thought it might burst, and a wave of energy wracked my body so hard that I dropped to my knees. The dome dropped and we rushed to her, while King Aldus and the mages of Hinch stood watching, mouths agape. Entriken just looked up at her in wonder.

Eventually, the wind died down, and she lowered back to the ground. Her face was as stunned as ours. The only person who didn't look surprised was Zell, who stood smiling at her and beaming with pride. But how had he known it would work? Is this why he had been pressuring us to use it as a wedding ring? Why now, when it hadn't worked before? And what the hell had happened to me?

Before I could voice any of those questions aloud, and before Cecilia could get settled back on her feet, King Aldus and the Hinch mages launched their attack. We immediately began to fight back—Caden running behind us to boost our magic as we fought. Kai stayed behind us as Entriken crawled toward him for safety, ducking under each magical attack. Fireballs, ice shards, and daggers of shadow flew back and forth in utter chaos. The loud bangs of each strike hitting magical shields was deafening, but the volley continued. Cecilia, however, wasn't struggling at all.

I watched as she shot a fireball straight at one of the mages aiming for her. It went through his water shield, struck him, and he turned to dust in an instant. As the rest of us continued our fight, she turned her sights to the next—a mage that had been engaged with me in the magical battle. She launched an ice ball that slammed through the mage's fire shield and took her head off.

Zell remained locked in a standoff with King Aldus as they exchanged blows that seemed evenly matched. It was clear that these two held contempt for each other from years of disagreeing, and I'm sure it felt cathartic to let it out. There were two mages left, one sparring with me and another now turning their sights from me to Cecilia. Hers was down in an instant. A knife flew from behind my head, following the trajectory of my shadows towards my mark. Kai's knife pierced my target, causing them to drop their shield, and my shadows inflicted further damage. With the mages down, we turned to our remaining target—the king. Realizing he was the only one left standing, he turned to launch a final assault at his daughter.

"Cecilia, look out!" Zell shouted. But it had been a ruse, and we all watched in horror as the king feinted a fireball towards the princess, but instead turned and threw it at his nemesis, then ran for his life.

Cecilia screamed as she tried to throw a shield up between the fireball and Zell, but she was too late. It blew a hole through his chest, and he collapsed to the ground. I had planned to run after Aldus, but Cecilia's cries pulled me back. She knelt beside Zell, covering his wound with her palms.

I knelt next to her and put my hands on him—attempting to heal his wounds—though I knew it would be a waste. This injury was far too serious to come back from.

Chapter 35

"I was hoping my new powers would let me heal him, but it's not working," I said through my tears.

Somehow, he was still able to speak, but not for long. "I'm so proud of you, Cecilia, just remember that," he sputtered, coughing up blood. "And tell your mother that I'm sorry. I promised her I'd escort you there, but I'm not going to be able to keep that promise. Just trust your instincts and follow the pull; you'll make it there."

"You kept your promise, you said you would keep me safe, and you have. It's me who let you down. I should've put that shield back up before they attacked. I wasn't fast enough. I'm so sorry, Zell. I'm afraid I can't do this without you, but I know we can't stop you from fading. How did you know the ring would work?"

"You could never disappoint me. I knew it would work because I knew the true interpretation of the prophecy. Imbuing alone wouldn't work. Light and dark had to be entwined in love. Working together. Though you had been in love with each other for years, it needed to be official. A wedding, and the ring on your finger. I thought the ring had to be on your finger during the ceremony, but it turns out even Original Gods can be wrong."

"I'm so sorry, Zell. I can't tell you how much it's meant to me that you've been by my side through all this. For once, I finally know what it would feel like to receive a father's love. I just wish I could've reunited you with your child so they could know what it feels like too."

He cupped my cheek in his hand as tears streamed down it. "I think she already knows. I just wish I had told her earlier how much I love her, and that giving her a better home had seemed like the right thing to do. What better life than that of a princess?"

What was he saying—that I was—no. I couldn't be. He couldn't be. I felt like my heart was going to explode and my mind was pulling me in a hundred different directions as my eyes darted around in confusion.

"But now she's starting to believe in herself. In how beautiful and powerful and strong she is. You have your mother's smile, but those eyes and fire are all me." His voice trailed off as his arm dropped to the ground and the light faded from his warm, blue eyes. Eyes I had never noticed before looked exactly like mine.

"Holy shit," Thomas said from next to me, pulling me out of my thoughts. "Zell was your father."

This kind, helpful, intelligent, selfless man had been my father all along. Not the monster who had taken away everything I loved. Losing Mac had crushed me, but this—losing my father the moment I had learned who he was—I feared I'd never come back from this, and the wound I felt forming in my heart proved it. A gaping chasm that I feared might never close.

"You can bring him back, Thomas. Your shadows are dark magic, surely you can reanimate him. Do it!" I yelled, desperate to have even one more moment with Zell.

Caden put his arm around me cautiously. "Do you realize what you're asking? There's a reason that dark magic is banned. I doubt he can do it, nor would he know how, but even if he could..."

"Who knows what it would do to Thomas, but Zell would almost certainly come back as something evil. Terrible. I beg you to think twice about that command," Kai added with pleading eyes.

You saw what it did to the stag, my queen. Do not ask this of your mate. Zell is at peace. He is returning to the earth, as is the cycle of life according to my master.

Thomas looked to me, ready to put up an argument he knew he wouldn't win, but they were right. I sucked in a deep breath and tried to compose myself. I had to ensure Zell kept his promise. "We need to bury him, then we need to find my mother."

Using my seismic and wind powers, I dug a deep grave for my biological father, tears streaming down my face the entire time. Ursin nuzzled his snout into Zell's face one last time before Kai, Caden, and Thomas carefully lowered him into the pit. I took one more look down at him, blew him a kiss, and created a gale to blow the dirt back in on top of him. Breaking off a piece of rock from a nearby boulder, I used my powers to etch the stone I placed above his head. "Here lies Zell. A beloved father and fire mage. An even greater man."

I stood up and dusted myself off, preparing to mount my horse.

"What about Entriken?" Thomas asked.

"I don't give a shit about Entriken. Leave him."

"But I'm your brother. These woods are dangerous."

"Half-brother. And our relation meant nothing to you when you stole that ring and brought it back to the asshole who raised me. Go running back to Daddy, you godsmearing little weasel."

I heard Thomas tell him to come with us anyway, because he was sure I would change my mind. I highly doubted that. He'd be lucky if I didn't wring his neck the next moment I saw his face.

Luckily, I had moonshine left from the trading post that I sipped as Ursin followed my directions, and we led the group in the direction I felt pulled. I needed to feel numb. I couldn't handle any more hurt or loss. The rage inside me needed to stay calm instead of boiling over through my magic. The alcohol never numbed how my magic felt, but it numbed my emotions and feelings like a salve.

Thomas caught up to me and tilted his head at the bottle I wasn't even trying to hide. "Do you really think that's a good idea? These woods are still dangerous, and we have no idea where your father is."

"I'm so fucking tired of less powerful men telling me what to do."

He held up his hands placatingly. "Whoa. I'm not telling you what to do. I'm just saying, you were upset the last time you drank when it affected our travels. I don't want you feeling that remorse again."

"And I wasn't ascended then, was I? I'll be fine."

"Okay. Do you want to talk about it?" he asked, giving me puppy dog eyes that made me want to melt.

I took a deep breath. I knew he was just trying to help, but it was infuriating that every time something bad happened, he kept pushing me to talk about my feelings. "I know you mean well, Thomas. But right now I just need to not feel anything. I promise I still love you—I just need to be alone for an hour or two, okay?"

He nodded and dropped back to his men and my brother.

Over the course of our trip, I had grown so close to Zell, and he had become like a father to me. Finding out he truly was my father and then losing him within seconds...I would never get this part of my heart back. I wasn't sure I would even survive this grief. My stomach felt full of lead and the urge to vomit was barely contained by my rage. The only thing that would soothe my aching heart was numbing myself to the pain. I wasn't going to let anything stop me from making sure he kept his last promise. I would find my mother, and then I was done. The kingdom and everyone in it could fuck right off.

I had apparently taken the drinking too far and impaired my ability to set up my tent when we stopped for the night. Caden put it up for me while I stood by and watched. Thomas and Kai were busy in conversation around Kai's tent.

"He's just worried about you. We all are. None of us want to change you or stop you from doing as you choose, but we're all here when you need us. I can promise I'll never force you to talk to me about what you're avoiding, but I can't say the same for those two," he said, tipping his head toward Thomas and Kai. "You want to glare at me in silence, that's fine too, but I'm never giving up on you. We all love you, Cece, but I get needing to feel numb to the grief. I don't talk about it, but I've been there. Kai was the one to get me out of it, but he had to be patient. And persistent. It was annoying as fuck, but I love him for it."

"I don't deserve him. I don't deserve a friend like you either."

"I disagree, but you don't get a choice. You're stuck with all of us. Shut us out all you want, but Thomas is having a hard time handling that. Maybe give him a pass, eh?" He nudged me with his elbow, and I almost fell over. He caught me by the arm and chuckled. "Want me to send him over to tuck you in? I think you need it."

"No, thanks. I just want to pass out and deal with it tomorrow."

Caden really was a good friend, and he proved it by keeping Thomas and Kai busy until I was fast asleep in the tent.

Thomas tried to comfort me the few times we stopped the next day, but I couldn't handle talking about it. And I couldn't handle the pitying glances from Caden and Kai. The heinous traitor trailed them by a few yards, and I wondered how long I'd be able to contain my profound need for violence.

The men organized a small camp, and I lit the fire for them without a word. I plopped down next to Ursin and leaned my head into his furry shoulder while I finished off my moonshine. When it was empty, I threw the jar into the fire and got up to scavenge through everyone's bags for anything else that might help fill the void in my soul. I found a bottle of wine in Entriken's bag and popped the cork with my magic before I started chugging. Entriken opened his mouth as if to stop me, but I gave him the middle finger and he snapped it shut again. He was lucky I had let him live. The least he could do was let me take his wine in peace.

"Are you sure that's a good idea, Princess? I know you're a goddess and all, but we're not safe yet, and we have a rough path ahead of us. We need to be formulating a plan for how to deal with the king after we get there as well," Kai said, assessing me with a sad smile and pitying eyes.

"We're going to be fine. We're close and I'm too powerful for anything in here to mess with me," I said, slurring more words than I had hoped. "The birds confirmed Aldus is racing back to Revell. I'm tempted to go after him now, but he would expect that. As soon as we find my mom, we go straight back to Revell and take him out when he's let down his guard and thinks he's safe. Then I'm done with all this shit."

"I agree we should take him out. No mercy with a trial, but I think we should regroup with the rest of my troops and the refugees. Collect them from their villages and storm the castle. He doesn't have many men left, and the four of us know every exit and entrance of that fortress. We can pick them up in Ursin's village and Yelen, and we'll be safe there to plan a solid offensive with a larger army," Thomas said and stepped closer.

"We don't need to plan. You saw how fast the coward ran. All his men are dead."

"*After* he took down Zell. He's strong, and he might have more. We can send scouts..." Thomas tried his hardest to convince me.

"And I'll kill them too!" Lighting flames in my hands, I started to hover inches off the ground as my voice boomed over our entire encampment.

Thomas held up his hands, letting shadows slowly wind their way out. "Easy, Princess."

"Queen. Remember? I am Queen Cecilia. Isn't that what you wanted? For me to take responsibility and take over the kingdom from the wretch who thinks he sired me?" The wind within the forest started picking up and circling us, swirling my hair around me. The dead and decaying trees creaked in protest as they swayed in the violent storm.

I glanced down at Caden, who had halted his brushing of Ursin, and Kai standing next to him. Both men dropped their hands to the belts that held their knives, like that was going to help them against either of us.

Ursin gave me a pleading look, the sweetest I'd ever seen the imposing bear appear. *Don't do something you'll regret, my queen. I fear the darkness of the forest is getting to you.*

"Shut up, Ursin!"

"I know you've had a lot to drink, but you're starting to sound an awful lot like somebody else I know," Thomas warned.

"Thomas, stop it. It's not helping!" Entriken argued. "This is what father warned me about."

My entire body lit aflame as my feet crashed back onto the ground. "What did you just say?" I gritted out.

Thomas drew my ire away from Entriken. "I think he's saying what I am. You're starting to sound an awful lot like the king, *Queen* Cecilia."

Before I could second-guess myself, I launched a fireball with one hand and a torrent of water with the other in Captain Lovelace's direction. "How dare you!" I shouted, before launching another assault his way, this time of wind and ice.

Shadows burst out of him to form a shield, preventing any of my attacks from hitting him, despite my godly power. Both of our jaws dropped. He was clearly as astonished that he could stop me as I was, but thank the gods he could.

When I turned to Kai, Caden, and Entriken, who were all shaking with fear, the adrenaline of the fight suddenly sobered me up. The ricochet of power had knocked all of them to the ground, and Entriken was holding his elbow. Now clearheaded, the realization of what I had done convinced me to halt my assault. I shook my head as I started to cry, realizing I had hurt somebody I cared about. I whispered, "I'm sorry," before I ran off into the woods.

What came over me? Who have I become? And how the hell was Thomas—thankfully—able to stop me?

Chapter 36

I wasn't surprised when Cecilia stormed off in a huff. She had been downing alcohol the entire trek. All of us worried about her, but she needed space. Nobody in the castle could avoid knowing about her binge drinking and sexcapades, but I thought she had grown out of that since we had started being together. With all her father's men dead and the king fleeing for his life after having witnessed his daughter's ascension, I knew she'd be safe on her own. These woods were dangerous, no doubt, but nothing compared to the powers of a deity.

"What the fuck was that, Captain?" Caden asked, looking after her with concern. "Why in the name of all the gods would you provoke her like that? Telling her she's like her father. That was a low blow, my friend."

"She was being ridiculous," Kai interjected. "We can't just storm in there, powers blazing, without a plan. Thomas was showing her reason."

"She could blow any of us off this plane of existence with a snap of her fingers, she *can* just go in there, powers blazing." Caden raised his voice, and it was the first time I had seen my two closest friends quarrel. They had been together almost a decade, and I'd never seen them so much as bicker.

Putting myself between them, I said, "Enough. Both of you. I appreciate your concern, but I think the forest's wickedness is seeping into all of us. I agree with Caden that I crossed a line, but I was just trying to show her reason. Who knows, maybe it wasn't my place, I just don't want her to do something stupid and get herself killed. I care for her too much." Both men nodded and backed off each other, and all of us took a deep breath to try to fight off the monsters warring to get inside of us.

"I'll go talk to her," Entriken whispered, picking at his fingernails.

"That might be the worst idea I've ever heard. She'll kill you on sight. Just let her have some space," Caden said and turned to the gigantic bear that had grown so close to her. "Ursin, can you tail her just to make sure she's safe?" Caden had also grown close to her animals, and I was grateful they listened to him as well.

The great bear nodded and sauntered off in the direction she had run.

"What the fuck happened, Cap?" Kai asked, sitting next to me as I sank to the forest floor.

"I think the dark magic in the woods is getting to her. There's no way that could've been just the alcohol. That wasn't her at all."

"I agree. I've been feeling unusually violent myself. The only thing that has kept me in check is knowing both of you could kill me instantly. But I meant, how the hell did you stop her? I'm assuming what we all witnessed with the ring was her ascension. That means she's a goddess." Kai looked off in the direction she had gone with wonder and terror warring in his eyes.

I scrubbed my face with my hands before I looked him in the eye. "I have absolutely no idea."

"Do you think you could be a god as well? Zell said something about you two being linked. If you weren't already a god, maybe the ring forced you both to ascend?" Caden asked.

I just shrugged and pondered in silence while Entriken looked on, apparently processing the facts in his head.

"I remember when your mother had you, and how doting

your father was. There's no way you were born of any god. I think Kai is right. I think the ring did this," the cowardly prince whispered.

"Don't get any ideas, Entriken. You try to take that ring again, and both of us will murder you," I said, my eyes piercing daggers through him.

"I don't think it will work for me anyway," Entriken added.

"You mean Thomas and Cecilia are more powerful, and you're more scared of them than Daddy now, huh?" Kai spat, glaring at him.

Entriken snorted a laugh, a sound I hadn't heard from him in years. "I really did run away from him to warn you guys. I brought him the ring out of fear, but it doesn't mean I love my sister any less. She's the only person who has ever cared for me or showed me any kindness."

"That's all it took for you to turn on your sister. Fear of your father?" Caden asked. The fact that my closest friends fought for my wife as fiercely as I did brought me so much joy.

"You have no idea what he's done to me." Entriken stood and lifted his shirt, and his entire torso was smattered with scorch marks and deep burns. While Aldus had busied Cecilia and I with torturing the enemy, he'd spent his time torturing his son apparently. Or he had commanded his other mages to do it.

"Why didn't you ever tell me or Cece?"

"I didn't think I could trust you. You were his favorite. And Cecilia...she didn't need another reason to go up against Dad. She was hanging on by a thread as it was. She would've attacked him and she might've ended up dead. Believe me or not, I do love her. But I know bringing him that ring was a mistake. One I'll never make again. I don't care if she never forgives me, as long as she's ok. She's my sister and she's all I have."

"Half-sister," Kai remarked.

Entriken shook his head and looked down at his feet. "It doesn't matter that we have different fathers. Our mother is who made us who we are, for better or worse. We grew up caring so deeply for each other when we were very small, but my father did his best to put a wedge between us after our mother died. I don't care what we learn, she'll always be my sister, and I'll always love her."

"Well, then I say we give her twenty minutes to collect herself before we all go find her and figure this shit out. What do you say, boys?" Caden asked.

Entriken and Kai both nodded. Caden's words about me possibly being a god rang in my head, convincing me of what I would never have otherwise believed. I tried to reach out with my mind. *Ursin, if you can hear me, Cecilia has twenty minutes before we come find her.*

Understood. But I'm still not calling you master.

I froze and my eyes widened. Kai and Caden both looked at me in concern.

"What's wrong?" they asked in unison.

"He heard me." Holy shit. Maybe the snap I had felt *was* me ascending with her. Maybe the guys had been right, and I was a god too.

Chapter 37

Cecilia

Running wasn't enough, so I used my wind to push me through the dark woods. A few minutes later, I came upon a cliff that appeared out of nowhere. A waterfall fell from it into a crystal clear pool of water. It was surrounded by the first greenery I had encountered since crossing into the dark wood. It was exactly what I needed.

I sat on the stone edge and kicked off my shoes. I briefly considered the warning we had been given about the water in these woods and realized I didn't care. When my feet entered the water, I heard a crash through the woods behind me and turned to see Ursin emerge. He looked around to ensure my safety, nodded at me, and stayed at the tree line yards away. Leaving me to wallow in my misery. I looked down at my reflection and let the tears flow—the dam breaking loose after holding them in for so long. Around the others I felt the need to put on a show of strength, but all my strength had failed me. I had lost too much, and now I was losing myself.

"I fought so hard not to become him, and it happened anyway. Entriken was right. Aldus was right. I'm just like him," I said to my reflection.

For a moment, the alcohol had me convinced that my reflection was morphing into the face of my mother, tutting at me for what I had become. Any restraint I had on my emotions snapped. If my mother could see me now, she would be immensely disappointed in me. My power trip, attacking people I cared about, and binge drinking when the fate of the kingdom was on the line. I had to do better. The reflection nodded as the waves morphed it again, mutating back to my face.

My disgust in myself and my drive to want to help my kingdom fought for dominance of my thoughts as I swished my feet through the water, taking in my first moment of peaceful thinking in ages. I felt nauseous and my heart tightened in my chest. Pondering over everything that had happened and what was still to come, I knew I had no choice. Fuck how I felt. I had work to do. Nodding once, I launched myself to my feet with undeniable resolve, surprisingly sobered up. I had people to save. This pity party would have to wait. Turning away from the pond, I marched towards the tree line.

I walked up to Ursin and gave him a big bear hug. "I'm so sorry, Ursin. I've let everyone down. Do you think I still have time to make this right?"

You do. We don't have long before they come looking for you though. Hop on.

He ran like lightning, but I gave a little push with my gusts of wind anyway. On our return trip, he let me know that Entriken hadn't been hurt as badly as I had suspected—he had just been caught off guard. We arrived back at camp just as the three men were packing up. Before any of them could speak, I confessed.

"Tonight, I did something I never thought I would do. I became Aldus. The thing I've feared most my whole life." I didn't even bother to stop the tears. I didn't care if I looked weak. They needed to know how genuine I was. "For decades, I rebelled against him because I knew what a monster he was. And now I've become the same. Our kingdom deserves so much better than me. Thomas, you're the only one kind and strong enough to lead our people. I'm just a fraud."

To my surprise, Thomas, Kai, Caden, Ursin, and newly arrived Ean bowed or knelt before me. Ursin must've called the large crow in for support.

"Get up. All of you. I've failed you. I'm not your queen."

Kai stood, holding his fist to his chest. "Your father was a dictator. A murderer. He let everyone starve while he did what was best for himself. You are not him."

Caden joined him and added, "You. Are. Not. Him. You lost someone close to you, and you're grieving. It's unfortunate that your grieving is far more dangerous than ours, but a little slip once in a while can be forgiven. Assuming you're sorry for it. We all know you are, and you're still our queen. We're all alive because of you. We're free because of you. We will not abandon you when you need us the most, my queen."

Entriken stood next, creeping cautiously towards me. He was lucky I was no longer in a vengeful mood. "I know you're mad at me, and you have every right to be. What I did was unforgivable and the act of a coward that was afraid to be tortured further. But these woods are a dark place, and they do things to your mind. That was not you tonight. We can all feel it. You mustn't let yourself believe you're capable of being as horrid as my father is. They're right, you are not him. You are so much better. Even he knows it, which is why he ran."

I was still pissed, but he was my brother. Half-brother. I hugged him tightly and pressed a kiss to his cheek, earning myself the first smile I had seen from him in years.

Only Thomas hadn't spoken yet, and despite having knelt to me, he now stood with his arms crossed. He was still livid over my attack—I was sure of it—and he had every right to be. I approached him and took his hands in mine, kissing his knuckles. "I'm so sorry I let it get that far. I can't tell you how ashamed I am that I attacked you."

"I'm not mad about that part, Cecilia. We all feel the darkness in this place, and nobody got hurt. What bothers me is that you felt like you had to drown your sorrows in alcohol. Like confiding in me wouldn't be enough. Confiding in us," he said, pointing to Caden and Kai. "We're married, Cecilia. You're my wife. And we're your family. You couldn't even come to me before hitting the bottle?"

"It's *my* grief, Thomas. You handle loss so much better than I do."

"Your grief is my grief—that's what our vows were about." He shook his head and sighed, then lifted my sinking chin to look back up at him. "Drinking can be fun. I'm not saying you have to stop entirely. What bothers me is that you felt like it would comfort you more than I could. That fucking hurt. Zell may have been your father, but he's been like family to me too. You're not the only one hurting, and we need to stick together. Get through this together."

Kai came over and threw his arms around both of us, squeezing us tight. "You're stuck with me as well."

"And me," Caden said as he joined in.

We all turned to Entriken, who was rocking side to side awkwardly. "Oh, get in here, you idiot," I said with a chuckle. He obliged.

Can I join as well? Ursin asked with a grunt.

"Sure, but I can't promise these three scaredy-cats won't run away," I said, turning my head to peek at him. The men realized who I was referring to and reluctantly broke the hug enough for Ursin to squeeze his way between us, and the men hugged his body as I wrapped my arms around his neck.

We spent the rest of the night discussing our options for after we found my mother. We debated whether to return to Revell and take down my father or to gather our people and start a new kingdom elsewhere, leaving my father to rot alone. The problem was that we had no idea if he had anyone else left on his side or if they would come for us, so we would need to figure out his status before we made any decisions. First, though, we had to find my mother.

After the guys had fallen asleep, I nudged Ursin and asked

him to escort me back to the pond under the waterfall, hoping to see my mother again. I didn't care that it had been my own muddled and drunken reflection. It had felt like I was speaking to her, and I pretended I was again. I dipped my toes into the pool below me as I sat on the cool, damp ledge.

"You would've been so disappointed in me today, Mother. I fear I was at my worst. But you taught me to never give up, and I know we're so close to finding you. I'm very fortunate to have such a wonderful husband, but I'm sure you already know that because you have seen every future path forward. You knew we loved each other before even we did. Even Entriken seems to be coming around. He says he came to warn us, and I want to believe him so badly. Things got so bad after you died. Aldus drove such a wedge between us."

I kicked my toes at my reflection, scattering it in hopes of it resembling her face again. I turned to Ursin, who nodded, urging me to continue pouring out my soul.

"Holy shit, I just realized...you've known all along Aldus wasn't my father and that Zell was. I understand what you saw in him though. He was a handsome man, and such a kind soul. I loved him so much, and I still can't believe he's gone."

The tears came again, but I didn't try to stop them. Instead, my bear sat next to me, and I leaned into his comfort and let them flow. When I had finally collected myself, I spoke once more.

"I can feel we're close. I should get to see you tomorrow. I've missed you so much, Mom. I know Entriken has too. I hope one day you'll be proud of me." I blew a kiss to the water, and Ursin and I headed back to camp for a restful night of sleep.

Chapter 38

Thomas

We had spent many nights together, but this was the tightest I had held Cecilia through the night. As we drifted off to sleep, she questioned how I had been able to stop her powers with mine, but that was something I couldn't answer. Kai and Caden were convinced the ring had turned me into a god as well. My ability to communicate with Ursin was hard to argue with. I was sure I hadn't been born one. I was the perfect blend of both of my parents' features, and there had been many witnesses to my parents' love for each other. But hadn't there been for Cecilia too? It was something I didn't want to think about.

Now that we weren't being pursued, we slowed our pace. We took breaks often and camped early each night, waking later in the morning than we ever had. This place was taking so much out of us, but our new schedule helped to keep the darkness out. It was also the first time we had felt at peace since making our escape, which was odd to experience when we were in such a horrible place.

The second day, we came to a bubbling creek too wide to jump across. When I dropped a leaf into it as I had during our trials for the ring, the leaf sizzled and disintegrated. We wouldn't be able to walk through it, and it was too much water for Cecilia to drain. It would just keep flowing. I sent Caden in one direction and Kai in the other to find a way across, but by nightfall they had returned with only bad news.

"I can freeze it, but we still run the risk of it harming us. And of course it will be slippery. That leaves us two options: I use my wind to float everybody over it, or we combine our powers and hope our shields make a strong enough bridge," Cecilia brainstormed aloud.

"Who wants to go first?" Caden asked with a snarky chuckle.

"My vote's for Entriken," Kai said, with just as much sass.

"It's the least I can do. Float me, baby sister," he said, closing his eyes and putting his arms out.

Caden gripped her by the shoulder to give her more power in case she didn't have enough. Her winds swirled around Entriken and he levitated off the ground. With a gust from her other hand, he started to float out just above the water. Halfway across, the winds sputtered, and he plunged closer to the water with a squeal. She shoved another gust his way and he landed safely in a heap on the other side.

"Whoops," she said, taunting him.

"Very funny." Entriken stood up and dusted himself off.

"Were you messing with him, or was that too much?" I asked her.

"Mostly trying to scare him, but I'm afraid I won't be able to move anything much heavier across like that. I think we need the bridge for Ursin, you, and Caden, but only you and I can form the shield. Let me get Kai and myself over there. Then you and I can make the bridge from opposite sides to get everyone else across."

"I don't weigh that much more than Kai," Caden said, clutching his chest in feigned hurt.

She snickered at him, and he rolled his eyes back at her before he joined Ursin, patting him on the head gently.

She levitated Kai smoothly to the other side without any

hiccups and then did the same for herself. She nodded to me from the other side, and we both shot our powers across the water a few inches above it to form a shield bridge. Caden, the lightest of those remaining, went first. He inched along without incident, falling to his knees and kissing the ground on the other side.

"You're lucky I'm busy or I'd hit you with a fireball, smartass."

Ursin went next and crossed the bridge in four large bounds, testing the limits of our powers as it bounced.

"Can you keep your shield up while you cross it?" Cecilia yelled from the other side.

"I guess we're going to find out," I shouted back. I placed one foot on our bridge, and it held strong. As I was about to place my other foot, my shadows started to wane and the walkway dipped closer to the water.

"Run for it!" Kai screamed, apparently fearing my powers would give out before I crossed. On the third step, my foot broke through my shadows and came so close to the water that the bottom of my boot sizzled before I was pushed backward by a gust of wind, landing on my ass.

"You're too drained of magic. I'm going to have to float you over. I'll lift you with the wind then toss you a vine. I can only push heavy things with my gusts, not pull."

I stood back up and nodded, closing my eyes and praying to all eight—make that nine—gods that she could do this. I was lifted off the ground, and it was the most surreal and utterly terrifying moment of my life. She held her winds firmly in one hand as she used the other to grow a vine long enough to toss to me. Though I had cracked my eyes open, I missed it. It landed in the water and crackled and faded into ashes. She regrew a second one and let Caden throw it this time. It landed straight in my hand, and I held onto it for dear life. They all hauled vigorously on it, but just as I was almost across the river, her winds sputtered and I plunged towards the deadly water, which turned to ice below me as I hit and skidded to a stop on the other shore.

Though it had mostly turned to ice, enough moisture

remained from my slide to do damage. I hurriedly ripped leaves off the nearest tree and wiped as much of the acrid water off my body as I could, but not before my skin was marred by steaming blisters. My powers wouldn't allow me to heal myself, but Kai did his best to patch me up with a salve from his pack. It hurt like hell, but it shouldn't get any worse. It hadn't been easy, but we had made it, and I was tempted to kiss the ground just as Caden had.

By the fourth morning, the very brave crow named Ean delivered Cecilia an update.

After listening while he sat on her arm, the bird flew off and she passed along the message to us. "Ean followed Aldus back to the castle. The Hinch mages were not with him, but when he got to the castle, he still had a few remaining council mages and soldiers left. All the servants have fled, so they are left to fend for themselves," she said with a chuckle.

"I'd pay a year's salary to see the king and his loyal idiots gather crops and prepare themselves a meal," Caden said with a smirk.

"Ean also says they're terrified. The paranoia that I'm right behind him is getting to them. They've been fighting and bickering since he returned. He thinks I'm coming straightaway to finish him off," she said with a confidence I hadn't seen since before we left the castle.

"Good. Let him stew in that. We'll stick to your plan. Find your mother first, meet up with the others, and get organized. By the time we're ready to hit him, maybe he'll have let his guard down—" I was cut off by the ground quaking. The trees rattled as decayed branches smashed the ground all around us and fissures split the dirt path.

"What the hell is that? Is that you, Cecilia?" Kai yelled.

"It's not me. Ursin says this is one of the traps of the Black Wood. We have to stick together. The fissures will worsen, and we can't be separated," Cecilia informed us, and we moved closer to her. Entriken grabbed one of her hands, and I grabbed the other, and Kai and Caden followed us as closely as possible. Ursin led the way with Cecilia right behind him as we picked up our pace.

The cracks widened and the ground fragmented around us, and I could see an idea formulate in Cecilia's mind. She halted and plunged her fingers into the dry and lifeless dirt like she had in the clearing with the ring. Her powers hadn't been able to sustain her efforts to regrow vibrant life in these woods, but that had been before we had the ring back. Before she had ascended. This time her powers permeated the ground, and the cracking and popping noises halted. A squelching noise began as the fissures closed, and small springs of water popped up and began irrigating the soil. Green vines emerged from all around us, decorating the area with blooms as they blossomed in a rainbow of colors around us.

She stood with a hopeful smile as we waited for the wither, hoping we were wrong. The fissures remained closed and the flora remained. We all cheered, because my goddess had done it. She had brought life back to the decayed Wood. It was only a small section, but the life remained. Ursin nuzzled her as I shook my head in wonderment. Aldus didn't stand a fucking chance.

Chapter 39

After weeks of tireless trekking, we could all feel how close we were. The seismic pulses grew stronger the closer we got. I could feel it in my heart, literally and figuratively. Whether my mother was actually here and alive still remained a mystery. The dark wood faded into green and gold—actual gold. About a third of the trees were covered in gold leaf and engraved with symbols I didn't recognize. The dark, decaying, and dreadful-smelling fungus was replaced with vibrant glowing mushrooms of all shapes, sizes, and colors, and there were birds, insects, and rodents flitting everywhere. The section of forest we approached was brimming and humming with life. Something that felt so out of place butted up against the dreadful forest we were finally escaping.

Two trees arched towards each other as they had where we had found the ring, and from that archway a mist drifted out, like wisps of smoke drifting from a chimney. Two humanoid figures emerged, one about my size with long, wavy hair, and another much larger. I squinted to make out their features, and my heart almost stopped when the beautiful face I had missed for the last two decades of my life finally solidified in front of me. My mother was alive and standing right before me, and holding her hand was Zell. My father. Alive.

Before they could reach me, my knees hit the ground and I buried my face in the lush grass below me. Judging by the gasps around me, the others were equally stunned. Probably mostly at seeing Zell alive and well, because we had expected to see my mother. My parents rushed to me and lifted me off the ground—checking to see that I was alright—and I scrambled to hug them both as tightly as possible, unable to speak through the tears consuming me. I never wanted to let go.

My mother gripped my face and stared into my eyes, and I could feel all the ice I had built up around my heart melt away. "Oh, sweetheart. I'm so proud of you. And look what a beautiful woman you've turned into." She looked over at Thomas before she turned back to me. "Your husband aged well too, huh?" she said with a wink.

A light chuckle escaped through my tears as I took deep, even breaths to calm my racing heart. "I wasn't sure I believed you were alive, but I'm so happy you are." Turning to Zell, I asked, "And you. How are you alive? And taller?"

A laugh bellowed from deep in his stomach. "That was only one of my mortal bodies, child. You can't kill an Original God that easily."

The jaws of our entire party dropped. It was rare enough for me to be stunned into silence, but even Caden was quiet. An Original God. I hadn't just been touched by a god—I had been born of one.

Mother took one of his large hands in hers and one of mine in the other. "Where did you think your powers came from, dear?"

"Honestly, I thought it was the ring that bound Thomas and I together. Does that mean Thomas was born of an Original God as well?"

"That is a complicated story," Zell said. "How about we all get inside the Divine Hollow, and we'll explain everything where it's safe?"

"Father ran for his life when she ascended. The animals have been watching him, so we're not in danger," Entriken interjected.

"You can never be too sure, can you?" Mother smiled fondly at my brother and held his face before she planted a kiss on his cheek. "My son, you look terrible. I'm so sorry I couldn't protect you from your father, but I can now. Come, let's get you something to eat."

When we passed through the veil, it was like the atmosphere changed color. In our world, the sky was a constant blue hue. Here, it was an orange-gold, like I was seeing the world through a piece of colored glass.

A group of bears sat in the distance, and Ursin turned to me for permission. I nodded and he loped off to greet them. Thomas, Entriken, Caden, and Kai walked to a table laden with a feast of meats, vegetables, cheeses, and baked goods. I hung back and took it all in. I had made it to my mother and had kept Zell's promise, only to find out that not only was he alive, he was an Original God. My mother stood next to me, witnessing my emotions while I looked on in wonder.

"I heard you, you know. At the pond. Both times."

Unable to look her in the eyes for fear of my dam of tears breaking once again, I whispered, "I had a feeling you might have."

"I am proud of you. And yeah, you made some lousy choices, but who hasn't? In the end, the darkness wasn't able to dig its claws into you like it did Aldus. He came looking for me here once, you know. He was never a good man, but he wasn't always the absolute monster he is now. He did always fear you, but when he came to the Black Wood in search of me, the darkness took root, and he couldn't fight it off. He spiraled out of control with paranoia, and it made him increasingly dangerous. You, on the other hand, made the choice to push it away, and you made the choice to fight to be a better person. Your heart is still pure."

I squeezed her arm and said, "Thank you for everything you did to make sure I lived through this. Sacrificing yourself. That was crazy, but thank you. And for making sure Thomas and Zell would protect me. If I ever have children, I hope to be half the mother you are."

"When, not if," she said with a mischievous sparkle in her eye, and we walked to the feast and joined the men.

"Ah, finally. My lovely daughter and the love of my life have decided to join us. Sit, eat, and let me tell you all about how my ring works. Ursin, would you like to join us?" Zell yelled over to our bear.

Yes, master, the bear ran back to join us as he responded, his answer almost causing my heart to stop.

"That's why he was nuzzling you! Holy shit! You're Memach!" My eyes widened in wonder. Not only was my father an Original God, he was also the creator of all mammals and birds.

"So...the ring was yours, and you couldn't give us a single hint?" Thomas asked, his tone gravelly and deep.

"There are rules that must be followed per the tribunal of Original Gods when it comes to passing on divine objects. I was not allowed to interfere in any way. The animal guides and protection were as far as I was allowed to go. She was also not allowed to take possession of the ring until she was at least twenty-five. But Captain Lovelace, perhaps you would like to hear about how it works. I'm sure by now you would have noticed some changes within yourself?"

From what I remembered, the tribunal was comprised of the eight Original Gods. Four masters of fauna and four masters of flora. They were each also blessed with a variety of elemental powers far stronger than the ones I possessed. My mother used to take me to their shrine in the courtyard, where each statue was evenly spaced in a circle. I remembered staring at each of their faces and would have sworn their eyes followed me as I played around them.

"I combined her goddess powers with my shadows. Was I also sired by a god?"

Zell smiled at my husband with fondness. "I'm afraid not. Though your parents were two of the humblest and kindest people I've ever known. They were good friends of mine. The prophecy Queen Isadora foretold confirmed that you were, in fact, the shadow and darkness that would balance out Cecilia's fire and light. You two were destined to be together from the beginning."

All of us sat and listened intently, hanging on every word from this larger version of Zell. Memach.

Mother rested her palm on his large bicep and added to the story. "If the king had found out about Memach and I, he would have had both you and I killed, my daughter. When godlings are small, their powers are weak, and he could have easily ended your life. Zell and I decided that since Aldus and I were already wed and had had Entriken before our tryst, it would be easiest to pass you off as a princess. It was the best path to keep you safe."

"It killed me to watch you grow up with no idea who I was, but your mother was right. It was the safest path. When your powers started to manifest, your father started to question her loyalty. The fire power could easily be passed off as genetic, but we had to hide any further powers from him. So I bound your powers to my ring and hid it where no human could easily find it. Only you and your Anamchara—your gods blessed soul mate— would be able to enter. I never expected you to be as powerful as you are without it, but being the stubborn woman you are, over time you had been draining the ring of your powers, despite your distance from it." Zell—Memach—took my hand in his and ran his thumb over my ring.

"For the record, I'm so happy that you're my real father. You have no idea how much it meant to me to grow close to you on the trip here."

"Likewise, Daughter. Now, as for you Captain," he turned his gaze to my husband, who was anxiously awaiting to hear his fate. "The prophecy and the ring have bonded the two of you, dark and light together, woven into one with the vows of marriage and the acceptance of the Anamchara bond. As such, your lives and souls are linked. You will both live an extended life, but when one dies, so will the other. With that bond comes godlike powers for you as well. You are both still half-human, but it has been eons since full gods have been birthed. There are no two creatures outside of this sanctuary more powerful than the two of you. Cecilia, being born part goddess, will, of course, be stronger, but the power that Thomas shares will still be immense."

"So, what do we do now?" I asked my parents.

"Now, you go end a king. You end the reign of terror. You remake the human kingdom into your own world," Zell said, crossing his arms and sitting up straight.

"And how do I do that?"

"Not that you need it, but with our help," Mother said. "Aldus came looking for *me* once before. I think it's time to return the favor."

Chapter 40

It had taken us weeks to make the trip across the kingdom through both the Blue Forest and the Black Wood. The trip back was already passing far faster thanks to the life that was slowly returning to the decaying forest and the combined powers of Cecilia and her real father. Since she had begun regrowing the flora on our way in, the power of the darkness threatening us had greatly receded.

I believed Memach and the other Original Gods in the Divine Hollow had been playing a part in the retreating darkness. Now that we knew who Zell really was, he assured us how disappointed he was that the Original Gods had let the darkness get so out of hand. It would take time to get the Black Wood back to a controllable state, but he was confident he and Cecilia would be able to improve it over the next few years. With the Divine Hollow no longer sealed, the other Original Gods were more likely to emerge and help heal the darkness as well. Our entire group had more energy. Some of Cecilia's—and Memach's—animals had returned now that the forest was no longer full of death and decay, and the horses met us halfway.

We collected my men in the small village near Ursin's cave, then proceeded to Yelen over a brief and uneventful five days. Our party was greeted by the original inhabitants of Yelen, along with refugees from many other places the king's bands of mages or guards had pillaged on their way through. It seemed the groups that had come after us weren't the only ones. The refugees from Revell, including Cecilia's closest friends, had been settling in nicely here. Each had made their provided house into a home and had taken up jobs and tasks to aid the community and the cause. Fortunately, the king and his men had avoided Yelen on their travels, or this village likely would have met the same fate as the others.

Cecilia—the pissed off queen and goddess that she was—strode into the village with a confidence that gave me chills. We had agreed it may not be best to let anyone else in on the whole goddess secret for now, or that she had not, in fact, been sired by the king. She walked straight up to the man in charge and said, "I'm so sorry to interrupt everybody's day, but would it be possible to gather everyone for a meeting?"

"Of course, my queen," he said before he scampered off. Within ten minutes, every last man, woman, and child were gathered in the square.

She nodded to me to begin, but I shook my head. They wanted to hear from their queen.

"Ladies and gentlemen, the time has finally come to fight back against the tyrant that has been starving you, using you, and treating you like a pawn in his ridiculous political games. My *father*—" she spat "—has pushed us too far. I know I have done little to garner favor with you, so it isn't fair of me to ask, but I am going to do so anyway. In three days, we march on Revell to overthrow the diabolical king. I will not force anyone to join me or fight by my side, but I will request it. I do not wish to be a dictator as he was, but I will gladly lead the people I care for to take back what is rightfully theirs. At this time, I'd like to ask for volunteers," she finished, wiping her sweaty palms on her dirt-stained skirt.

The entire gathering dropped to one knee and held their

hands to their chests, even the smaller children. The smile that spread across my face could've lit the entire village for weeks. Cecilia looked back at me with wide eyes. I had told her not to expect any backlash, but she was still struggling to believe how much the people loved her. She had said she had done little to garner their favor, but the truth was that she had been the only person to show them any care since her mother had passed away. I glanced over at her mother, whom we had attempted to hide under a hooded tunic. The pride that radiated from her was infectious, and I was grateful she was here to witness the legacy her daughter had been carrying on in her name. In secret. Her clandestine mission—or destiny.

Now it was my turn. "Suffice it to say, Princess Cecilia, you'll have a full army. As captain of the future queen's guard, only men —and women—over the age of eighteen are permitted to join us. If you are hurt, sick, sore, or elderly, we do not expect you to fight. There is no shame in supporting the cause without putting your life on the line. All those who will join us, please meet us in the square tonight at dusk for a briefing and to be supplied with weapons and any protective gear we can scrape up this afternoon."

Alwyn and Amelia approached us as the rest of the crowd scattered to finish their business in preparation for the life-changing events. They engulfed her in a warm hug, and the tears began to flow before anyone could get a word out. Zell—Memach —and Queen Isadora approached—the former not disguised at all, as we assumed none here would have heard of his death. Ursin and a slew of other animals followed behind them, coming out of hiding in the woods to help us formulate a plan.

Isadora dropped her hood as she neared, and Alwyn's face paled. He covered his face with both palms for a moment, then dropped them as joy and shock warred in his expression. Once he had regained his composure, he launched himself at her, and they embraced like they would never let go. When he pulled away, he took her face in his hands before he caught himself and dropped to one knee. "You're alive! But, how?"

"That's a long story, my friend. We should all get out of sight and chat. We have a lot to catch up on and a battle to plan."

Amelia's eyes scanned Zell before she caught a glimpse of the rings on mine and Cecilia's fingers. She shrieked and jumped into Cece's arms for a huge hug. When they were done squealing, she turned to offer what I assumed would be congratulations to me as well. I was wrong. "If you hurt her, I'll fucking stab you."

I laughed so hard that the others turned to make sure everything was okay. "Noted, Amelia. But honestly, Cecilia scares me way more than you do."

"Good," she said with a smirk. "Then I'm happy for you. And I told you so. Also, is it me, or is Zell taller?"

Chapter 41

Cecilia

The two days it took to ride to Revell from Yelen felt like both years and seconds at the same time. This confrontation had been a long time coming, but my emotions still warred within me. He was an evil man, but he had raised me. He had taught me things. He had housed and fed me even though I wasn't technically his, even if he hadn't known that. When we finally arrived, I didn't want to wait any longer.

When we had almost reached the edge of the woods, Ean landed on my shoulder.

The bands of remaining mages, councilmen, and guards have returned to your father and are outside the walls of Revell. He has scrounged up additional soldiers from other kingdoms as well. Thirty of them are all that remain.

"Thank you, Ean." I patted the bird on the head, and he launched back into the sky to keep watch. I relayed the information to Captain Lovelace and the seventy-five others that had gathered with us. Though we had stronger numbers, they still had powerful mages. "Wait here. I'd rather not risk anyone else's lives if I don't have to."

Connecting to my divine powers, I let my winds lift me stories off the ground. Although my wind powers had previously been strong enough to levitate me, only the Original Gods were able to fly like this. The remaining men and women loyal to my father were lined up in three rows, ready to strike, but the cowardly king was nowhere to be found. Our army was also in lines, remaining just barely hidden from Revell behind the tree line. Of those who had witnessed my ascension, only my father and my closest friends remained alive. I took great pleasure in watching everyone below me react to my new powers.

Our entire rebel army hit their knees and put one fist to their hearts as they bowed their heads to me. On the other side of the field, the jaws of the handful of remaining council members and mages dropped like boulders thrown off a cliff. Most fled, and the others hit their knees like my army had. Those that fled were pursued by my birds, who would keep an eye on them until we could capture them.

"We're not here to hurt any of you," my voice boomed down from the sky. "I'm here to end the villainous reign of King Aldus, and that's it. Hand him over, and we'll leave."

One brave mage stood his ground, throwing a water shield around himself. In his other hand, he formed a ball of darkness and fired it up at me. I deflected it into the sky and shot a fireball back at him, turning him to ash.

"Anybody else?" I asked. Not a soul moved. "I'll ask again, where is King Aldus?"

The king's men pointed at the highest tower in the center of the castle. The tower where his council had presided. The tower where my rooms were. The tower he had held me captive in for so long. The tower my mother had jumped from to escape him and protect me. The place where it had all started. And where it would end. Today.

"Of course, hiding like the coward he is. Is there anyone else left in the castle?" I asked one of his other captains. The man shook his head, eyes dropping to the ground in either embarrassment or regret. It may be a huge dishonor to turn your back on your king, but it was even more disrespectful to lie to a god. This was an internal struggle I knew many of them would experience.

"What should we do?" Thomas asked from below me.

"Double-check that the castle is clear, and get the rest of his army out of here. The animals believe all the servants have fled, but I want to be sure. Save as many of the books as you can—anything that will help us rebuild: farming, architecture, whatever you can grab. There won't be much left when I'm done. I'm burning the castle to the ground. Starting with the highest tower." As I flew over the castle walls, the few men remaining on the balustrade ran for their lives, and not a single one took aim at me as I headed for Aldus.

I landed on the ledge and gripped the stone, sending a seismic wave throughout the tower. The rock split and crumbled from the pulse. I closed my eyes to sense the life around me and pulled the vines climbing the outside walls toward me, directing them at the falling rock—securing the stones in place, sealing up the doorways to the tower, and isolating Aldus with no escape. I did a double check to ensure nobody else was present as I waited for Zell and Thomas to evacuate the rest of the castle.

There was no sound or movement within the tower. Aldus was staying rooted wherever he was hiding, but I was tired of waiting. Now that I knew Zell could also speak to animals, communication across a distance was simple. I whistled, and my crow landed on my shoulder.

"Tell Thomas I'm going in, Ean. I've waited long enough. I've got Aldus trapped alone in the tower. I'll make sure the damage doesn't spread until they confirm their mission is complete."

Yes, my queen! Ean took flight to deliver my message.

Carefully, and with a fireball in my palm, I climbed through the window. I contemplated whether he'd jump out the window to end his own life or jump from the roof like my mother had. No. He was too cowardly for that. I was sure I'd find him quaking on his throne of lies.

I checked my rooms first, and a small part of me expected an ambush or attack to come at any moment. Or even a booby trap. Nothing. My room had been ransacked. I assumed he had been looking for any hints as to what I knew about the ring. No. I had been right. He was going to go down on his throne.

Could I just open the door? Sure. But that wouldn't be good enough. I wanted him to fear for his life. I wanted him to feel trapped like he had made me feel all those years. To feel at someone else's mercy about whether he'd get to live another day or eat another meal. To understand how every person in the kingdom had felt under his thumb. In a fusion of fire and ice, I blasted the doors off their large metal hinges and sent them flying through his council room, where they annihilated the table that he had had his minions sit around, making all the wrong decisions for Revell's future.

He sat on his throne, attempting to put on a tough façade. The way his fingernails were digging into the wood and his knuckles were turning white sent another message. "Ah, the prodigal daughter returns."

"And yet, she is not your daughter. The best news of my life. Did you know?"

"I suspected. Which is why Entriken was to be my heir. I have no idea who your whore of a mother chose to father her beastly daughter," he said in an even tone.

I scoffed at his insult, but I didn't need to use my ungloved hands to prove he didn't mean it. The entire kingdom had adored her. "You loved her, there's no hiding that. You still do, I'm sure."

"Did. She decided to take her own life to escape me."

My cackle filled the room, and he was visibly shaken before he regained his composure.

"And yet you claimed it was my fault. You know, I was just going to kill you right here. But I think there's something you need to see first. Tell me, Aldus, would you like to meet my real father? I say meet, but you know him well already. He comes bearing a surprise for you." I whistled again for Ean, who entered and landed on the remains of the destroyed council table.

"Ean, please send for my father. Make sure he brings our... guest with him."

The crow nodded and was off again.

"You can talk to animals? That explains why your mother refused to let you have a pet. That bitch knew so much more than she let on. How many of your powers did she know of?"

"All of them. She foresaw everything. Given who my father is, though, one could deduce it easily. Have you heard of Memach?"

"One of the Original Gods. Creator of mammals. One of the first history lessons for you and your brother."

"He also loved my mother deeply."

"The Original Gods locked themselves away in a divine location eons ago."

"They did. But sometimes they take human form and engage in human activities. I'm sure it will all make sense when they—" I heard the crunch of loose gravel under large feet coming from the hallway.

Zell entered alone at first, and Aldus's face reddened into a deep maroon. He gripped the chair even tighter, and for a moment, I thought he would attack. "You!"

"Yes, me. What better place from which to keep an eye on my lovely daughter than your council chamber, *Your Highness*," he said with a mocking bow.

"And you've convinced the child that you're Memach, an Original God, and her father? What's in it for you? Hoping she'd find the ring for you so you could steal the power that would be mine? Her mother is conveniently too dead to prove her parentage."

"That's where you're wrong, Aldus," Isadora said as she strode into the room, kicking a few stones across the floor with her heeled boot.

The king's jaw dropped, and for the first time in his life, he was silent. For the first time in his life, his eyes welled with tears. His throat bobbed and his skin grew paler.

"What's wrong? Nothing to say to your wife, Aldus?" she teased.

"But how—I saw you—your body— I heard rumors, but I didn't believe it."

"Yes, I did die. But when your lover is immortal and your suicide intentions pure, exceptions are made, and resurrection is possible. Of course, due to what I had foreseen, it was best to keep that hidden from you and Cecilia until she was older. I know you came looking for me. You entered the Black Wood knowing how high the risk was of it poisoning your soul."

Aldus hit the floor on both knees and began to weep into his palms. I guessed the weight of all the truths must be too much to bear. When he finally caught his breath, he answered. "Your body disappeared before we could bury you. One of my mages had heard a of a place deep within the Black Wood that may be where souls like that went. I needed to see for myself. But I never caught a glimpse."

We didn't have time for this. I couldn't endure it. I needed this to end before I changed my mind.

"I'm thrilled about the family reunion and all, but I came here for a reason. I just wanted to rub the truth in a little before I complete what I came here to do." I spat.

He turned to my mother one last time. "I'm so sorry. After I lost you, I just snapped."

"And you think that was a valid excuse for how you treated me?" I stalked closer to him to make him look me dead in the eyes. "I was a fucking child. You made me torture people and locked me away. Constantly threatened me. The only positive thing you ever did was push me closer to Thomas."

As I said his name, Thomas entered the chamber and took in the scene before updating us. "The entire kingdom is evacuated, and we've taken as many books as we can, my queen."

"Thank you, my love. Father," I said sweetly, turning to Zell, "please escort my husband and mother from the tower. I'll finish this."

Zell tipped his head in acquiescence, then looked at Aldus one last time, pointing an accusing finger at him. "Many times I tried to turn you from this fate, Aldus. Pushed you in the right direction. You had so many chances to do the right thing, and you failed this kingdom at every turn. The rightful queen will now take her place."

Aldus looked at my mother once more, but she just shook her head in disappointment and left with Zell, hand in hand.

Thomas remained. "It's one thing what you put me through, but for decades I listened to you demean Cecilia. Insult her. Keep her hidden away. You pushed her further and further down every chance you could get. You made me believe she was a worthless brat. Nothing could be further from the truth. If you had embraced her, she could've helped you build a beautiful and successful kingdom. Instead, you're meeting the fate every single person in Revell has wished upon you. A slow and painful death. I hope the power was worth it, *my king*," he said with one last insulting bow, and left the room.

"What of your brother?" Aldus asked in a whisper after Captain Lovelace had left the two of us alone.

"He's fine. He won't be coming to your rescue. You may be terrifying to him, but I'm a fucking goddess. That's just a little scarier, don't you think?" I lit a new fireball in one hand and produced a ball of ice surrounded by a whirling tornado in the other. "Any last words for the would-be daughter you drove to murder you?"

"You deserved better, and I'm sorry."

"I did. I do. And I have it. No thanks to you. And that sorry bullshit," I walked up to his throne to look him dead in the eyes. "It doesn't work with me. Enjoy hell."

"Force the truth from me. Do it. You need answers. You need closure. I was a shit father but let me give you this."

Forcing the truth from him hadn't been part of my plan, but the opportunity to inflict some torturous pain on him before I ended his life was too sweet to turn down. I extinguished my powers and gripped his wrist, forcing my power into him, and waited for the writhing that didn't come.

"The day you were born, you were the most beautiful thing I had ever seen. You looked just like your mother, but you were mine. At least, I thought so. You were so tiny. So fragile. With so much life ahead of you. I watched you grow with a heart full of pride, until the day your mother took her own life. Every day after that, I blamed you for her death. I knew you hadn't harmed her. It wasn't your choice either. But I knew she had done it to protect you, and I resented you for it. I couldn't stand looking at your face anymore. Her face. And I pushed you away, hoping I could heal the anger and hurt inside me. I kept you away from Entriken because that's what the darkness wanted. For you to feel alone. Isolated. Powerless."

He took a deep breath, like saying all of it was difficult to get out. Like something was fighting him.

"Somehow, the darkness knew of your mother's prophecy. I could feel it. Many have tried to kill me over the years, but I can't explain to you why they failed. Whether it was some divine force or fate, I'm not sure. When the darkness consumed me, it made me even stronger. Almost invincible. Except against you. The darkness knew you needed the ring to finish me off, and it hoped that me having it instead would make me stronger. I was so glad when it didn't work for me."

A single tear rolled down my cheek as he sat peacefully, with no attempt to resist my power.

"Entriken could never hold a candle to you when it came to education or strength, but I knew he would be much easier to mold. Keeping you locked away was the only path I could see to my healing. Then I heard a rumor that your mother might be in the Black Wood. The love of my life, resurrected. I'd watched her body disappear with my own eyes. Maybe with our family whole, I could mend things with you. By then, you had spiraled out of control with drinking and the constant parade of men in and out of your wing, but I prayed it wasn't too late."

"I was never as bad as you assumed, Aldus. Most nights, I wasn't up late drinking. I was stealing your food and bringing it to the villagers that you were starving." Pushing my powers in, I felt another force trying to work its way out. Angry. Annoyed. Eager for vengeance. It tried to penetrate my skin, so I pushed harder.

He shook his head and almost smiled. "Of course you were, Queen Isadora's offspring at her finest. I'd wondered where it had all been going. But let me finish. When I entered that wood, that's when the darkness overtook me. It wound its way into my soul and my heart, blackening it. I collapsed and only made it back alive thanks to my men. I wasn't strong enough to fight it, but I couldn't let it overtake you. You were the only hope left for our kingdom, if only you would come around and realize your power. But the darkness, it wanted more."

He pinched his eyes tightly and squirmed on the throne.

"It wanted death. Torture. Pain. I gave it pain through your brother in beatings, limiting them as much as I could control. The darkness made me love the power I was gaining and left me hungry for more. I took it out on any mongrel who tried to sneak into my kingdom, but I couldn't let it have my sweet girl. I knew she'd be queen one day when she was strong and brave enough to end me. It's the only way, Cecilia. You have to end me. It's your destiny. You may not be my daughter, but I loved you like you were. I always will."

I had never expected to cry for the man before me, but I was being proven wrong. "You're not going to fight back, are you?" I asked quietly.

"I'm tired of fighting. This is your destiny, my dear. And for what it's worth, I'm so proud of you." He sat back in his throne and sighed, closing his eyes.

The dark force pushing its way out of him managed to permeate my skin before I let go of him. A chill wracked my body, and I could feel it. The need for vengeance. The angry fire trying to consume my heart.

"Believe it or not, even after everything you put me through, I love you too." The dark force crawled around in my forearm like a worm as I examined it.

He nodded. "It's ok. The darkness will make it easier, but I know you'll be able to fight it off. Do better than I did."

I took a deep breath to convince myself that completing my mission was still the right thing to do. The parasite within me made it easier, as he had said. The screams began as the room went up in flames. Aldus's feet were stuck to the ground in frozen cubes, his hands bound to his sides with vines as cracks began to spread across the floor of the room. I hovered above and watched the flames consume him, along with all the pain he had caused me and those I cared about. There would be no mourning today, but my traitorous tear ducts disagreed.

*Kill them all...*I heard resounding in my head.

"No. There's only one more death I need. Yours." Forcing the darkness out of me, I strangled it with my vines and froze it into a neat little cube. I doubted it would survive, but even if it did, nobody would ever find it inside the wreckage.

I blasted a hole in the ceiling to create an exit for myself and to aid in the rapid burning of the building that held every terrible memory in my lifetime. Aldus's head tipped back, and his mouth opened—a dark cloud of mist shot out of it and escaped through the hole in the ceiling. Like a dust cloud being sent back to hell, his blackened heart had been freed from the pained grip the darkness had had on him.

I flew out feeling as though an immense weight was lifted from my shoulders and approached my awaiting army. Caden shivered as I landed next to my family and friends. Together, we watched the kingdom we had never loved burn to the ground.

Chapter 42

Cecilia

We stood on a marbled cliff, overlooking the ruins of what had been Revell before we had decimated it a month ago. Thomas and I came back here weekly to remind ourselves of what we had been through and why we needed to work to keep from becoming Aldus.

Thomas kissed my hand that was joined with his. "I think the council made the right call. It's not worth rebuilding. Too many bad memories for all of us."

"Trust me, I agree with the unanimous vote. Let Revell rot. A reminder of what letting the darkness in can do."

From where we stood, we could also see our friends helping Gunther rebuild the small village outside of the fortress. Over the past month, we had built small villages around the fortress. Each had their own communal garden and selection of livestock. Trading posts had been set up on the routes between them for the exchange of goods, but nobody would be left to starve in order to feed the royalty.

"You don't miss living in a castle?"

Snorting, I gave him a side-eye. "Do I miss being detained in a giant stone prison? No. I love being outside among the flowers and animals. Breathing in the fresh air. Traveling from place to place and meeting everyone in our kingdom. Seeing what we can do for them. This is what we were destined for. I can feel that here," I said, tapping my heart.

"All I feel is the tug to you, my love."

"Kiss ass," I joked. Thomas and I were now king and queen, but unlike previous royalty, we lived a more nomadic life. We maintained small residences in a few of the villages, but we spent our time hopping between them as needed. Contributing where we could.

"You're handling it all well, my queen. These last few weeks of rebuilding have been exhausting, but overall, everyone seems much happier. Except for Caden. For some reason, he's been growing distant. I'm worried about him. If anyone can get through to him, it's you. Last week Kai asked if any of my shadows had gotten into him."

My brow furrowed as I turned to my husband. "Why is this the first I'm hearing about this?"

"It didn't seem like a big deal at first, and you had a lot to handle. But he's getting worse."

"He's also one of my best friends. Why didn't he come to me? I'll go see him now."

Using my tornado powers, I flew myself to the village where he and Kai had been building their cabin. The same village where my former maid Amelia and Chef Alwyn now lived. Kai was outside hammering wooden shingles to their cabin.

"Thomas just told me—where's Caden?"

"Grumpy is inside taking a nap so I don't wring his neck. I know we joked about him being worried about Thomas' shadows entering him when he boosted his energy, but that couldn't do this, right?"

"I fear it's worse than that. Stay out here, I'll go check on him." Entering the house quietly, I snuck up the stairs to where I assumed the bedroom was. When I nudged the door open, Caden sat up with his arms crossed and glared at me. Like he had known I was coming. I lit a fireball in case self-defense became necessary, but I could see the anger, fear, and sadness warring in the jarred expressions on his face.

"I can't fight it anymore, Cecilia. You need to do something. I'm going to harm someone. It keeps taunting me to hurt. Kill. I keep distancing myself, but it's only a matter of time. Please. I have no idea what this is."

Sighing, I pinched the bridge of my nose. "I do. It's not the captain's shadows. It's pure evil—the darkness that had entered King Aldus in the Black Wood and consumed him. I think it entered you the night I killed him. I destroyed a small piece of it. I can do the same for you, but I need you to trust me. You have to fight it for a few more minutes, okay? Don't let it overtake you to harm me. Can you do that?"

"I'll try," he barely got out between gritted teeth, his hands now gripping the sheets in agony as his body started to writhe.

If I wasn't quick enough, one of my best friends might die. I lunged for his arm and forced my truth powers into him as I had with Aldus. The dark force began to work in opposition, just as it had last time. This time, I let it penetrate my skin as it left Caden's body. I could feel its claws start to dig into my heart, trying to force its darkness into me, but I had too much to fight for. I was too strong for it, just as I had been last time. I knew that now. Once the darkness had fully left Caden's body, I forced it out of me and into the corner of his bedroom.

My vines tangled around it as my fire singed it, corralling it into a tighter and smaller puff of darkness. Finally, I blasted it with my ice powers, freezing it into a deadly cube. I clenched it, pondering where to put it to prevent this from happening again.

I turned back to Caden and found him collapsed on his bed. "Are you okay?"

He began bawling like a small child, and something inside of me snapped as I watched my strong, fierce friend break down like that. I kept the cube afloat with my wind powers as I went to him, checking him with my truth touch one last time before I embraced him. "It's okay. It wasn't *you*—we all know it. You're free now."

"I'm so sorry."

"It's not your fault, Caden. It's mine. I watched that darkness escape the keep, and I thought we were in the clear. I should've known. Should've been more vigilant. Get some rest, my friend. I'll send Kai in to take care of you. I need to get rid of this."

"I love you, Cecilia. I mean that. You're the best friend I've ever had. The best queen this kingdom could ask for. Thank you for saving my life."

"I love you too, my friend. Now sleep. You have a lot of hard labor ahead of you, since Kai's been pulling all the weight this week," I joked, winking at him.

He chuckled as I left the room to explain everything to a terrified Kai.

We had allowed the mages of Hinch who had surrendered to live, and they had fallen in line quickly. King Aldus had long held them in place with the threat of his power, which he had built up far more than he could prove. Once he had seen my ascended powers, he didn't stand a chance of holding on to that dream. But I couldn't trust them to help me secure this dangerous item. Only the gods would know what to do.

Each week, I had been returning to the Black Wood to push more life back into it, and I had even been joined by some of the Original Gods when doing so. Each of them had been horrified to see how out of control the darkness had become while they had been sequestered away in peace. It was getting increasingly difficult to tell where the Black Wood started, but the air there was no longer stifling. The path to visit the gods had been restored, and some of them had even come to visit our realm to witness the rebuild. My parents had come and gone from the Divine Hollow to aid with the rebuild and to visit with us, observing how our rule was going. My mother—ever the seer—met me halfway with my father as I rushed through the woods with the frozen darkness.

"You did well, Daughter. You're shaping up to be an excellent ruler," my mother said.

"Isadora already informed the other Original Gods. We'll secure the darkness and make sure it doesn't seep out any longer. Now that we're back, there's no need to keep the dangerous woods around us to hide the hollow."

Seeing the two of them together and happy filled my heart with so much joy. It was such a vast contrast to what I had thought love was as a child. The man who had raised me had been angry and not affectionate, but Zell worshipped the very ground my mother walked on. My own relationship with Thomas was very similar, which gave me hope for the future of our kingdom.

"How is Entriken?" My voice came out in a whisper. He hadn't left the Divine Hollow to join us in battle out of fear of my father. A part of me also thought he might have felt guilty for having betrayed me, but Zell pointed out how little help he had been during our travels and said he thought Entriken had stayed behind to prevent any of us from having to save him.

"He's healing. I'm sure once he's feeling himself again, he'll be ready to come help you rebuild. For now, the hollow feels safe to him. Something he hasn't felt since I left."

"Well, I'm glad the mama's boy has his mom back," I said to her with a wink. I dusted off my hands and tossed my small pack of supplies onto my back.

"Are you rushing back?" my father asked.

"I'm afraid so. We held elections last night for leaders from each village and animal class to sit on our council. We're meeting for the first time today to discuss meeting location rotations and how this whole law- and decision-making thing should go."

"Please tell me Ean and Ursin won," the proud mammal god said.

"Of course they did. I'm still angry your council refuses to bring Mac back, but his sweet Luna was elected instead." My eyes welled with tears at the memory of my kind and hairy friend.

"We told you—it doesn't work that way with animals," my mother said in a consoling tone.

My heart broke every moment that Mac wasn't there with us. I had hoped to see him in the Divine Hollow, but the monster that had ended his life had used dark magic, which prevented Mac from entering the plane of existence there. I'd get to see him again when I fully crossed over, but I hoped that was a long way off.

When I made it back to Yelen—where the first meeting would be held—a much livelier Caden greeted me outside. He dropped to one knee and put his arm over his heart, his head bowed in respect. "Get up, you fool," I said, lifting him. "How are you feeling?"

"I'll be feeling much better once you and Thomas give me a little niece or nephew to play with. I know you were working on it during our trek, so you had better be working harder on it now."

I whacked him playfully. "We are, but our dual ascension will make it harder. I'm trying not to think about it so I don't go into a depressive spiral. Besides, things are too complicated for children just yet."

A large, beautiful wolf emerged from the inn where our meeting was to be held. *If you wait until the timing is perfect, you'll never try for it. Life is always a mess. You just have to make the best of it as it comes.*

"Or keep your husband away from crazy princesses who get them killed."

Mac died an honorable death for the queen we all believe in. His children are so proud of his legacy. His sacrifice brought about all of this, she added, looking around at the bustling town full of citizens from every kingdom and animals of every class.

"Regardless, I'll spend the rest of my life trying to make it up to you."

She bared her sharp teeth in a haunting smile as more members of our new council, Thomas, and Kai approached.

We sat around the large wooden table, which brought to mind my father's council. Except this wasn't just a bunch of old, powerful men. It was men and women of all classes and professions and even animals. As I listened to the discussion in this first session, something became very clear to me. The people and the land were prospering under our rule, despite me feeling like a fraud. I had no idea what I was doing, but with the support network I had, that didn't matter. I would learn to be the leader everyone thought I could be. I cared too much about my friends and this world to let them down.

Our fight was over, but this wasn't the end for us. The rebuilding was just beginning.

Please Review

As an indie author, reviews are extremely important to my career. If you could, please leave a review on whatever platforms you are able to. I would be so grateful!

Acknowledgments

It wouldn't be right to start these out without thanking the person whose book prompted me to have the dream that inspired this project. Thank you Chelz for inspiring the magical and steamy scene that kicks this baby off.

I also have to thank Bestie for the second book in a row for coming up with the most clever title that fit my book perfectly. It's also so uplifting to chat about my writing with you, and having you in my corner to cheer me on is what gets me through it.

There is also no way this book would be getting published without the assistance of my incredible beta readers and writing partners, who have become family to me.

Jude, I'd be lost in writing and life without you. I'm so glad fate intervened and pushed us together because I can't imagine not having you in my life. The countless times I've bounced ideas off of you and you've brainstormed some brilliant ideas that perfectly matched my voice have been integral to this story, and I don't have enough words to tell you how much that means to me.

AJ, you found every plot hole and helped me improve this story so much. Your advice really took it to a whole new level I didn't think was possible, and the comments made me chuckle and gave me life. I don't think I'll ever publish a book without asking you to look through it first.

I also want to immensely thank my writing family, the hedgie house, for supporting me all the way through and making sure I always believe in myself.

Jen, one of my favorite memories of working on this book will always be when we were brainstorming cover ideas and laughing our butts off as I named all my ideas weird things. There have been so many ways you've helped me at every stage of getting this book out that I probably can't even remember them all to list, but know how much I value our friendship and your assistance every step of the way.

Tamara, thank you for keeping me honest this book and helping me see things that readers would that I didn't. You made time to help me even in the midst of your busiest schedule ever, and that has always meant the world to me. One day, I'll force a love of fantasy books on you whether you like it or not.

Feya, whenever I start to crumble, you're always there to pick me back up, reminding me of my value. Every part of the process I've shared ideas with you and bounced things off you and you've been so gracious and helpful every single time.

A big shoutout to my amazing editing and design team for all their help! You were all delightful to work with and I'm so grateful for your professionalism and hard work!

Copy/Line Editing—Juicy Details Editing, especially Monica and Maria. From the moment I found you all on Instagram, I knew we were meant to work together. I can't tell you how thrilled I am to have you to coach me and to finesse this into something I'm so proud of!

Proofreading/Formatting—Hope E. Davis, I think all of bookstagram knows how dear you are to me, but I can't say it enough. Meeting you in person finally and instantly clicking made me so happy that fate brought us together to be book buddies.

Book Cover Art — Ruxie, I can't tell you how much I adore you and your fantastic skills. You were such a pleasure to work with and I'm so honored you took on the task of bringing my characters to life.

Also, a big thank you to other hedgies who have motivated or inspired me on a daily basis and for being such wonderful and supportive friends. I'm also very grateful to the bookstagram community for showing so much support on my debut, as well as this second book, and it's been an honor having you along for this wild ride!

About the Author

Growing up in upstate New York, I rarely saw females in STEM fields. While earning my B.S. in Mechanical Engineering from Rensselaer Polytechnic Institute, I was often the only woman in the room. Those experiences now fuel my stories, featuring fierce female protagonists who aren't afraid to prove their worth in male-dominated spaces. Because let's face it—we've all had that moment when someone assumed we were the secretary instead of the engineer in charge.

When I'm not building worlds or crunching numbers in my infamous spreadsheets (yes, I'm that kind of organized), you'll find me hiking with my beloved Corgi, Kieran (named after the

FBAA character—fellow book lovers, you know who I mean!). My other passions include experimental cooking (my crispy smashed potatoes are legendary) and tending to my vegetable garden.

Fair warning: My characters share my enthusiasm for good food and great coffee!

As an author and a STEMinist, I believe in transparency and supporting others on their journey. Whether it's demystifying sci-fi for newcomers or sharing insights about the indie publishing process, I'm here to break down barriers. My stories blend accessible sci-fi with fantasy, featuring relatable heroines who combine technical brilliance with real-world awkwardness (internal banter included!).

I currently reside in upstate New York with Kieran, who insists on proofreading all my manuscripts with his approval.

Love and Other Alien Concepts (a sci-fi romance) was my debut novel, Touch of Clandestiny being the first in my dip into Romantasy. I'm currently drafting a witchy murder mystery romance (title not yet announced) and plotting a sci-fi mythology-themed series.

You can follow me on:

Instagram: @catiereadsandwrites

Website: https://catie1024.wixsite.com/catieoneillauthor

Goodreads/Amazon: Catie O'Neill

www.ingramcontent.com/pod-product-compliance
Lightning Source LLC
Chambersburg PA
CBHW020145310726
48970CB00006B/2020